ENTE
A

Books by Judy Duarte

MULBERRY PARK

ENTERTAINING ANGELS

Published by Kensington Publishing Corporation

ENTERTAINING ANGELS

JUDY DUARTE

KENSINGTON BOOKS
http://www.kensingtonbooks.com

KENSINGTON BOOKS are published by

Kensington Publishing Corp.
119 West 40th Street
New York, NY 10018

All Kensington titles, imprints, and distributed lines are available at special quantity discounts for bulk purchases for sales promotion, premiums, fund-raising, educational, or institutional use.

Special book excerpts or customized printings can also be created to fit specific needs. For details, write or phone the office of the Kensington Special Sales Manager: Kensington Publishing Corp., 119 West 40th Street, New York, NY 10018. Attn. Special Sales Department. Phone: 1-800-221-2647.

Kensington and the K logo Reg. U.S. Pat. & TM Off.

ISBN-13: 978-0-7582-2016-5
ISBN-10: 0-7582-2016-2

First Kensington Trade Paperback Printing: May 2009
10 9 8 7 6 5 4 3 2 1

Printed in the United States of America

To Karen Solem, who encouraged me to reach higher and dig deeper. Thank you for your incredible support along the way.

And to John Scognamiglio, for his belief in me and in the Mulberry Park novels. Without you and your editorial vision, these stories would still be a dream.

Do not forget to entertain strangers, for by so doing some people have entertained angels without knowing it.

—Hebrews 13:2 NIV

Chapter 1

Renee Delaney trudged along the sidewalk on her way to the bus depot, her leather soles scraping against a layer of city grit on concrete.

It was too bad she hadn't put on her wannabe Sketchers when she'd left the house, but she'd been in a hurry and had slipped into the only other shoes she owned—a pair of worn-out brown sandals that had been resting near the cot in the back room where she'd slept. Now her toes were cold, and she had a sore spot just below the inside of her ankle, where the frayed strap had rubbed the skin raw.

The chill in the air caused her to shiver, and she drew her fists into the sleeves of her sweat shirt, which she'd chosen to wear because the extra-large garment hid the growing bump of her stomach. She'd never been fat in her life, but she wouldn't stress about that now, or she might freak out at the thought of how big she was going to get.

Up ahead, a man wearing a tattered gray trench coat with a dirty, red-plaid lining pushed off the wall he'd been slumped against. As he approached, he grinned. "Hey there, little girl."

Her stomach clenched, and her heart rate spiked. She knew better than to look away from him, so she eyed him warily and continued walking at the same pace.

As he approached, his smile broadened, revealing discolored teeth, the front one chipped. "Where you goin', girl?"

Yeah, right. Like she really wanted him to know. She narrowed her eyes in a don't-mess-with-me glare, which worked—sort of. He did walk past her, but his arm bumped her shoulder in the process.

He reeked of stale cigarette smoke and sweat on top of sweat. Cheap booze, too. And the horrible smell lingered, even after he passed her by.

She suspected he was homeless, just like she was.

Oh, God, she thought. Don't let me end up smelling like that guy.

She blew out a sigh. She might not know where she'd end up tonight, but it would definitely have a bathroom and shower.

Speaking of a bathroom, she'd have to find one before she boarded the first bus leaving town.

She fingered the swell of her belly through the thick, cotton sweat shirt and caressed the bulge where her baby grew.

Just last week, she'd purchased a couple of blousy tops at the thrift shop, but that was before Mary Ellen, her mom's second cousin, had dropped the bomb about moving out, and Renee had realized she was going to need every bit of cash she could get her hands on.

But who cared? She'd been homeless before—lots of times. Besides, this was only temporary. She'd get a job before the money ran out.

It would have been nice if Mary Ellen had let her stick around until the baby was born, though. But earlier today, the older woman had flipped out at the news.

"Pregnant?" Mary Ellen had slapped her hands on her pudgy hips. "How could you be so stupid? You're no better than your mother."

Renee had wanted to argue, but how could she defend a woman she'd never really known?

"You'll just have to get rid of it," Mary Ellen had said.

Justin Detweiler, the father of the baby, had been blown away by the news, too, and had suggested the same easy solution.

But Renee had given both Justin and later Mary Ellen the same answer. "I can't."

She hadn't explained why. For one thing, she wasn't exactly sure—she just couldn't do it, that's all.

"Well, I'm not going to marry you or anything," Justin had said. "I've got plans for college."

Renee had plans for college, too, since she figured an education was her only hope to make something of her life. Of course, the academic option had poofed the moment that pink dot had formed on the home pregnancy test.

When they first hooked up, Renee had thought Justin was going to be some kind of knight in shining armor, but his body language had quickly put the kibosh on that. So did the way he'd stepped back from her, letting her know that their budding relationship had just taken a dump, and that it was all her fault. The jerk.

"I've got some money in savings," he'd said. "So I can pay for it."

At that point, she'd realized she'd better take whatever he gave her, even if she wasn't going to use it for what he'd intended.

She'd tried to tell herself that she didn't care about not having a boyfriend anymore—*and* not having a place to stay tonight—but that wasn't true. She never had liked being alone, especially when it was dark.

"I'm not running a flop house," Mary Ellen had said, her pinched face growing red. "I agreed to let you stay with me after your last placement didn't work out, but I'm not taking on a baby, too. Get rid of it or I'll call the social worker and have her put you back in foster care."

That had scared Renee more than anything. Not for herself, but for the baby.

What if they took the poor kid away from her and put them in separate foster homes?

She couldn't risk letting that happen. For some reason, she felt an almost overwhelming sense of responsibility for the baby. Who else was going to love it and make sure it wasn't sad or lonely?

So she'd packed up her things and headed out the door with all the courage and pride she could muster, her chin up, her shoulders straight. Well, at least for the first block or two.

Now, as the sun began to slip into the west and she neared the bus depot, she wasn't so sure about anything anymore.

She shifted the shoulder strap of the gray backpack that held the most valuable of her possessions: the three hundred dollars Justin had given her—less the cost of a cheeseburger and fries—a fake ID, some baggy clothes, a plastic sports bottle filled with water, and a couple of granola bars she'd been hoarding in the closet-size bedroom that had, until earlier today, been hers.

Now she was on her own.

As a long line of parked buses came into view, a tall, shaggy-faced man turned the corner, heading in her direction.

He wore a baggy green shirt, faded blue jeans with a frayed hole in the knee, and a dusty pair of Birkenstocks that looked as though he'd had them since the '60s. She suspected he was homeless, too. Or maybe he was just a leftover, drugged-out hippie.

He smiled, and his eyes—the prettiest shade of blue she'd ever seen—zeroed in on her. She tried to give him the same back-off message she'd given the last guy who'd crossed her path, but for some reason, she wasn't able to.

"How's it going?" he asked.

Before she could turn up her nose or respond in a way that would tell him to go on his way, footsteps sounded at a pretty good clip. She glanced up to see another dude rounding the corner at a dead run, a black vinyl handbag tucked under his arm.

Renee tried to get out of his way, but instead of watching where he was running, he was looking over his shoulder.

Bam! He slammed into her like an out-of-bounds running back bowling over a cheerleader on the sidelines.

With her hands still tucked in her sleeves, she couldn't break her fall and landed hard on the sidewalk. The purse snatcher stumbled, but caught himself and kept running.

"Are you okay?" The hippie-guy reached out a hand to help her up, and she pushed a fist through the sleeve opening and took it, surprised at the warmth of his touch.

She nodded. "Yeah, I'm fine."

"How about the baby?" he asked.

The *baby*? How did he know she was pregnant?

Renee wasn't showing all that much yet, especially in the bulky sweat shirt. So she cocked her head to the side and furrowed her brow.

"The baby," he repeated. "A tiny little girl, with curly black hair and green eyes."

He was a hippie all right. And strung out on some kind of whacky weed or sugar cubes or something.

Renee managed the hint of a smile. "Yeah, she's fine, too."

"Good." He nodded toward the bus depot. "You leaving town?"

Something told her to keep that info to herself, yet for some dumb reason she nodded.

"My name's Jesse," he said, as if wanting to be friends.

But she didn't respond. He didn't need to know who she was.

"Where are you headed?" he asked.

It wasn't any of his business, so she should have shined him. But for some reason, she shrugged instead and said, "San Francisco maybe. I'm not sure yet."

Actually, it might be nice to ride a bus all night long. That way, she'd end up in a new city and still have a whole lot of daylight left.

"Fairbrook is a better choice," he said. "You know where that is?"

She nodded. It was another San Diego suburb, not far from here.

"The Community Church runs a soup kitchen," he added, "so I'll probably end up there."

She didn't need to hear his sob story. Not when she had one of her own.

Jesse offered her another smile that crinkled the skin around those pretty blue eyes. "You'll find everything you need in Fairbrook." Then, instead of heading toward the buses, he walked in the opposite direction.

Weird, she thought, as she continued on her trek out of town. Jesse, the hippie guy, was probably crazy, but he'd offered her the first bit of kindness and respect she'd received in a long time. Especially from a stranger.

If he was right, and Fairbrook had a place where she could eat some free meals, she'd be able to conserve the money she had. And that was a top priority right now. She'd had her fill of foster homes and shirttail relatives like Mary Ellen. And it was time to make it on her own.

Fairbrook was as good a place as any.

The engine of the ten-year-old Ford Taurus sputtered again, and Craig Houston bit his tongue, holding back a profanity that wasn't considered appropriate for a pastor to say. But the blasted car had been skipping and chugging ever since he'd left his granddad's home near Phoenix. And as he neared the California line, he was growing more frustrated by the minute.

If his life had been part of some master scheme, he suspected his day would have gone a whole lot smoother than it had. So it seemed only natural to question the validity of his "call" to the ministry—or at least his assignment as an associate pastor to what he'd been told was "a fairly small congregation in a lovely beachside community in southern California."

The car skipped again, and Craig let his temper slip just long enough to slam his hand on the dashboard. At this rate, he was never going to reach the Fairbrook city limits.

As he'd done several times since leaving Scottsdale, he pulled into the closest service station and asked if they had a mechanic on duty.

"Hey, Pete!" one guy yelled to a burly man in his late forties who wore a pair of grungy coveralls.

Twenty minutes later, Craig got the same answer from Pete that he'd been getting all day. "I can't find anything wrong under the hood."

"Honest," Craig said, "it's running hard and skipping like crazy."

Pete agreed to take the car out for a test drive, only to come back ten minutes later and say the same thing three other so-called experts had said earlier.

"It ran like a charm for me." Pete handed the keys back to Craig.

That figured. Instead of some master game plan, this was beginning to feel like one divinely inspired practical joke.

"Do you have a pay phone?" Craig asked, wishing he knew where he'd left his cell. He'd had it when he'd started out this morning, but somewhere along the way, he'd misplaced it.

Pete pointed to the back wall of the shop with a beefy, grease-stained hand.

"Thank you."

While striding toward the telephone, Craig reached into the front pocket of his dress slacks and pulled out all the change he had, as well as the stick-it note with the name and the number of the couple awaiting his arrival.

When the line connected, a female voice sounded. "Hello?"

"Mrs. Delacourt?" he asked.

"Yes."

"This is Craig Houston. I'm really sorry about calling like this. I know you've prepared dinner for me, but I've been having car trouble and have no idea when I'll arrive."

"Where are you? Can I send someone to pick you up?"

"I'm still in Arizona, so there's no point coming to get me. I just called to let you know I'd be late and to tell you that I'll pick up something to eat along the way."

"I'm sorry you've had so much trouble."

So was Craig.

"Is there something my husband or I can do to help?"

"I'm afraid not." He'd just had the fourth mechanic in a row insist there wasn't anything wrong with the engine, but that definitely wasn't the case. Unless, of course, Craig was losing it and imagining some reason to go home and revamp his future.

"You take care," Mrs. Delacourt said. "And don't worry about the time you arrive. My husband and I stay up late."

"Thanks." Craig hung up the phone, then sighed.

What a lousy way for the new associate minister to introduce himself to the couple who'd offered to take him in until his place was ready.

He could, he supposed, resort to prayer, asking for smooth sailing the rest of the way, but he and God weren't exactly on speaking terms lately.

Of course, from all he'd been taught in seminary, he suspected that was his own fault.

But under the circumstances, taking all the blame didn't seem entirely fair.

As the sun dropped low in the western sky, and the transit bus drove off, blasting Renee and two other disembarking passengers with a diesel-fueled roar, she surveyed her new surroundings.

A self-serve gas station that offered a mini-mart and a car wash sat on the corner of a street lined with trees covered in purple blossoms, which made the city seem prettier than the one she'd just left. At least you knew it was spring here. Maybe Fairbrook had been a good choice.

She didn't take anyone's advice very often. Not because she was stubborn or anything. It's just that most people she came across—young or old—hadn't done a whole lot with their own lives and didn't seem to know what they were talking about.

And those who did?

Well, they just didn't understand the reality Renee lived with.

She'd talked to the high school guidance counselor about it once and tried to explain.

Well, sort of.

Mrs. Brinkley had seemed to think that all Renee had to do was keep out of trouble, buckle down, and study. Then, somehow, like magic, a scholarship and financial aid would make everything okay.

Some of what she'd said was true, but buckling down wasn't so easy to do when there were people in and out of the apartment at all times of the day and night. Or when the lights went out while Renee was reading *A Tale of Two Cities* for English class because Mary Ellen hadn't paid the electric bill. Or when the goofy guy who shared a wall with Renee kept his radio turned up high all night, listening to whacky AM talk shows where callers reported alien abductions and discussed a government conspiracy to keep them quiet.

Or when her stomach growled so bad it was hard to focus on 2+2=4, let alone 3x-5y=z, and the only thing in the fridge was a six-pack of beer, a jar of salsa, and a hunk of dried-out cheese.

So while it seemed a bit wild to follow the advice of a homeless hippie-guy, the need to conserve her cash and the promise of a soup kitchen had been key to Renee's decision to go to Fairbrook.

Now all she had to do was find a place to stay for the night.

A gray-haired lady dressed in teal-blue slacks and a cream-colored sweater began a slow shuffle along the sidewalk. A worn black tote bag hung from the crook in her arm.

"Excuse me," Renee said, easily catching up with her. "Can you tell me where I can find the community church?"

The woman cocked her silvery head to the side and squinted, as though she was new in town, too. Then she lifted her free arm and pointed a gnarled finger in the same direction she was heading. "This is Main Street. Follow it down about eight or ten blocks. You'll come to Applewood. Turn left. That'll lead you to Mulberry Park. The church is on the same side as the playground, although the entrance is actually on First Avenue."

Renee wasn't all that good with directions, but she figured a park and a church would be tough to miss. "Thanks."

She continued to tag along until the older woman turned down one of the side streets, and Renee trudged straight ahead. The sore on the side of her foot burned and stung something awful, and she found herself limping.

She counted blocks as she went, and while it seemed as though it took forever to reach Applewood, it had probably only been a few torturous minutes. Fortunately, the little old lady knew what she was talking about. The park lay straight ahead.

Renee glanced beyond the playground and easily spotted the church, one of those white, old-fashioned types that had stained glass windows, a bright red double door in front, and a bell tower with a steeple on top. Trouble was, the parking lot was practically deserted, and Renee felt like kicking herself for being so dumb and listening to a bushy-faced hippie.

An old guy wearing a pair of denim overalls and a blue plaid shirt was sweeping the grounds with a push broom. When she asked about the soup kitchen, he told her it was already closed for the day.

"Come back between eleven and two tomorrow," he added, while he continued to sweep.

She wasn't all that hungry yet, but she would need to eat something by tonight. She still got a little pukey sometimes, and it helped to have food in her stomach.

But after buying the cheeseburger and the bus ticket, her three hundred dollars was dwindling fast.

She ran a hand through her hair, her finger snagging on a snarl. She wished she'd taken time to comb it better this morning and to pull it back or something. But she wouldn't stress about that now. Not when she needed to find a place to sleep. A place that wouldn't cost very much.

As the old man continued to stroke the sidewalk with his broom, she called out to him again. "Excuse me. Sir?"

The swish-swish of his movements paused, and he turned around to face her. "Yes?"

"I'm looking for a motel, and I was wondering if you could tell me where I can find one."

"The Happy Hearth is on Fourth Avenue, just past the post office. And the Welcome Inn is on Bedford Parkway."

"Thanks." She bent over, something that wasn't quite as easy to do as it used to be, and ran her finger along the frayed edge of the sandal strap, where the skin on the inside of her ankle had started to bleed. If she thought the old man might have a first aid kit on him, she'd have asked him for a Band-Aid. But she doubted he did. So instead, she asked, "Which of the motels is closest?"

He stroked his chin with the hand not holding the broom handle. "The one on Bedford, I suppose."

She bit down on her bottom lip.

"You new in town?" he asked.

For a moment, she was afraid to admit it. But if he got too inquisitive or mentioned her age, she always had the fake ID to back up her story, and it was a pretty good one. So she nodded. "Yeah. Just arrived today. I'm looking for a job, too."

He studied her for a moment, as if really looking at her—inside and out—which was something most people never did.

So she stood tall, tried to conjure an aura of self-confidence and maturity, and smiled. "I'm a hard worker. And I can do just about anything. So if you know of anyone who's hiring . . . ?"

"Not off the top of my head." He rubbed a hand over his thinning hair as if trying to joggle his memory. "But if you're in a hurry, you can cut through the park. The jogging path that runs past the ball field is a shortcut to Bedford. Just head east. When you reach the street, hang a right."

"Thanks." She took a step, then froze. "I don't suppose you know what the rates are?"

"I had to put my brother-in-law up there a couple of years

ago, and it cost sixty bucks a night. But I suspect it must be more now."

Renee nodded, forcing her expression to remain positive and upbeat while her spirits were sputtering by the minute. Her money wasn't going to last a week. But what else could she do?

More scared and desperate than she dared admit, she limped across the street and made her way to the park. Before crossing the newly mowed lawn, she removed her sandals and carried them.

The soft, cool blades of grass massaged her aching feet, as she continued on her way. She scanned the tree-dotted grounds, the empty playground, the baseball field, where a preteen boy pitched to a man squatting behind home plate.

It was a nice park, she decided.

If she knew where she'd be sleeping, she might have hung out for a while. But night was closing in on her, and an imaginary time bomb was tick-tocking in her head.

Could her life get any worse than this?

Yeah, it could.

If she ran out of money before she got a job, she'd really be in a fix, especially with a baby to think about.

Up ahead, a great big tree grew in the center of the park. Underneath the shade of its branches, a concrete bench rested, offering a seat to a weary traveler.

It seemed like she'd been walking since early this morning. Her legs ached, and she needed a rest.

What would it hurt if she sat down to rest for just a minute or two?

Instead of hurrying to find the motel, she padded to the bench, removed her backpack, and plopped down.

She'd known that her decision to have the baby meant that she was on her own, but she hadn't realized how scary that might be, especially since it would be dark soon.

If she was a religious person, she might pray at a time like this. But she didn't know what to say.

She'd gone to Sunday school with one of the foster families she'd lived with, but she couldn't remember too much about it. Just that they sang songs, listened to stories, ate oatmeal cookies, and drank a lemonade-based punch that was yummy.

Still, she was running out of options at this point, so she clasped her hands, letting them rest in her lap, and bowed her head.

She didn't close her eyes, though. She just stared at her toes and the red, angry wound on her foot, felt the tears sting her eyes and clog her throat.

"If you're there, God—" She looked up through the dancing leaves in the tree, spotting a dappled glimpse of the sky. Oh, God, please be there. She glanced back at her feet and sighed, hoping her words didn't fall on deaf ears. "I don't know where to go or who to trust. And now I've got a baby to look out for."

No answer.

A story she'd heard at Sunday school came to mind, and she wished that she could remember all the details now. But it was about a bunch of people who'd been in the wilderness for forty or fifty years. And God had sent a cloud to show them the way to go. He'd given them some kind of heavenly food to eat, too.

What she wouldn't do for her own personal cloud and a decent meal right now.

So she took it a step further. "Can you please help me? I need to find a cheap place to live and a job."

She waited for a while, as if some big booming voice would shout out from the heavens and tell her exactly where to go and what to do.

Still no answer. But then again, she supposed she really hadn't expected one. Over the years, Santa Claus, the Easter Bunny, and the Tooth Fairy hadn't meant the same to her as they had to other kids, and she'd learned to deal with it.

Of course, God was supposed to be real—at least, to a lot of people.

So, in spite of a niggling doubt, she cleared her throat and gave it a parting shot. "If you won't do it for me, then would you do it for the baby?"

A light breeze kicked up, and tree leaves rustled overhead. It wasn't the James Earl Jones impersonation that she'd been expecting, but it sure beat the silence that had mocked her before.

Aw, come on, Renee, she chided herself. Shake it off. You're wasting what little daylight you have left.

So she stood and slipped her arms through the straps of the backpack, adjusting her load for comfort, then made her way to the gray block building that she hoped was the public restrooms.

When she spotted a door that said WOMEN, she muttered, "Oh, thank God," but not to anyone in particular. Then she grabbed the handle, pulled it open, and stepped inside.

There were two stalls to choose from and a table for changing babies. But her gaze immediately dropped to something pink on the floor—a hooded jacket that had been discarded. She picked it up, felt the white fur-like lining that was almost new.

She checked the tag, looking for a girl's name in it. Some mothers did that. Put a label or marked in their kids' coats and stuff.

While growing up, Renee sometimes had articles of clothing that still bore the name of the kid who'd gotten them firsthand.

Gretchen, whoever she was, had once owned a hand-knit sweater with a tag that said it had been lovingly made by her grandmother. Renee didn't know if Gretchen's mom had given it to the Salvation Army because it had been outgrown or if it was because of the ink stain on the sleeve. Either way, it was cool to think someone's grandma had made something that ended up in Renee's drawer.

But the jacket she'd just found didn't have anyone's name on it.

It was a little too small, and while she probably could still use it herself, she carefully folded it and placed it on top of the paper towel dispenser. Then she chose a stall and did what she came to do.

After flushing, she went to the sink, where she washed her hands then dried them on a paper towel. While standing near the trash can, she noticed a bluish-green plastic Wal-Mart bag leaning up against the wall. Out of curiosity, she reached for it and peered inside, spotting a couple of empty Tupperware containers, a plastic fork, a child-size box of apple juice with the little straw still attached, an orange, and a package of un-opened graham crackers.

She placed the sack on the sink and rustled through it a bit more, then gasped at what she found.

Wow. Too weird.

She pulled out one of three Band-Aids, the designer kind with cartoon characters on them.

If she didn't know better . . .

But she did know better. Someone had left the remnants of a picnic lunch in the bathroom. And either that same person or another girl had left behind a jacket when packing up to go home. No need to think of it as a miracle or anything. It had just been a losers-weepers kind of day.

But it still seemed like someone had placed these things here—just for her.

"Thank you," Renee muttered to the cold gray walls or to Whoever might be listening.

Again, silence followed, which was just as well. She'd probably freak if some booming voice said, "You're welcome."

She grabbed a couple of towels from the dispenser, then used them to wash the wound on the inside of her foot and to dab it dry. When she was satisfied that it was clean, she applied a Nemo Band-Aid.

On the way out, she paused at the door. Normally, she didn't take things that didn't belong to her. But it was beginning to look like the jacket might be part of a heavenly gift package, so she went back for it, thinking it could come in handy if it got any colder before she reached the motel.

She took time for a quick drink from the water fountain and refilled her sports bottle. Then she slipped on her sandals and started her trek once again, crossing the park and following the jogging trail on her way to Bedford and the motel, just like the old man at the church had told her. But she hadn't taken more then five or six steps when a flash of light caught her eye.

Squinting and using her hand as a shield, she tried to determine where it was coming from.

Somewhere in the canyon that lay beyond the park, she guessed.

The reflected light continued to shine and flicker as if someone was sending a message in Morse code. She tried to ignore it, but couldn't. Maybe God didn't always use clouds to show people the way.

Okay, this was probably just a fluke and way too weird to contemplate, yet in spite of her better judgment, she cut through the brush, drawn to the light like a moth.

About twenty yards in, she found a path that seemed to lead right to the source, a big tree with a wooden structure built in its branches. A bicycle rim hung over the small doorway—some kind of ornament or decoration, she guessed. Apparently, the chrome had picked up a sunray and shot it at her.

Her curiosity now appeased, she turned to go, then froze in her tracks. She'd asked for a cheap place to spend the night, and an abandoned tree house wouldn't cost her a dime.

She glanced up at the sky. "I don't suppose you meant for me to stay here tonight."

No answer.

Slowly turning around, she made her way to the tree, surveying the sturdy structure and pondering the possibilities. Seven or eight wooden steps had been nailed to the trunk to allow entrance to the little house.

Just think of the money she'd save.

And six feet above the ground, she'd be safe from snakes.

She placed a foot on the bottom rung and began to climb until she reached the opening. Inside, two fringed throw rugs— one blue, the other green—covered the floor. Both were frayed and had seen better days. They were dirty, too. But she could shake them out.

There were a couple of comic books in the corner, as well as a ball of string and an old red coffee can.

On a wooden ledge about eighteen inches from the ceiling, three red candles, each used to various degrees, sat upright, held in place by globs of melted wax.

Well, the place definitely had possibilities.

And it wasn't far from the park, so she had access to a bathroom and running water . . .

Renee pulled herself through the opening, then removed her backpack and, with the bag of stuff she found, began to settle in for the night.

What was it Jesse, the hippie guy, had said?

You'll find everything you'll need in Fairbrook.

Maybe he'd been right.

But two hours later, as darkness huddled over the canyon and a pack of coyotes yipped and howled just steps away from the tree, Renee wasn't so sure.

Chapter 2

Just as Craig neared Fairbrook's city limits, the Ford Taurus rumbled one more time, then groaned and shuddered to a complete stop.

Giving in to temptation, he finally let loose and swore under his breath, a reaction he'd been holding back for the past two hundred miles.

Ain't nothing wrong under the hood, nearly a legion of mechanics had told him time and again.

Which meant what? That the problem was behind the wheel?

Craig glanced at the clock on the dash. 10:36.

Unable to help himself, he looked heavenward, rolled his eyes, and slowly shook his head.

Deciding he'd better push the car to the shoulder of the road and walk the rest of the way to town, he threw the transmission into neutral and climbed out of the driver's seat.

With the door still open, he placed one hand on the steering wheel and began to push with the other.

"Need some help?"

Craig nearly jumped out of his skin at the sound of an unexpected male voice. He turned to see who was there. Darkness separated them, yet footsteps crunched on the gravel at the side of the road at his approach.

Moments later, the man stepped into the light of the headlamps. His hair was long and shaggy, and he wore a bushy, silver-streaked beard.

If Craig were a gambler, he'd wager that the guy was homeless based upon his appearance and his clothing—a baggy dark shirt and jacket, frayed jeans with a gaping hole in the knee, and a pair of bulky leather sandals.

Continuing to maneuver the rattletrap hunk of metal and tires out of the road, Craig thanked the stranger for the offer. "It's all right. I've just about got it now."

The guy nodded toward the city lights. "I'm heading to Fairbrook, too. Would you mind giving me a lift?"

Was he blind? Strung out on something? This car wasn't going anywhere unless it was attached to a tow truck.

The pent-up frustration that had been building over the past few hours called for a retort, yet everything Craig had been taught at the seminary tamped down a snide comment. "I wish I *could* drive you into town, but I'm afraid we'll have to walk."

"Mind if I take a look?" The man nodded toward the hood of the car.

Who was this guy? A down-on-his-luck mechanic?

"Sure. Go ahead." Craig crossed his arms over his chest, shifted his weight to one hip, and watched the man release the latch, then lift the hood and peer inside.

He didn't do much, just wiggled a wire or two. Then he lowered the hood with a bang and brushed his hands together. "Why don't you give it another try now?"

Craig blew out a sigh. With all the trouble he'd been having with this vehicle, he was ready to throw up his hands. Or to stomp his feet and shake his fist. The hold on his temper was stretched to the limit.

Since none of the service station mechanics who'd taken a look could find anything wrong, it seemed futile to think that this shabby stranger would have any more luck with a lot less effort.

But whatever.

Craig slid behind the wheel, turned the ignition, and pumped the gas pedal. The engine started right up.

The stranger came to the passenger side, opened the door, and peered across the seat at Craig. "How about that ride now?"

Speechless, Craig nodded and waited for him to get in. Then he put the transmission in gear and pulled back onto the pavement, the engine purring as though the car had just rolled out of a dealer showroom.

"My name's Jesse," he said.

Craig introduced himself and added, "I'm the new associate minister at Parkside Community Church."

"You don't say. That's a noble profession."

Craig, who didn't feel very noble right now, supposed that in some cases it was. "My granddad was a missionary for about thirty years. Now he pastors a large congregation in Phoenix, so it seemed like a natural decision." And one that had certainly pleased his family.

Jesse nodded, as though taking it all in. Then he pointed to the radio on the dash. "Do you mind if I turn that on for a minute or so? I'd like to get the baseball scores."

"Go ahead."

Jesse pushed in the button, turning on the power, then tuned into an AM station and sat back in his seat. "Do you follow any of the teams?"

"No, I'm afraid not. I don't have time for sports anymore."

"That's too bad."

Yeah, it was. Craig did his best not to stew about it, though. At one time, baseball had been his whole life, and giving it up had nearly killed him.

He glanced across the seat at his passenger, a guy who didn't appear to do much work—or play—then continued to watch the road ahead.

As the radio announcer rattled off the scores of tonight's

games, including a win for the Padres after a grand slam in the bottom of the ninth, Craig stole another look at Jesse, who was smiling, a glimmer in his eye. If Craig didn't know better, he'd think Jesse had hit the winning homer himself.

"Did you have money on the game?" Craig asked.

"Nope. I'm not a gambler." Jesse crossed his arms. "But just before the game, Dave Ellings stopped by Children's Hospital and promised a kid named Joey that he was going to hit one out of the park for him."

"Oh yeah?"

"The kid's going to have surgery tomorrow morning. The odds are against him waking up, but he'll pull through."

Craig didn't pay the homeless man any mind until the radio announcer said, "Before we cut to the next commercial, I'd like to share a bit of news that was just leaked to our producer. Dave Ellings's homer went way beyond the left field fence tonight. It seems that just this afternoon, Ellings learned that Joey Grabowski, a ten-year-old baseball fan who's in Children's Hospital with a brain tumor, is facing surgery tomorrow morning—a surgery that's both delicate and dangerous. And while the other team members gathered at Petco Park, Ellings risked a fine by making a surprise visit to Joey and promising to hit one out of the park—just for him. What a heartwarming bit of news. My hat's off to you, Dave."

Craig looked across the console at Jesse. "How'd you know about that?"

The man shrugged. "I guess you could say that I've got a . . . gift."

Craig believed people sometimes had gifts, but he wasn't so sure about this particular guy. If Jesse had been blessed with something special, it hadn't appeared to have taken him very far.

"There's an all-night diner on Bedford Parkway," Jesse said. "Would you mind dropping me off there?"

As much as Craig wanted to drive right to the Delacourts'

house, he figured he owed Jesse the ride he'd requested. He'd probably still be walking if the man hadn't tinkered with the engine. "I'll need directions."

"No problem. Just turn left on Applewood. It's a couple of blocks beyond Mulberry Park."

Craig followed his instructions. As they drove past Parkside Community Church, he gave the old-style clapboard structure a once-over, since that's where he'd be working. It was also where he'd be meeting the senior pastor and the board of elders tomorrow morning.

But it was the park across the street that drew his attention, especially the empty ball field, with the lights still illuminating it. The green and black scoreboard indicated that the home team had won five to two.

A couple of young men in matching red T-shirts walked away from the dugout toward a white pickup. One carried a black canvas duffle bag—filled with baseball gear, no doubt.

Seconds later, the lights faded to black, and Craig returned his attention to the road.

"There it is." Jesse pointed to a small restaurant on the right side of the street.

Craig stopped in front, double-parking, and glanced at the restaurant window that was trimmed with white café-style curtains. Bold cursive paint on the glass read: *Debbie's Diner*.

"Thanks a lot," Jesse said, as he climbed out of the car and shut the door.

Craig was just about to pull away when he saw Jesse reach into his pocket and begin counting coins. It was clear to see that the man was down on his luck and probably had been for awhile.

Using the control panel on the side of the door, Craig lowered the passenger window. "Hey, wait a minute." Then he reached for his wallet and pulled out one of the few twenties he had to last him until he received his first paycheck, and handed it to Jesse. "Let me buy you dinner tonight."

"Thank you. I appreciate that." Jesse took the cash. "Before you go, do you mind if I give you a piece of advice?"

"What's that?"

"Things aren't always what they seem around here, Pastor. You'll need to look beyond the obvious and dig deep within yourself if you want to make a difference in this town."

At one time, when a pro ball career was no longer possible and Craig had resigned himself to the ministry, he had hoped to make a difference in the world, but here he was—stuck in Fairbrook.

Still, for a moment, he clung to what the homeless man had said. Then he let the words fade into the night air.

A guy like Jesse couldn't possibly have made all the right choices himself. If he had, he wouldn't be lacking a car, a job, and enough money to buy his next meal.

"Take a left at the intersection," Jesse added. "And if you follow that road down a mile, you'll be back on track."

Craig did as the man instructed and, just before eleven o'clock and nearly six hours late, he arrived at Tuscany Hills, the gated community in which the Delacourts lived.

After providing an ID to the guard, Craig was allowed inside and followed the winding road to 2316, a newer two-story house with a well-manicured yard. He parked at the curb, then grabbed his canvas carry-on and a vinyl garment bag from the backseat and headed to the front door, where he rang the bell.

He waited until a man in his late forties to early fifties answered.

"Mr. Delacourt?" he asked.

"Yes, but call me Daniel." His host reached out his hand in greeting. "Please come in, Pastor Houston."

"I apologize for being so late."

"Those things happen." Daniel led him through a travertine-tiled foyer. "How's the car working?"

"Actually, it seems to be running better now. I'm not sure

what was wrong with it, but I'll get it serviced first thing in the morning." As he followed the man inside, he glanced at the interior of the house, which had been tastefully decorated in shades of beige, brown, and blue. He was too tired to note much more than shutters on the windows.

An attractive blonde, tall and slender, greeted him at the entrance to the living room, her hair neatly styled, her makeup still fresh. "Pastor Houston, I'm Cassandra. Welcome to our home. Can I get you a cup of coffee? Perhaps a piece of cake?"

"Thank you, but I'm going to have to pass." Craig just wanted to get settled in his room and let the couple turn in for the night.

"We'd planned to put you in our guest house," she said, "where you'd have more privacy. But I'm afraid it's being re-modeled and isn't quite ready yet. So I made up the Murphy bed in the office. It has a private bath, so you should be comfortable there."

"No problem." Craig wasn't fussy, but in a house like this one, with everything in its place, he suspected the office would be just fine.

"You'll be surrounded by Daniel's collection of baseball memorabilia," Cassandra added.

Great. Just what he needed—a reminder of what his life might have been like.

Nevertheless, Craig managed a smile and a nod.

"I'll show you the way," Daniel said.

As Craig began to follow his host through the living room, he noticed a large portrait of a teenage girl hung over the fireplace. She was dressed in pearls and a white dress, her hair swept up in some kind of a twist. She resembled Cassandra, only more petite, more delicate. And a few decades younger.

His steps must have slowed to a snail's pace because he found the young woman in the picture . . . remarkable. And not just because she was attractive.

Daniel, who'd noticed him lagging behind, turned and smiled. "That's Shana, our daughter."

"Pretty girl," Craig said.

"Yes, she is." Cassandra looked at the portrait as though it were a work of art. "She's a real sweetheart. We've really been blessed."

"*Twice* blessed," Daniel added. "We nearly lost her to leukemia when she was twelve. But thank God she pulled through."

"Shana is finishing up her last semester of college in Australia," Cassandra added. "In May she'll graduate with a master's degree in biology."

As Daniel led the way to the den, Craig stole one last glance at the girl.

The artist had captured something in her eyes—a memory? A dream? A Mona Lisa secret of some kind?

Craig wasn't an expert, but he suspected a painting like that could make an artist famous.

Of course, fame wasn't something he cared to think about, especially at bedtime. It made falling asleep next to impossible.

Kristy Smith had no idea how many times the telephone had rung before the sound ripped through the night and drew her into a conscious state. Once? Twice?

She fumbled for the receiver that rested on the nightstand by her bed, hoping she could answer before the sound woke her six-year-old son or her disabled grandmother.

"Hello?"

"Hey, it's me. Shana."

Kristy rose up on an elbow and squinted at the lighted dial on the alarm clock that sat on the bureau. 3:15. Then she cleared her throat, hoping to dislodge the sleep from her voice. "What's up?"

"Did I wake you?"

She blinked a couple of times, then scanned her darkened bedroom. Shana obviously hadn't considered the time difference when she'd called. It must be important. "Yeah, I was asleep, but that's okay. Is something wrong?"

"No, something's right. I've got good news. I'm getting married."

As pretty as Shana was, she didn't date very much. So her announcement came as a surprise.

Kristy threw back the covers and sat up. "Wow. What did you do? Let an Australian hunk sweep you off your feet?"

"Actually, he's a Southern California guy. Guess who it is."

Kristy didn't have a clue. And at three in the morning, she wasn't up for games.

Fortunately, her best friend took pity on her sleep-deprived state and answered, "Brad Rensfield."

Bits and pieces of the past flickered like a short circuit in Kristy's sleep-deprived mind—the Rensfield estate, tiki lights, alcohol-laced punch. An unchaperoned party. A fair-haired Romeo who'd completely swept her off her staggering feet.

He'd told her his name was Matthew, but that was about all she knew of him. Even Brad, who'd introduced them, had somehow forgotten any identifying details afterward.

She squeezed her eyes shut, trying her best to blink back her shame while wrapping her mind around the unexpected news.

"I don't get it," she said. "I thought Brad was attending law school here in California."

"He was. He *is*."

"Then how did you two . . . ?"

"We've kept in touch through e-mail, but about two weeks ago, I noticed a change in . . . Well, in his tone. And as soon as I'd answer one, I'd get another."

So their relationship blossomed over the Internet?

"Then this weekend, Brad took a break in his studies and flew out to visit." Shana laughed, the familiar lilt in her voice just as sweet as ever. "We spent a wonderful evening together, and you'll never guess what happened."

Kristy could certainly connect the dots, but she wasn't sure she wanted to.

"We stayed up all night talking," Shana said. "And then we watched the sunrise together. And that's when he proposed. It was so sweet, so romantic, that I couldn't help but accept. We've set the date for August twenty-fourth."

Kristy found it difficult to focus, let alone speak. But what was there to say? *I think you should slow down?*

She couldn't do that. Shana and Brad were totally suited for each other. They were both golden children destined for a fairy-tale life. Yet a wave of uneasiness turned her thoughts on edge.

Maybe it was because Brad hadn't been very helpful seven years ago when she'd told him she needed to find the mysterious Matthew, that she needed to talk to him. "I hardly know the guy," he'd said. "He was a friend of a friend."

She'd asked all the other guys who'd been at the party, trying to find out who'd brought him. But none of them gave Matthew up. She'd even asked the few girls who'd been there, but since she and Matthew had immediately hit it off and left the group, the girls hardly remembered even seeing him. So she'd gone back to Brad and swallowed her pride.

"I'm pregnant," she'd admitted. "It happened that night at the party."

"That's too bad. Having a kid will really mess up your life."

At sixteen? And with a disabled grandmother to take care of? He'd had that right.

Since he hadn't been able to provide her with any contact information, he'd offered to spring for an abortion.

At the time, she'd seriously considered the offer. She'd been pedaling as fast as she could to keep up with her schoolwork and to take care of Gram. But something about his gesture had rubbed her the wrong way. Maybe because it was too much like him hiring a cleanup crew to come onto the Rensfield estate after the last drunk teenager had gone home so he could hide the evidence of the party before his parents arrived.

But this wasn't about Kristy.

It was about Shana.

"Brad loves me," Shana added. "Can you believe it?"

Yes. Brad was bright, relatively good-looking, although not what you'd call handsome. And he was the heir to the Rensfield department-store chains. All in all, he was every woman's dream, every parent's sigh of relief.

Yet Kristy couldn't shake her skepticism. Something just didn't feel right, but at three in the morning, she couldn't quite put her finger on what it might be.

It certainly wasn't jealousy. She neither liked nor disliked Brad. Nor had she ever dated him, even though he'd come on to her a few times.

Kristy had been searching for a prince among teens back then, and Brad, who'd been making notches on his bedposts, clearly hadn't been what she'd been looking for.

But there was more to it than that.

His attitude toward problem solving, she supposed.

But that didn't seem like a good enough reason to dash Shana's hopes and dreams.

Maybe the engagement was a good thing. Maybe Brad had grown up and realized that, besides being born rich and raised with the proverbial silver spoon in his mouth, Shana was the best thing that had ever happened to him.

"That's great news," Kristy finally managed to say.

"Off and on since eighth grade, I've had a crush on him—you know that. And it seems he'd had one on me, too."

Maybe so, but Kristy had never noticed Brad giving Shana the time of day while they were in high school. He'd actively pursued the girls more likely to put out.

And that was another thing. Talking all night long didn't seem to be part of Brad's MO. What had triggered his romantic and noble turnaround?

"This still seems like a big surprise to me," Kristy said.

Shana's breath caught, as if she was going to say something

else, then she slowly let it go. "Well, let's just say Brad and I have a history."

In all their late-night, lay-your-heart-on-the-line chats, Brad's name had never really come up. Sure, there was the junior high crush, but they'd never really discussed him after that.

Apparently, the two best friends hadn't been entirely open with each other.

Still, Kristy wouldn't rain on Shana's parade. "Congratulations. I hope you'll both be very happy."

"Thanks. But my biggest reason for calling you was to ask if you'd be my maid of honor."

She *had* to be kidding. How was that for luck? Just when the whispers had finally died down.

Kristy's first inclination was to say, "No way," but friends like Shana Delacourt came along only once in a lifetime. And a true friend would be more supportive.

Yet they also looked out for each other.

Kristy's fingers tightened around the receiver as though she could mentally send her reservations about taking such an active—and prominent—role in the ceremony over the telephone line. "Are you sure you want me to be that involved?"

"Of course, I'm sure. I love you. You're my best friend. So how about it? Will you be my maid of honor?"

The Delacourt/Rensfield nuptials were bound to be Fairbrook's equivalent of a royal wedding and surely the social event of the season. If Kristy agreed to stand up with her . . .

But how could she not?

"So what do you say?" Shana asked. "I can't imagine having anyone else."

Kristy opened her mouth, yet it took a beat for the words to finally come out. "Okay, but promise me something. If you ever, for *any* reason, have a change of heart and want someone else to slip into my place, you'll let me know."

"Why would I want to do that?"

"Because . . ." Gosh, Shana could be so naïve. Kristy let

out a wobbly sigh and tried to figure out how to explain to someone who probably wouldn't get it. Someone who hadn't had to face public humiliation and whispers that weren't always the quiet, behind-her-back kind.

"Get over that party, Kristy. It's been almost seven years, for goodness sake. You met a guy and things went too far. Mistakes happen. No one's going to hold that over you."

She made it sound so simple.

"Okay, I'll be your maid of honor, but just be honest with me. If things get . . . awkward, I'll hand over my bouquet to someone else—no questions asked."

"I promise. If that happens, I'll speak up. But I need you to do something else for me."

"What's that?"

"Since I'm stuck over here until mid-May, you'll need to do some of the footwork. We'd like a small, intimate wedding, and I don't want my mom to get carried away."

Uh-oh. Another potential crisis. There was no way Mrs. Delacourt would take a backseat on planning her only child's big day. "I'm not sure I can help out there. Your mom is going to insist upon calling all the shots."

"I know. And that's what you're going to help me prevent."

Shana never had been able to stand up to her mother, and Cassandra Delacourt could be pretty intimidating when she put her mind to it. In fact, Kristy wasn't looking forward to bumping heads with her, but she would—for Shana—if push came to shove.

So she relented. "All right, I'll help. And I'll keep you posted."

"Good. Then I'll let you get back to sleep. I'll talk to you in a couple of days, okay? And thanks a million, Kristy. I really appreciate this."

"No problem." But as she hung up the telephone, a bevy of goose bumps shimmied over her, and she ran her hands along her arms to chase them away.

What had she gotten herself into?

* * *

Renee sat in the center of the old green throw rug she'd slept upon and yawned. She'd stayed awake for hours last night, until exhaustion chased away her fear of the dark.

Now she had a crick in her neck, and her back hurt.

As the rays of the morning sun peered through the cracks of the wooden walls, dust motes danced and glistened in the beams like fairy dust.

Weird, huh? And it was even weirder to think of a tree house as her home, but for a girl who'd never really had a bedroom to call her own, it was actually kind of cool. A memory she'd have to tell her baby about some day.

She wondered what time it was. Seven o'clock? Eight? Too bad she didn't have a watch. She knew it was Wednesday, though.

Reaching into her backpack, she dug around until she found the last granola bar. She hoped it would be enough to take the edge off the hunger pangs she'd woken up with, but even if it wasn't, she planned to be first in line when the church opened the soup kitchen at eleven. Then she would eat her fill, making it her big meal of the day.

After nibbling on the bar and making it last as long as she could, she grabbed a toothbrush, a nearly empty tube of paste, and a comb from her backpack. Then she shoved them into her pockets so she could use both hands while climbing to the ground.

She planned to freshen up in the park restroom, then hit the city streets, looking for a job. There were a couple of cutesy-looking shops and eateries on Applewood, across from the park. Maybe one of them was hiring.

As she began to climb out of the tree house, holding on to the doorway and carefully placing her feet on the wooden steps, a young voice sounded behind her. "Hey! What are you doing?"

She glanced over her shoulder, where two kids stood. The bigger one, a dark-haired boy about nine or ten, had his arms crossed. He nodded to a faded, hand-painted sign on the side of the tree house. "Can't you read?"

Before finishing her descent, Renee glanced at the scrawled words she'd disregarded yesterday: **No Grils Allowed.**

Great. Now she was getting evicted. If she had a quarter for every time that had happened to her, she wouldn't be living in a stupid tree.

Once on the ground, she turned to face them. "Is this your fort?"

"Yeah." The smaller boy, a younger kid with light brown hair, used his finger to push his glasses along the bridge of his freckled nose before looking her up and down. "Who are you?"

"My name's Renee." She offered him a smile. No need to make any enemies. In her old neighborhood, some of the kids could be really mean. "I was just checking this place out. It's pretty cool—for a tree house."

"Yeah, it is," the smaller boy said. "That's what we thought when we found it."

"So you didn't build it?"

"Nope. But it's ours. And it's got our stuff in it."

Well, it had her stuff in it, too.

"You know," she said, "I've been wanting to find a fort like this for a long time. Would you guys mind if I used it for a few days?"

"Heck, yeah, we'd mind." The older boy, his thick dark hair in need of a trim, chuffed. "What good is a secret fort if people know where it is and can use it whenever they want to?"

"Besides," the smaller boy added, "you're a girl."

There was that. She supposed she could figure out something else to do, find somewhere else to spend the nights until she got a job, but there was still the money issue. "What if I paid you to let me use it for a few days?"

"You mean you want to *rent* it from us?" the younger boy asked. "With *real* money?"

She nodded. "I guess you could say that. I'll give you five dollars if you let me . . . uh . . ." No need to tell them she was actually going to live in it. ". . . if you let me use it and keep my stuff in it for a while."

The younger boy looked to the older boy for direction, his expression hopeful. "We could buy that kite we saw down at that store that sells beach stuff, Danny."

"Not with five dollars. It's not enough."

What was this? A major real estate negotiation? Renee crossed her arms and shifted her weight to one foot. No way was she going to pay them more than that. Not when she might luck out and find a real place to stay in the next day or two.

They seemed to be at an impasse, so she came up with an idea that might please them all. "How about a dollar a day?" If she found a place soon, she'd spend even less than the five bucks she'd originally offered them.

"Hey, we could make thirty dollars if she used it for a month," the younger boy said.

Renee grimaced at the thought. She didn't even want to think about living in a tree house that long. "But here's the thing," she said, tossing out a stipulation. "You can't tell anyone that I'm using it. If you do, the deal is off."

The boys looked at each other. The older one—Danny—shrugged at his friend before nodding in agreement.

She kind of liked negotiating with them and wondered how far she could push. "You know, I'd throw in an extra fifty cents each day if the place was furnished."

The younger boy seemed to be doing the math, while Danny narrowed his eyes. "What do you mean by *furnished*?"

"Well, for one thing, I could use a blanket and pillow in case I ever need to . . . you know, take a nap or rest." Again she thought about what might happen if they told anyone about this. "But like I said, if you can't keep a secret . . ." She let the threat hang between them.

"No one is better at keeping their mouths shut than us," Danny said. "Me and Tommy took a blood oath when we found this place. And if one of us breaks it, we'll die."

Renee figured it was in her best interest to let them believe in the dire consequences of breaking a blood oath, so she held her tongue.

Finally, the younger boy seemed to shake off the threat of death and spoke up. "Hey, you know what? My mom has a whole bunch of junk in our attic that we don't ever use. She'll never know it's even gone."

"What else do you need beside a blanket and a pillow?" Danny asked.

Renee bit back what she really wanted, like a front door with a deadbolt lock and a bathroom with warm running water, instead figuring she'd better take what she could get. "I'd like whatever else you can find that would make this place comfortable." Then she had an Oh-wow! moment.

She had no idea why she hadn't thought of it first. "You know, a flashlight and some extra batteries would be great."

"All right." Danny held out a hand for her to shake. When she took it, and the deal was cinched, he turned his palm up. "Where's the money? You'll have to pay us first."

Apparently, the two little wheeler-dealers didn't trust her. But hey. She couldn't really blame them. Like her, they'd probably been burned before.

"You'll never find anyone more honest than me," she told them. She just hoped she could say the same thing about them when she was ready to move on.

She reached into her pocket and withdrew a dollar bill and two quarters.

She hoped her money wouldn't run out before she landed a job and found a real place to live.

If it did, she and the baby would be in a real fix.

Chapter 3

As Craig dressed for his meeting at Parkside Community Church, he looked through the open bathroom door and scanned the Delacourts' den, where he'd slept the night before.

He'd been too tired to do anything other than give the room a cursory glance last night. But this morning, when he woke to the sunlight filtering through the cracks in the shutter, he took a better look at his surroundings and realized just how impressive the display of memorabilia actually was.

There were framed shirts and photographs hanging on the walls, as well as autographed balls—one by Hank Aaron and another by Babe Ruth—lining a polished oak bookshelf.

"I hope you like baseball," Cassandra had said.

Craig did. Or, rather, he used to. Ever since his injury, he'd been hard-pressed to even watch a game.

A knock sounded lightly at the door.

"Pastor Craig?" Cassandra asked.

"Yes?"

"Breakfast is ready."

"Thank you. I'll be right out." He tucked the tails of his pale blue dress shirt into his black slacks, then buckled and adjusted his belt. He also put on a tie, something he would have to get used to wearing.

Before leaving the bathroom, he took one last look in the mirror, making sure that, other than the piece of toilet paper he'd stuck to his chin to stop the bleeding of a razor cut, he would be putting his best foot forward today.

His sports jacket was still hanging in the den closet, so he grabbed it and slipped it on. As he made his way to the door that led to the hall, he took time to make one last perusal of several old black-and-white photos, each matted and professionally framed, that were hanging on the wall. One picture in particular caught his eye, a shot of Lou Gehrig standing before a microphone at Yankee Stadium, giving his farewell speech.

As a kid, Craig had watched Gary Cooper's portrayal of the baseball great in *Pride of the Yankees* over and over again. He could recite the poignant words by heart.

"People all say I've had a bad break," Cooper as Lou Gehrig had told the solemn crowd back then. "Yet today I consider myself the luckiest man on the face of the earth."

Shoving aside thoughts about bad breaks and sad endings, Craig let himself out of the room he'd slept in and made his way to the living room. There Daniel Delacourt, one of the partners at a local law firm, sat in a wingback chair, reading the newspaper.

Upon hearing Craig's footsteps, Daniel folded the paper, set it aside, and stood. "Good morning, Pastor. How'd you sleep?"

"Great. Thanks."

"How about some breakfast?"

"Sounds good."

As Daniel led the way to a modern kitchen with black granite counters and stainless steel appliances, he said, "My wife and I received some good news this morning. Our daughter, Shana, called to announce her engagement. She'll be getting married in late summer."

Cassandra, who was dressed in a linen pantsuit, stood beside a trendy-style coffee pot. She looked up and smiled, her green eyes bright and expressive, her makeup highlighting the best of her features. "You can't imagine how delighted we are. The young man is Brad Rensfield, and his parents are wonderful people."

"Congratulations," Craig said.

"Coffee?" Cassandra reached for a white mug before Craig was actually able to utter a Yes, please.

"Cream?" she asked. "Sugar?"

"Just black."

Cassandra handed him a cup of the fresh morning brew. "I have muffins, too. Bran, blueberry, and banana nut."

"Thank you. I'll have the blueberry."

Cassandra nodded, then pulled a small plate from the cupboard.

"The Rensfields own a chain of department stores," she added, as she removed a muffin from the platter, put it on a small plate, and handed it to Craig. "So it's nice to know that Shana won't have any financial worries." Then she addressed her husband. "I think I'd better talk to the special-events coordinator at the country club this morning. An outdoor ceremony will be nice in August. I just hope they aren't completely booked."

"Don't forget about Kristy," Daniel said. "Shana insisted that she be involved with the planning."

Cassandra frowned, creating a furrow that marred her forehead. "I realize that. But there are a lot of things I don't need help with. And certainly not her help."

Daniel took a seat next to Craig. "Shana was adamant about not leaving Kristy out."

Cassandra sighed. "I never have understood that friendship."

Craig peeled the paper off the bottom of his muffin, wondering if he should be privy to the conversation and wishing he knew how to politely excuse himself. But before he could figure out a way to graciously do that or to change the subject, Daniel turned to him, drawing him in even further. "Shana and Kristy have always been close. In fact, when Shana had leukemia, Kristy used to come by every day to visit."

Cassandra handed her husband a cup of coffee, then poured one for herself.

"You have no idea how much my wife and I appreciated that," Daniel added.

Cassandra removed a quart-size carton of nonfat milk from the refrigerator, a huge built-in model that was fully stocked. She added a dab to her coffee, then put it away. "Her kindness came as a big surprise, though."

Craig couldn't refrain from asking why.

"The poor child had been living on the streets before moving in with her grandmother." Cassandra carried her cup and muffin plate to the table, then took a seat across from Craig. "I would have expected her to be . . . Well hardened, I suppose. More self-centered."

Daniel slowly shook his head and clicked his tongue. "I can't believe she's the same girl. Back then Kristy had been a gangly child with wild, leprechaun hair, big green eyes, and a chip-toothed grin. The first time she showed up at the front door, she was almost afraid to come inside the house. But I have to give her credit. She came every afternoon to visit Shana, bringing homework, notes from friends, and a bit of sunshine that lifted a worried father's spirits, too."

Cassandra stirred her coffee slowly, then tapped the spoon lightly on the rim of the china cup. "I have to admit she was truly a godsend back then."

Unable to steer clear of a situation he probably ought to tiptoe around, Craig asked, "So what changed?"

"Kristy was a year older than most of the girls in her class, probably because of a transient lifestyle and getting a late start in school. And while she was somewhat homely and gangly, she developed early. She grew into those long legs and tamed her hair." Cassandra paused, as though wondering how to best finish her thoughts when talking to a minister.

But Craig got the picture. The ugly little redheaded duckling had morphed into a leggy, auburn-haired swan.

"By the time she hit high school," Daniel added, "the boys had taken a real shine to her."

Cassandra crossed her arms, wrinkling the crisply-pressed blouse she wore. "Kristy was a wild thing, just like her mother. And she got pregnant during her junior year. God only knows who fathered her baby, and it completely ruined her only chance to make something out of her life."

"Cassie," Daniel said, "I'll admit I wasn't happy about that friendship from the get-go, but the two girls have an unexpected closeness."

"Yes, I realize that. But they had very little in common back then."

Daniel pushed his chair away from the table and got to his feet. After walking to the pantry and pulling out a to-go cup, he transferred his coffee and left his mug in the sink.

"Nevertheless," he said to his wife, "I plan to honor their friendship. Those bouts of chemo used to knock Shana for a loop, yet Kristy never blinked an eye about it. She read to her when she was too tired or too nauseous to play. And she never once mentioned the hair loss. That's something I'll never forget."

"Neither will I, sweetheart." Cassandra tore a piece from the top of her bran muffin. "But they still don't have anything in common. And even less so now that Kristy is waiting tables at Paddy's Pub and Shana is working toward a master's degree."

"But they've still maintained a friendship," Daniel said.

"Yes, honey. I know. And of all the people in Fairbrook . . ." Cassandra's words faded, and she focused on the muffin she was nibbling at piece by piece.

"Shana has pulled away from a lot of people," Daniel said to Craig. "Even her mom and me, although I suppose that's to be expected."

"She's still close to *you*," Cassandra told her husband.

Silence followed, leaving Craig to wonder if there was trouble in paradise.

Things aren't always what they seem, Jesse had told him.

But Craig shook it off. The last thing he needed to do was place too much stock in the ramblings of a homeless man.

Besides, he had his own problems to deal with.

Kristy had the early shift today, and since the car was on the blink and she would have to take the bus to work, she wanted to give herself some extra time.

"Honey?" Gram called out.

"Yes?" Kristy made her way to Gram's room, where antique furnishings and crocheted doilies couldn't mask the hospital bed that lurked near the window.

"Are you leaving for work now?" the elderly woman asked.

"I'll be going soon." Kristy approached the adjustable bed that made lifting the partially paralyzed woman easier. As she leaned to place a kiss on Gram's cheek, she caught a whiff of gardenia mingled with Bengay.

"What time is it?" Gram turned her head toward the clock on the nightstand, revealing the curls crushed and tangled by repeated contact with the pillow. Gray roots she used to hide with the help of Lady Clairol and frequent visits to the beauty shop on First Avenue tugged at Kristy's heart.

"Nearly ten o'clock," Kristy answered, even though the woman had looked for herself.

Gram took a deep breath, then let out a brittle, bone-weary sigh.

Eager to give her grandma something to look forward to, Kristy said, "It looks like we'll need to color your hair again. Why don't we get you all prettied up tomorrow? I can give you a manicure and a pedicure, too."

Gram rolled her tired eyes. "I can't see any reason to fuss about my looks. I don't go out. And other than Pastor George, I don't get many visitors."

"I have a feeling it's because you run them off."

Gram furrowed her wrinkled brow. "What do you mean, I run them off?"

"Well, it's not as though you tell them to leave or throw bedpans and pill bottles at them. But people who love and care about you have a difficult time when you talk about wanting to die and discuss the funeral arrangements you've already made."

"Why shouldn't I? I'm practically dead already. The Good Lord just wants to punish me and keep me here on earth, useless and unproductive. A burden. For goodness sake, I can't paint. I can't work in the garden. I can't even look after Jason while you work."

"I doubt God would punish a good, kindhearted woman who'd once been active in church and in the community."

If He was punishing anyone, it had to be Kristy.

Each time she saw Gram lying in that bed, imprisoned in a body that was failing, she was reminded of her negligence.

If she'd been home the night her grandmother suffered the first and most devastating stroke, instead of at that party at the Rensfields' estate, she might have called the paramedics and gotten help for Gram sooner. But Kristy hadn't snuck in until the wee hours of the morning. And her grandmother had spent most of the night on the living room floor.

The memory was as clear today as it had been when she'd opened the door and found Gram lying on the drab, olive-green carpet, unable to move, unable to speak. The distorted mouth. That cold, glassy stare.

Oh, God, she pleaded again. *Make it go away, will you?*

But the scene never faded, the memory never went away. And she'd have to deal with the guilt for the rest of her life.

Still, she wished Gram would just accept the reality they all had to live with. Didn't she realize that Kristy was emotionally pedaling as fast as she could?

She did the best she could to shake off the negativity and the resentment that crept in whenever she let down her guard.

"You're too young to have to be burdened by me," Gram said.

"Don't even go there. When my mom ran off, you stepped in. And from that day on, my life changed dramatically. You have no idea what it was like, begging for handouts with her at intersections, crying myself to sleep in homeless shelters."

"It was the drugs that made your mother that way. I'm sorry that she failed you."

So was Kristy, although she couldn't—no, make that *wouldn't*—blame drugs for it. And her mom's abandonment still hurt, if she let it.

"But *you* didn't fail me," she told Gram.

And that was a fact.

In her grandmother's care, Kristy had gotten a room of her own, three home-cooked meals a day and a magical cookie jar that seemed to always stay filled. And even though Gram had been nearly sixty, she'd been a loving guardian who'd jumped right in with parents half her age. There wasn't a field trip that she hadn't driven on, a school program she hadn't attended. A PTA meeting that she'd missed.

And how had Kristy paid her back?

By being as wild as her mother had no doubt been. But those days of foolish, teenage rebellion were over. Kristy would take care of her grandmother, just the way Gram had always taken care of her.

And she wouldn't complain—ever—although that didn't mean she liked listening to death wishes.

She mustered a smile and tried to change the subject. "Hey, I forgot to tell you. Shana Delacourt is going to get married in August. To Brad Rensfield."

Gram managed a smile—something Kristy rarely seemed to see these days. "The Delacourts ought to be ecstatic. The Rensfield boy is as rich as old fury and a fine catch."

Without thinking, Kristy muttered, "I'm not so sure about that."

"What do you mean?"

Kristy hadn't meant to broach her thoughts about that with anyone, let alone her grandmother. "I really didn't mean anything by that comment. It's just that he's a bit spoiled. And he's sowed so many wild oats that his folks ought to invest in a granary."

"Oh, well. Boys will be boys. Now that he's grown up, he's probably gotten that tomfoolery out of his system."

Kristy sure hoped so.

If anyone deserved to be happy, it was Shana.

Gram shifted in bed, undoubtedly trying to find a comfortable spot, and grimaced.

Kristy took her frail, liver-spotted hand and gave it a gentle squeeze. "Do you need to go to the bathroom?"

"No, not yet." The old woman blew out another feeble breath. "I wish that you didn't have to ask, that I didn't need help. I'm sorry for being so much trouble."

Kristy pushed the button that lifted the head of the bed, then helped her grandmother sit up a bit. "I love you. And you're no trouble."

"Oh, for crying out loud, Kristy. Look at me. I'm worthless like this. Why couldn't I have just died that night?"

"You're the one with all the faith, Gram. Maybe God has a reason to keep you here."

"Humph. And just what would that be?"

"You'll have to ask Him," Kristy said, only too glad to pass the buck on spiritual and philosophical issues and change the subject.

When Gram humphed again, Kristy asked, "Do you think we have enough time to pull off an August wedding?"

Gram paused, as though weighing the benefits of stewing in self-pity or answering Kristy's question. "Mildred Walker's granddaughter started planning her wedding more than a year in advance."

"That's the kind of time frame I was thinking of. But Shana's determined to get married this summer. And since she's in Australia and can't do much in preparation, she asked me to help." Kristy drew open the drapes to let in a bit of sunlight. "I suppose I'll have to hustle, but I don't mind."

"I remember my own wedding day," Gram said, her faded gaze wistful. "My sister Grace did most of the work. And she even baked the cake."

"Well, I'm not sure what I'm getting myself into. Shana asked me to help with the planning, but I have a feeling I'm going to butt heads with her mom." And that wasn't something she was looking forward to, especially when the woman had never thought Kristy was good enough to be her daughter's friend.

Of course, it wasn't as though she'd ever been mean. She just had a way about her that shouted out her objections loud and clear.

"Cassandra Delacourt can be a bit fussy, but she's got a good heart. And she's done a lot of charity work over the years. In fact, Pastor George mentioned that she planned a fashion show last fall, and the proceeds went to fund the soup kitchen."

Kristy had heard that. And she suspected the money was helpful. But she couldn't imagine Cassandra donating her time at the kitchen.

Of course, who was Kristy to criticize? She didn't have the time or the means to support the kitchen at all.

And attend a fashion show at fifty dollars a head?

In her dreams.

The doorbell rang, and Kristy stepped away from the bed. "That's probably Barb. I'd better let her in."

Barbara Crenshaw, the licensed vocational nurse, had been a godsend, especially since she looked after both Gram and Jason while Kristy worked, eliminating the additional cost of daycare.

"Can't Jason get the door?" Gram asked.

"He went out to play with Danny and Tommy," Kristy said, as she turned to leave the room.

"Well," Gram said, "if I don't see you before you leave, have a good day."

Kristy stopped and glanced over her shoulder. "You, too."

The look in Gram's eyes said that a "good day" wasn't likely.

If Kristy could have conjured up an upbeat response, she would have. But if truth be told, she wasn't expecting a good day, either.

Chapter 4

Renee sat on a swing at the playground in the park, the toes of her sandals shoved into the sand.

She gripped the chains, leaned back and looked at the sky, trying to gauge the position of the sun. It was late morning; she knew that for sure.

Since she had no way of knowing when it was eleven o'clock, she decided to sit in the park and wait until she saw people heading toward the church across the street.

That was another thing she should have asked the boys to provide—an alarm clock so she could tell time. What if she had a job interview or someplace else to go to?

Her stomach growled, and she placed a hand on the bump where her baby grew, rubbing it gently. "I'll get you something to eat as soon as I can."

She could, she supposed, just hang out in front of the church until the soup kitchen doors opened, but she didn't want to draw any more attention to herself than necessary. All she needed was for some do-gooder to turn her in to social services, thinking they were looking out for her best interests.

"Having fun?" a man asked.

She glanced to the edge of the playground, where Jesse, the hippie guy, stood. He was holding a small, brown paper bag in one hand.

He looked pretty much the same as he did yesterday, when he suggested she come to Fairbrook. He still wore the same baggy green shirt, the same faded jeans—she could tell by the frayed hole in the knee.

It seemed safe to guess that he was homeless and didn't have access to a shower.

At least she'd managed to clean up this morning and change her clothes. But she wouldn't hold that against him. She could end up in that same situation if she wasn't careful.

"Hey," she said. "I see you made it."

He nodded. "I got in last night. So what do you think of the place so far?"

"It's okay." She tightened her grip on the chains, pushed back with her feet, and set herself in motion. "I'll feel better when I get a job, though."

"Something tells me you'd be better off in school."

She stopped pumping, felt the swing slow, then kicked again—determined to blow off the remark as ridiculous. "Why would you say that?"

"You look pretty young to me."

"Well," she said, pumping for all she was worth, "just so you know, youngness runs in my family."

"Oh, yeah?"

"My second cousin is going to turn fifty on her next birthday, and she looks like she could be my sister."

"You don't say." Jesse made his way toward the swing set. "That's unbelievable."

Actually, it ought to be, since it was a flat-out lie. Mary Ellen had lived a pretty rough life. And all those cigarettes she'd smoked and the booze she'd drank hadn't helped. With that mousy gray hair and all those wrinkles around her eyes and mouth, most people thought she was way older than she really was.

The dishonesty tweaked Renee's conscience, but she continued her story. "I know, but it's cool, huh?"

She hated liars, mostly because she hated it when people lied to her. But she couldn't risk having anyone learn the truth. What if someone found out she was a pregnant minor living in a tree?

Of course, Jesse the hippie guy didn't appear to be a run-of-the-mill do-gooder, so maybe she didn't need to worry about it.

But for safe measure, she added, "We've got good genes in our family."

Jesse, who now stood only feet away from her, lifted his sack. "Have you had breakfast yet?"

"Yes," she said, stretching the truth. "I had oatmeal."

Hey, everyone knew granola bars were made out of oats.

Jesse opened the brown sack he had, reached inside, and pulled out an apple. He handed it to her. "Here, then. Have a snack."

Cool. She slowed the swing to a stop, then took the fruit from him, looked it over, and rubbed it on her shirt, like she was trying to shine it. "Thanks. I love apples."

Actually, she wasn't all that big on them. And if given the choice, she preferred the tart, green ones. But her stomach was beginning to gnaw on itself, and she figured the baby could use the vitamins and nourishment.

She tried to be ladylike when she took the first bite, but it was so juicy, and she was so hungry, that she was afraid she would end up wolfing it down.

A couple of bites into it, she tried to get the focus off her. "Have you had any luck finding a job?"

"I'm not worried about it. Work has a way of finding me. How about you?"

"Not yet. I'm going to stop by the soup kitchen, then I'll start job hunting. Hopefully, I'll get one soon."

"Do you have a place to stay?" he asked.

Her mouth was full of apple, so she nodded. And when she'd finished chewing, she said, "I'm renting a room. It's upstairs and has a great view."

"It's always a relief to know where you're going to sleep each night."

She nodded. He had that right.

"Do you know what time it is?" she asked.

"Close to eleven, I think."

Good. She figured he was waiting for the doors to open, too. "Are you going to the soup kitchen?"

"Not right away." He placed a hand over his eyes, shading them from the sun, then glanced off in the distance. "I've got something to do first. I'll probably drop in before they close at two."

She wanted to ask what he was going to do, but she figured it wasn't any of her business. It's not like she and Jesse were friends.

A wistful shadow crept over her.

She missed Megan and Danica, the friends she'd made in San Diego. Friends she'd had to give up when Mary Ellen had kicked her out.

For a minute, she wanted to blame Mary Ellen for screwing up her life. But that wasn't true.

She'd done that all by herself.

At eleven o'clock, Craig sat inside the cozy, book-lined library of the Parkside Community Church. He'd just met with the board of elders and the senior pastor, George Rawlings, a short, stocky man in his late fifties.

The group had seemed pleasant enough, although a bit on the stuffy side. And, overall, the meeting had gone as well as could be expected.

Just moments ago, one of the elders announced he had a luncheon date, and the board had quickly dispersed, each one going his own way.

The only two left were the pastors.

"You came highly recommended," George said. "And the fact that you're related to Wesley Houston is a real plus. You've got some big shoes to fill."

"Yes, sir. I know that."

Before assuming leadership of Desert Fellowship, a large and growing congregation in the Phoenix area, Craig's granddad had written a book about his experiences as a missionary, which had become required reading in seminaries all over the country.

"You'll probably find that Parkside Community Church is much smaller and less dynamic than you're used to," George said, "but we're growing and reaching out to the community. We have a lot to be proud of."

"I'm sure you do." Craig offered the man a smile. He was determined to make the best of his new position in Fairbrook, even though he'd been hoping to get a bigger, more prestigious assignment, one that would have provided him a better opportunity to make a difference in people's lives. At least, that seemed like a good way to validate his ministry.

"You'll be heading our youth group," George said, "as well as our home visitation to shut-ins. And, of course, whenever I'm out of town or unavailable, you'll give the sermons and cover for me."

Unfortunately, being a bench warmer had never held much appeal. But win or lose, Craig had always been a good sport. So he put on his best hey-it's-just-a-game smile, nodded at George, and tried to conjure the proper enthusiasm for the job.

"Why don't you let me give you a tour of our church buildings," George said.

"Thanks. I'd appreciate that."

The senior pastor led Craig out of the library and past the official church office, where they'd met earlier. Then he pointed out his private study, with its own wall-to-wall bookshelves and polished oak desk.

It was small, Craig noted, but impressive.

Two doors down, George stopped at a room that was smaller yet. "And this will be your office. We've ordered a desk, but it hasn't arrived yet. I'm afraid you'll have to make do until then."

"No problem."

The house, which had been promised as part of Craig's salary package, wasn't ready for him to use either, which made him wonder if Parkside Community needed an associate minister as badly as the bishop seemed to think they did.

Again he couldn't help but think there'd been some kind of mistake, maybe even on his own part, because in spite of telling his family that he'd been called to the ministry, he hadn't heard a peep.

Their next stop was the sanctuary, with its stained glass windows, padded wooden pews, and the hand-carved altar. "That's the original pulpit," George said.

"How long ago was the church built?"

"Actually, it used to be located in Encinitas. At the turn of the last century, it was divided into pieces and brought to Fairbrook by horse and wagon."

"No kidding?" Craig studied both the structure and the interior of the sanctuary a little closer, trying to get a feel for the history.

"Come with me," George said. "I'll show you the fellowship hall."

Craig followed him to a large room, where about fifteen to twenty women had gathered to sew.

"They're stitching quilts together," George said from the doorway. "When they're finished, we'll raffle them off at the community bazaar in July. The proceeds will help fund the soup kitchen."

After introducing Craig to the ladies, each of whom smiled warmly, George motioned for him to head out the door first. Then he followed him outside.

"We also offer the fellowship hall for community events," George said. "In fact, the Boy Scouts will be meeting here this afternoon. And there's an A.A. meeting tonight."

Craig was glad to know that the church reached out to others who weren't members of the congregation.

"Come on," George said, "let me show you the grounds."

Once outside, Craig scanned the property, noting the numerous trees that provided shade and a retreat-like setting.

George pointed across the street. "That's Mulberry Park. Each December we host a community event called Christmas Under the Stars. It's always a huge hit. We provide hot cocoa, tea, coffee, and homemade cookies and other goodies. We sing carols, and there's a reading of the Christmas story. Next year, we plan to add a live nativity scene."

"How many people attend?" Craig asked.

"Hundreds. And we seem to get more and more each year."

"Sounds fun."

"It is. And during vacation Bible school in the summer, we take the kids over to the playground and have outdoor activities on the lawn. There's also a men's softball league, which reminds me. Are you interested in playing?"

"We'll see." Craig offered a smile, but the fact was, he'd rather play another kind of game—fast ball, hard hitting, competitive. College level or beyond . . .

"Last but not least," George said, "I'll take you to the soup kitchen, which is another thing you'll be in charge of. I'd like to introduce you to the Randolphs."

Craig followed George to a modular building that had been placed at the edge of the parking lot.

"The kitchen has an advisory board," George said, "which includes Dawn and Joe Randolph, the couple who are in charge of the day-to-day operations. Dawn and Joe are a real blessing. I don't know what we'd do without them."

George opened the door, then waited for Craig to step into the room, where rectangular tables stretched end to end. Only a few of the chairs were occupied.

"We serve meals between eleven and two," George said, "so people will be coming and going until then."

A tall man in his late forties, who'd just walked out of the back room, grinned when he spotted George, and strode toward them. He wore a navy blue T-shirt with white block letters that said Fairbrook Fire Department.

"Joe," George said. "Let me introduce you to Craig Houston. He's the new associate minister and will be working with you and Dawn."

When the big man reached out, Craig shook his hand. "It's nice to meet you, Joe."

"Likewise. My wife and I are looking forward to working with you. I hope you'll be an active part of the soup kitchen."

"I'm sure I will be," Craig said.

"Joe is a paramedic with the fire department," George added, "and whenever he's off duty, he helps out. But Dawn is here every day."

"Speaking of Dawn," Joe said, "she's been eager to meet you. If you'll excuse me, I'll let her know you're here."

"Before you do," George said, "how are things going?"

Joe crossed his arms and scanned the room. "It's business as usual. The big rush usually comes around one."

"Did that electrical short ever get fixed?" George asked.

"Yes, but now we've got another problem." Joe placed a hand on the senior pastor's shoulder. "I heard a rumor that there's a group of homeowners planning to attend the city council meeting next Tuesday night. They'd like our soup kitchen moved."

"Where to?"

"It doesn't seem to matter, just as long as it's outside city limits."

"What good will that do? Most of the people we're trying to feed don't have transportation or the means to drive back and forth across town each day."

"Apparently, there's a group that's complaining about the bad element we draw to the church. And since we're so close to the park, a place where families with small children often gather, they're worried about safety issues."

George shook his head and sighed. "Sometimes we even feed entire families. The parents, whether single or married, are often between jobs or on temporary disability. They can bring their kids here for a warm, nutritious meal. And afterward, they're able to take them to the playground for a while, which is what Dawn usually suggests. That way, for a couple of hours, they get a chance to enjoy themselves and forget their troubles."

"I tried to explain that to Ralph Gleason when he complained about the bad element," Joe said. "But some people can get awfully hardheaded when they think they're right."

George's gaze locked on Craig's. "I suppose you'd better plan to be at that meeting and represent the church. Hopefully, Joe and Dawn can go with you. But if not, they can fill you in on some of the politics we'll have to face."

Craig nodded, realizing his job just got a bit more important.

To be honest, he didn't mind overseeing the soup kitchen. Whenever his parents had taken him to visit his grandfather in India, he'd seen how poor some of those people had been, how helpful the church had been in providing for more than their spiritual needs.

He'd only been six on his first visit, so it had been awkward for him at first, trying to connect with kids who had been raised in a different culture. But he'd learned that they had a lot in common at playtime.

Not that this was the same thing, but it did give him an opportunity to practice some of what he'd learned in his missiology classes.

"How's Dawn holding up?" George asked Joe.

"She's doing okay. Losing her mother unexpectedly was tough, but she's got a lot of faith."

"I know," George said. "It seems as though she's had more than her share of disappointments over the years."

As the two men chatted, Craig found himself surveying the

room, noting the various people who'd gathered to eat. Two elderly women sat nearest him. He wondered if they were homeless, or if they were just living on a limited budget.

Either way, he could see that the church-sponsored meals could certainly help senior citizens stretch their social security checks.

He made a mental note to keep that in mind when he addressed the city council.

A couple of men, one of whom wore a Veterans of Foreign Wars cap, sat a few tables away. He'd gotten rather animated as he talked to the men next to him.

One young woman sat alone. She was bent over her plate, her long, stringy hair falling forward and hiding much of her face. Her elbows were on the table, and her arms were circled around her plate, as though she was trying to protect her meal, as though someone might snatch it away before she was finished eating.

He watched for a while, as she practically shoveled in her food.

Meatloaf and baked potatoes, he noted. Green beans. A scoop of . . . peach cobbler? It all looked pretty tasty, and he figured they had Dawn Randolph to thank for that.

"We'll need to make another run to Costco," Joe told George. "We're running out of paper plates again."

Craig figured he probably ought to pay attention to the conversation, yet he found himself drawn to the people in the room.

"Do you mind if I spend some time introducing myself to our guests?" he asked the senior minister.

"Not at all. That's a very good idea. Go right ahead."

Craig made his way to the gray-haired gentleman with the VFW cap. Ever since he'd lost his father in Operation Desert Storm and the local American Legion had reached out to him and his mom, he'd held a soft spot for veterans.

Each Memorial Day, they used to hold a special event for kids who'd lost a parent in the war. And while it was tough being fatherless, he'd appreciated the legionaries who'd been so understanding, so supportive of his mom.

"Do you guys mind if I interrupt you for a minute?" Craig asked the three men.

The tall, lanky fellow with the VFW cap smiled. "Not at all. Have a seat."

Craig sat next to a short, heavy set man wearing a pair of blue coveralls. "My name is Craig Houston, and I'm the new associate minister here. I don't mean to bother you, but I wanted to tell you that I appreciate your service to our country."

They seemed to light up at his comment, and the one wearing the cap stuck out his hand to shake. "I'm Ward O'Sullivan. A veteran of Korea."

Ward went on to introduce his buddies, Jacob Porter, a marine who'd fought in Vietnam, and Harold Schlictning, a medic who'd served in Europe during World War II.

They talked a few minutes, then Craig excused himself and strode toward the two elderly women who were seated together. When they looked up, he introduced himself.

Kathryn Ellings shared that she was on a fixed income, and that the soup kitchen had been a real blessing to her. Her friend, Ellie Rucker, whose hair was matted in back as if she hadn't used a comb in a while, didn't say much.

Craig chatted with them for a moment, then excused himself to speak to the only one he had yet to meet—a teenager, he suspected. But by the time he started toward her, she'd cleaned her paper plate and was carrying it to the trash can.

He watched as she scanned the buffet line, where a woman wearing a red plaid apron had just added an insulated carafe next to a pitcher of lemonade.

"There's more coffee," the woman announced, before returning to the kitchen.

The girl, who'd been standing next to the buffet line, snatched a couple of rolls and shoved them under the ribbed hem of her sweat shirt, causing her belly to pooch out.

Stocking up for dinner? he wondered.

When she turned toward him, her hands holding the hem of her bulky shirt against her stomach to hold the bread inside, he averted his eyes so she wouldn't know that he'd seen what she'd done.

As she drew closer, he allowed himself to look at her and smile. "Thanks for coming."

She nibbled on her bottom lip, as though her conscience might be at some sort of impasse, then returned his smile. "Thanks for having me."

"I'm Pastor Craig," he added. "And you're . . . ?"

"Renee Delaney."

He didn't even consider offering a handshake. No need to embarrass her if those rolls fell out. Instead, he said, "It's nice to meet you. I hope to see you back here again sometime. Maybe tomorrow?"

"Yeah, maybe. The food was really good, so you probably will. Unless I get a job."

"You're looking for work?" he asked.

"Yeah. I can do just about anything. So if you know anyone who's hiring . . . ?"

If Craig had a home of his own, if he'd managed to stockpile a couple of paychecks already, he'd offer her some kind of employment, even if it was just to mow the yard or wash windows.

"I'll keep you in mind," he said. "Do you have a phone number? In case I need to get ahold of you?"

She bit her bottom lip again. "No, not yet. I just moved here."

"Me, too." He offered her another smile.

Her feet seemed to do a little shuffle, and she nodded toward the door. "Well, I guess I'd better go. I'll see ya around."

"Okay." He watched as she strode out of the soup kitchen, her head up, yet her shoulders slumped.

Poor kid.

"Pastor?"

Craig turned to see George heading toward him. He had a woman with him, the middle-aged brunette who was wearing the red plaid apron.

"This is Dawn Randolph," George said. "Our soup kitchen would have shut down months ago if she hadn't single-handedly stepped in and volunteered to do all the grocery shopping and cooking."

Dawn had a scatter of freckles across her nose, making her look younger than she probably was. As she reached out to greet Craig, a smile lit her brown eyes. "It's nice to meet you."

"I guess we'll be working together," he said.

"That's what I heard. I'm looking forward to having your help."

"Your husband mentioned that there's a group of people trying to get the church to move the kitchen out of town," he said.

She tucked a curly strand of hair behind her ear. "Sometimes, when the problems in society are hidden, people don't see the need to fix them."

"Do you get a lot of homeless?" He wondered about Jesse, the man he'd met last night. Did he know there was a place he could get a hot meal each day?

"Yes, we do. And we try to do whatever we can to help them get back on their feet. The Ladies Aid has been gathering secondhand clothing. And when they find something that would be suitable for a job interview, like a suit and a matching shirt and tie, they have them dry-cleaned or one of the group launders and presses them. Then they place a coordinated ensemble in a plastic garment bag."

"That's a great idea."

"We also provide the homeless with the church's address and a phone number with voice mail in case they need to fill out a job application."

Craig thought of the young woman who'd just walked out.

"There was a girl here earlier," he said. "A young woman, I guess. She's looking for work, but doesn't have a phone number. If I'd known that, I would have passed the information along."

"You mean the little blonde with straggly hair?" Dawn asked.

"You noticed her?"

"I notice all of them, especially the young ones."

"How old do you think she was?" Craig asked.

"It's hard to say. Sixteen maybe?"

"That's what I thought. I wonder where her parents are."

"Who knows? Hopefully, working. I try to be friendly and welcoming at first. I hate coming on too strong. Some people aren't happy about needing charity, so I take a little time to get to know them. But my heart always goes out to the kids."

Craig could understand that.

"I plan to get to know her better next time," Dawn said. "That is, assuming she comes back."

"She'll be back. I have a feeling she isn't used to getting regular meals."

"For the most part, the majority of those we help are down-and-out adults. Some of our regulars are senior citizens trying to make ends meet during the last days of the month before their social security checks arrive. And then we get some people who are homeless and will probably stay that way for various reasons."

"Drugs and alcoholism?" he asked.

"That certainly is a problem for some of them. And unless they're willing to get help, it's difficult to force it on them." She crossed her arms and sighed. "I'm afraid there are a few who will never get back on their feet. But that doesn't make them any less hungry."

"Does it ever get to you?" he asked. "Working with people who don't always want to be helped?"

"Yes, but a lot of the people who utilize the soup kitchen

just need a foot up. A boost. A little love and compassion."
Dawn slipped her hands into the pockets of the apron she
wore. "It's really tough when I see families that have been up-
rooted. I try to do whatever I can to help. In the evenings at
home, when Joe is on duty, I make stuffed animals and rag
dolls. I keep them in a box in the kitchen, then pass them out
to the occasional children who stop in for a meal with their
parents."

"Do you have any success stories?" he asked, thinking he
might want a few of those to relate during that city council
meeting.

"Quite a few of them, actually. And that helps us keep our
perspective."

The elderly women, who'd picked up after themselves,
stopped by to say hello to Dawn.

"I loved that meatloaf," Kathryn said. "It tasted almost as
good as my mother used to make."

Dawn smiled, yet her eyes grew watery. "It was my mom's
recipe, and today was her birthday. So I fixed it in her memory. I'm glad you liked it."

The other woman, the one whose hair was matted in back,
patted Dawn's upper arm. "No baby yet?"

"I'm afraid not, Ellie."

"Well, I'm still praying for you."

Dawn offered the woman a warm but wistful smile. "Thanks.
Prayers are always appreciated. But Joe and I have resigned
ourselves to not having children."

"That's too bad," Ellie said. "Everyone needs a family when
they get older."

Craig wondered if Ellie had a family. And if she did, whether
they took time to visit, to invite her for home-cooked meals.

Dawn slipped an arm around the stooped woman and gave
her a gentle squeeze. "You're right about that, Ellie. But don't
worry about Joe and me. You and the others who come to
eat here each day are our family."

Craig scanned the tables, noting those who'd gathered for a free meal.

Would these people ever feel like family to him?

He looked forward to working with them and helping them any way he could, but he didn't think he'd go so far as to claim them as friends and family.

Chapter 5

Paddy's Pub was really hopping, which was typical for a Wednesday. The happy-hour patrons who had been gathering since about four o'clock were quenching their thirst and grazing on Irish potato wedges and Belfast buffalo wings.

Some of them were also morphing into jerks.

"Get me two house chardonnays and a Guinness," Kristy told Randy, the bartender.

"You got it."

While she waited for her order, she slipped off her right shoe and rubbed her arch against the built-in footrest on the bar. She didn't need to look at her watch to know it was time to clock out. But she wouldn't get to for a while.

On days like this, she hated her job, hated the blisters on her feet, the ache in her back.

She'd only been working at Paddy's since the grand reopening a few months back, and if the pay wasn't better than the diner where she used to work, she would have quit by now.

At one time, Paddy's was just a seedy bar, but a year or so ago, a couple of investors bought the place and remodeled by expanding the kitchen and adding a dining room. There'd been a few changes to the outside, too, but the biggest improvement had been within. The walls were now covered with mock white plaster and trimmed with dark timber beams.

The primary decorative focus was a rock wall that displayed a large, open fireplace, complete with grate, bellows and a suspended cast iron kettle. Next to it, wooden benches and settle seats provided the patrons a place to sit amidst the Gaelic ambiance.

When Kristy had learned the employees would be required to dress in period clothing, which was intended to add to the ambiance, she'd almost backed out of the job offer. But the new owners explained that they were providing lockers in the break room, where the hired help could keep their street clothes and personal belongings.

It would have been a pain to trek through town dressed as a seventeenth-century tavern wench.

Even though no one had said anything, Kristy suspected her red hair had been a real selling point when it came to landing the job, but that was okay with her, especially if it meant more tips. She needed the money to make ends meet.

Still, she preferred to work the dining room, which was easier and less stressful. She'd already put in more than eight hours serving food today, but when Sandra Billups had called in sick, Kristy had been asked to move over to the bar and cover until a replacement came in.

The tips were much better on this side, so she accepted the change without complaint. Still, she didn't like dealing with drunks, no matter how much money they threw around, no matter how important their jobs were and how much stress had driven them to Paddy's to unwind.

"Hey, baby," a patron in the corner who'd grown increasingly annoying hollered. "Why don't you put down that tray and come over here? I could sure use some company."

The guy had been pretty quiet and uptight when he arrived. But he'd been downing Irish whiskey since before four, and his sobriety had been deteriorating steadily.

His discarded jacket, which he'd hung over his chair earlier, had slipped onto the floor. And his tie rested on the table in a pile of silk.

It was time to cut him off.

Where was Ian, the bouncer? Flexing his muscles and flirting with that busty blonde he'd sidled up to earlier, no doubt.

What a crowd this was.

The new owners might have done their best to cater to a higher-class patron, but the old pub regulars continued to show up night after night, hunkering down and digging in until closing time.

There seemed to be an imaginary line down the middle of the bar, giving it both a shady and a respectable side. But as far as Kristy was concerned, there wasn't much difference between the two groups once they'd thrown back a couple of shooters or downed a few beers.

Every now and again, she would hear one of the old crowd complain about how uppity everyone had gotten now that they were putting on the ritz.

Still, to her, the new and improved Paddy's Pub wasn't *that* nice, and neither were some of the people who hung out here. Just working in the bar was enough to reinforce her vow to never touch a drop of alcohol again.

As she turned to take the tray of drinks to table seven, she nearly bumped into a dark-haired man clad in worn jeans and a white polo shirt.

She spouted out a blanket apology, while trying to balance her load. When their gazes finally met, she recognized an old friend.

Ramon Gonzales slid her a slow smile. "I didn't mean to sneak up on you."

Kristy didn't usually enjoy running into any of the people she'd gone to school with, but Ramon was one of the exceptions, and she returned his grin. "I usually work on the restaurant side, but they were shorthanded in here."

It had been an excuse. An attempt to make him understand why Kristy, who had a history she wished she could rewind and replay with a different outcome, would work as a cocktail waitress. She supposed, after seven years, she still struggled to right her reputation, especially when it came to a guy who'd always been nice to her.

She probably hadn't needed to explain. In school, Ramon had been a shy and introspective guy who never used to talk about people behind their backs.

Dark Latino eyes bore into hers. "How's it going?"

"All right. How about you?"

He gave a half shrug. "I'm okay. Business is good."

Ramon's dad had been the groundskeeper at the Rensfield estate ever since Kristy was in the sixth grade. She remembered because Ramon had been the new kid in school, and all the girls had a crush on the cute, dark-haired boy who didn't speak English.

Actually, she realized, even after learning the language, he still spoke very little.

When most of the other graduates had gone on to college, Ramon had started a mobile landscaping company with an old, beat-up Toyota pickup and tools he'd picked up at an estate sale. From what she'd heard, he was building a reputation for being more than a guy who just cut lawns and pruned hedges.

Kristy adjusted the heavy tray in her hands. "I saw the garden you created around the fountain near the playground at the park. It's beautiful. You've got a real eye for color to go along with a green thumb."

"Thanks." He looked at her as though he had something on his mind, on his heart.

When they were still in school, she'd noticed a similar expression at times, a puppy-dog gaze that was hard to read. She wondered if anyone ever took the time to look beyond the silence.

Ramon nodded toward the tray-load of drinks she carried. "Can you take a break? I'd like to talk to you."

For a while, during their junior year in high school, Ramon and Shana had a thing going, but then Mrs. Delacourt had flipped when she got wind of it. Shortly after that, the relationship ended. Shana hadn't wanted to talk about it much. She'd been pretty sullen for the rest of the school term, then had finally rallied, around the end of summer. Of course, at that time Kristy had been caught up in her own problems—an unexpected pregnancy and her grandmother's debilitating stroke—so she hadn't been very supportive of Shana.

Still, the Ramon/Shana thing had seemed to work itself out.

Kristy glanced at her watch. "Sure. I've got a minute or so. Let me drop these off and I'll be back. It's been a long time."

"Yeah, it has."

Ramon took a seat that faced the doorway, then watched as the attractive redhead delivered drinks to a couple of women near the window.

He'd always liked Kristy. Years ago, when they'd been in high school, he'd been struggling in chemistry. She'd approached him and asked if he wanted her to tutor him. Embarrassed that his difficulty with the subject had become public knowledge, he'd almost declined. But then he'd reconsidered and swallowed his macho pride. They'd met at the library at the end of the day, and she'd explained things in a way old man Winslow hadn't been able to.

Kristy had been an academic whiz, and Ramon had always figured her let's-party reputation was due in part to boredom, since school came so easy for her. Too bad she hadn't been able to go to college and on to medical school, like she'd planned. She probably would have made a great doctor.

Ramon stretched out in his seat and contemplated skipping out before she returned. Instead, he sat tight and berated himself for buckling his hard-nose stance when it came to Shana Delacourt.

Whatever had given him the idea that he ought to quiz Kristy about a stupid rumor?

And why did he even give a rip?

He and Shana were through years ago. Maybe even before their first date.

When Kristy returned, she asked if he'd like a drink.

"Got any Coronas?"

"In here?" She laughed and glanced at the shelves behind the massive, hand-carved bar. "We've got just about every Irish ale and malt ever made, but my boss refuses to carry any other kind of beer on principle. You should have stopped at El Toro Loco instead."

He sat back in the wooden chair that wasn't nearly as comfortable as the seats at El Toro Loco and tossed her a smile. "Yeah, well you don't work there. And I wanted to ask you something."

"What's that?"

"I heard that Brad flew to visit Shana in Australia."

The smile on her face shifted, as her brow furrowed. "You heard right."

He glanced down, fiddled with the wooden holder on the table that advertised malt whiskeys and ales, then returned his gaze to her. "Is there something going on between them?"

She folded her arms, wrinkling an oversized Irish peasant blouse that didn't do a thing for a woman who'd once seemed to enjoy displaying a dynamite shape, then shrugged. "They're getting married in August."

The news slammed him in the chest, nearly taking his breath away, but he managed to nod. He didn't understand his compulsion to quiz Kristy. Why couldn't he just let thoughts of Shana go, like he'd always done in the past?

He supposed the idea of her marrying anyone would have bothered him, but something didn't feel right about her and Brad Rensfield. For one thing, he'd never really liked the spoiled rich kid. So just thinking about him and Shana together gnawed a hole in his gut. Shana was too sweet for Brad. In fact, she was too good for most guys, which is why Ramon hadn't put up a fight when she'd broken up with him.

Well, that and the fact she'd wanted to keep their relationship low-key, if not a complete secret.

Ramon's pride hadn't let him accept terms like that.

"So, what did you hear?" Kristy's gaze drilled into him.

"That Brad made a visit to Tiffany's for a ring before boarding the plane."

"Boy, news sure travels fast."

"Especially through the Rensfield employee grapevine."

Kristy didn't appear to be enthusiastic about the gossip, and since she and Shana had been best friends for years, he wondered if the Brad thing had seemed to blindside her, too.

"You don't seem excited," he said.

She shrugged. "It's just a little sudden. That's all."

Ramon didn't reveal his hand very often—to anyone—and even if he wasn't afraid to share what was on his mind and in his heart, Kristy had enough stuff to worry about, a big enough load to carry, what with a kid and her grandmother and all.

He crossed his arms, now wishing he hadn't arrived on the scene—especially since Kristy didn't appear to know any more than he did. "The news just seemed to come out of the blue, I guess."

"Yeah, I know."

So Ramon wasn't the only one with qualms about the surprise engagement. But since Kristy wasn't doing much talking, he couldn't very well prod for more information than he already had.

He looked at Shana's best friend, really looked at her. She'd been pretty in high school—a knockout, actually. She'd played up her looks back then, using makeup and her choice of clothing to enhance her best features and attributes.

But now she played them down, and he suspected he knew why.

She'd never talked about the night that Brad had thrown the first of many parties he had hosted when his parents were out of town. Nor had she talked about the father of her baby.

The truth was left for speculation and gossip, which was

too bad. The guy who'd gotten her pregnant should have come forward and been a man about it; he had to have known.

"Hey, Red," some drunk in the corner called out to Kristy. "Did you forget about me?"

She grimaced and rolled her eyes. "I hate serving guys like that."

Ramon nodded, took her hand and gave it a quick, gentle squeeze. "You ought to be in med school, Kristy."

"Yeah, well things don't always work out the way we want."

No, they didn't.

Something in her gaze—sympathy, understanding?—told him she knew about him and Shana. But she didn't say a word, and he didn't want to resurrect old memories.

She pulled her hand free and offered him a wistful smile. "I can get you a list of the brews we have."

"Don't bother." The chair legs scraped the floor as he stood. "I've got beer at home, and I think I'd rather spend a quiet evening alone."

"So would I." She blew out a wistful sigh. "But I can't clock out for another hour or so."

As she turned away, Ramon reached into his pocket and pulled out a twenty-dollar bill. He left it on the table.

A tip, he supposed. Or maybe it was payment for a couple of tutoring sessions that had gotten him a B in chemistry, rather than a D.

Then again, he suspected it might be penitence for keeping quiet about where she might find the guy who fathered her baby.

Craig had spent all afternoon getting a handle on his new job. He'd figured that the best way to give it his best was to jump in and get started. So, after the soup kitchen had closed at two, he'd helped Joe and Dawn clean up and prepare for the next day.

Then he'd gone back to his office, which had probably been a broom closet before his arrival. He'd checked out the phone jack and the electrical sockets so he'd know how to set up things once the desk arrived. Then he'd worked out a calendar in his day planner. He would have put his schedule into the computer, but apparently, that was on order, too.

He'd talked to Lorena, the church secretary, and had compiled a list of all the youth in the church. Then he'd called each one, introduced himself, and invited them to a pizza party on Saturday night. He said they'd be doing something special in the weeks to come, but he'd yet to figure out just what. He decided he had plenty of time to come up with something clever and fun that would appeal to teenagers.

Next, with Lorena's help, he'd created a list of the shut-ins, church members who weren't able to come to services on Sunday. Then he'd blocked out time to meet each one.

"That one's a real pistol," Lorena told him, as she tapped one name with her finger. "From what I understand, she was a sweetheart before her stroke, but she's not very pleasant to be around now."

"Why is that?" he asked.

"It's her attitude. I think she's angry with God, and she seems to take it out on anyone who stops to visit."

"Who's been going to see her?"

"To be honest, I think most of the women from the Ladies Aid took turns going to see her for a while, but she practically ran them off. So as far as I know, Pastor George is the only one left."

And that meant Craig would be his successor.

As much as he'd like to move Lorraine Smith to the bottom of the list, he bumped her to the top instead. Not that he was a glutton for punishment. It's just that he usually liked to get the worst over first.

Before he knew it, five o'clock rolled around, and he called it a day.

Ten minutes later, he returned to the Delacourts' house and, using the key Cassandra had given him earlier, let himself in the door. Even though Daniel and Cassandra had done their best to make him feel welcome, he still felt awkward walking into the house without knocking. And the hearty aroma of dinner—roast beef, maybe?—didn't soften his discomfort.

"I'm home," he called out as a courtesy.

"Oh, good," Cassandra said, meeting him in the foyer with a smile. "Daniel isn't home yet. I'm afraid he's working late tonight—again. So I'll just set a plate aside for him. That way, we can eat whenever we want to."

"I'm afraid I have to go out this evening," he said.

Her smile seemed to droop, although he couldn't be sure because, if she'd been disappointed, she quickly recovered.

"I can put dinner on now," she said, "if you'd like. Or I can save you a plate, like I'm doing for Daniel."

Craig wasn't particularly hungry, since he'd eaten a late lunch—the meatloaf that had been left over from the soup kitchen—but something told him not to mention it.

"I wouldn't mind having dinner before I go, if that's okay," he said, glad to see her smile return.

"It'll just take a minute."

Moments later, after washing his hands, Craig shed his jacket and hung it in the den closet. Then he joined his hostess in the formal dining room, where a rose bowl filled with yellow buds served as a centerpiece.

She held a tray with two plates, although he realized she'd set the table for three and noted that she'd used china, crystal, and silver. He wondered if she was trying to make him feel special, or if she always went to this much trouble for a family dinner.

He supposed it really didn't matter.

She asked him to have a seat, and he complied. Then she placed a plate in front of him that had been filled with roast beef, new red potatoes, and glazed carrots.

He reached for his linen napkin, as she served herself. She asked him if he minded saying grace, and after he did, he reached for his fork.

But he held off on digging in. "Everything looks delicious, Cassandra. Thank you for going to so much trouble."

"You're welcome. I love to cook and entertain." She glanced at the empty setting across from her, then looked back at him and smiled. "It's always nice to have someone appreciate my efforts."

He wondered how often Daniel had to work late and guessed that it was probably too often.

"So," Cassandra said, reaching for her linen napkin. "Where do you have to go tonight?"

"To visit Lorraine Smith. Do you know her?"

Cassandra placed the napkin in her lap. "Yes, I do. She's Kristy's grandmother."

"The maid of honor in the upcoming wedding?" he asked.

"Yes." Cassandra reached for her fork. "Lorraine suffered a debilitating stroke about six or seven years ago, followed by several others. Now she's confined to bed, which is a real shame. She used to be very active in the church. She was also an artist. In fact, she painted the portrait of Shana in our living room."

That was nice to know. Craig could use that information as an icebreaker. "I'll have to compliment her on her work when I meet her this evening."

"I'm sure she'd appreciate that. She took up painting relatively late in life, and when my husband and I were looking for someone to commission for our daughter's portrait, Shana insisted we have Lorraine do it. I must admit, I wanted a professional with references, but Daniel gave in to Shana." Cassandra speared a carrot with her fork. "He always does."

"I'm not an expert," Craig admitted, "and I haven't met Shana yet, so I can't tell if it's a good likeness or not, but that's a great portrait."

"Yes, it is. And in retrospect, I doubt that we could have found anyone else who would have done our daughter better justice."

They continued to eat, the only sounds an occasional clink of silver upon china, yet Craig found himself curious about the Smiths and finally broke the silence. "Does Kristy live with her grandmother?"

"Yes, ever since she was twelve."

"Where's her mother?"

"I have no idea. As far as I know, neither Lorraine nor Kristy have heard from her in years."

"What happened to her?"

"From what Lorraine told me, Susan was always wild and rebellious, which I thought was surprising, under the circumstances. Lorraine and her husband had tried for years to have a baby, but they'd been unable to conceive. So they were thrilled when the opportunity to adopt Susan came up. But instead of appreciating her new parents and loving home, the girl rebelled and was constantly in trouble." Cassandra lifted her crystal water goblet and took a sip. "You know, drinking, smoking. Drugs, too."

"That's too bad."

"Yes, it was. Stan, Lorraine's husband, died of an aneurysm when Susan was in high school, leaving Lorraine to deal with the girl on her own. From what I heard, Susan often ran away for days at a time."

"That must have been tough on her." Craig appreciated having some background information on Mrs. Smith, although it didn't make him feel much better about the visit. He suspected it was going to be awkward either way.

"Lorraine was beside herself with worry and frustration." Cassandra picked up her knife to cut her meat. "Not long after Susan turned eighteen and moved out for good, she told Lorraine she'd gotten married and was pregnant. You'd think Lorraine would have been worried sick about that, but she actually thought motherhood would change her daughter and make her settle down for good."

"I assume it didn't."

"No, I'm afraid not. Somewhere along the way, Susan's husband died of a drug overdose, and as a result, little Kristy spent her elementary years in and out of homeless shelters."

Craig couldn't help feeling sorry for the elderly woman who'd been dubbed a pistol by the church secretary. But he sympathized with Kristy, too. It sounded as though her early years were rough.

"Did the state step in and take Kristy away from Susan?" he asked, suspecting that had probably been the case.

"They didn't for the longest time, which I never understood. But one night, Susan left her alone in a shelter and never returned. No one knows what happened to her. It's possible that she got tired of being a mother and ran away."

"Did anyone consider that she might have met with foul play?" Craig asked.

"It's possible, I suppose. Shana always insisted that, in spite of the substance abuse, Susan adored Kristy and never would have abandoned her, which I'm sure is what Kristy had told her. Shana also said that Susan had quit using drugs after she got pregnant with Kristy, but that's impossible."

"Why do you say that?"

"Because she couldn't seem to stay out of homeless shelters."

Craig wasn't sure if he could buy it, either. But he suspected there were a lot of reasons some people were homeless, and they didn't all have to be drug- or alcohol-related.

"Either way," Cassandra said, "Kristy was abandoned as a child. And she'll have to deal with that issue for the rest of her life."

"A lot of people are able to overcome dysfunctional homes and families," Craig said.

"I suppose, in your business, you need to be optimistic. And I hope you're right." Cassandra lifted her napkin and dabbed her lips. "It's just that I hate to see Shana get caught up in all of that. She's very softhearted and always believes the best about people."

"That's not a bad thing."

"No," Cassandra said, "but since her father and I have tried our best to shelter her, I worry that someone could take advantage of her innocence and good nature."

"College has probably been good for her. I doubt that she's as naïve as she used to be."

Cassandra placed her napkin on her plate, covering the traces of food she apparently wasn't going to eat. "I hope you're right, Pastor, but I wouldn't know. Shana and I aren't as close as we once were."

Craig wasn't sure what he was supposed to say to that, so he opted to remain quiet until he finished his meal.

"I made apple pie for dessert," Cassandra said as she stood and began gathering their plates.

"That sounds wonderful, but I'd better pass."

"It's homemade," she said, her expression sober, her tone hopeful.

"It's not that. I really ought to head over to the Smiths' house before it gets any later."

Cassandra managed a smile. "I understand."

"You know," Craig said, "I wouldn't mind having a big slice of pie when I get back. Would that be okay?"

"Yes, of course. I have vanilla ice cream to go with it."

"Great." Craig placed his own napkin on the plate, then scooted his chair back. "I won't be long."

As he headed for the door, he had the urge to turn around and check on Cassandra.

For some reason, he got the feeling she was more fragile than she appeared.

He let himself out the front, closed the door, and headed for his car. He hadn't gotten two steps when Jesse's words settled over him.

Things aren't always what they seem.

Craig looked over his shoulder at the house, and the light peeking through the cracks in the shutters.

Chapter 6

After changing into her street clothes, Kristy exited the pub through the back door, then headed for the bus stop. It had been a long, grueling shift, and she'd been especially glad to clock out.

Too bad she couldn't just get in her car and go home, but the transmission was going out on the twelve-year-old Chevrolet Impala that had once belonged to Gram, and Kristy didn't have the money to pay a repairman before Friday, which was payday. So now, like she'd done for almost a week, she was taking the bus home.

A dog howled in the distance, and the streetlight nearest Paddy's Pub flickered. For a moment, she felt uneasy.

The new owners might have renovated the bar and added a dining room in hopes of making Paddy's a more family-friendly place, but they hadn't been able to do anything about the crummy neighborhood in which it was located.

She could have hung out a little longer in the pub, but she'd grown tired of the rowdy crowd, the noise, and the smell of booze. So she strode along the sidewalk, watching the cars go by. It seemed that each one was heading home, and she envied the fact that they'd get there way before she would.

When she reached the bus stop, which was little more than a bench on the corner of First and Canyon Drive, she took a seat. She'd only waited a moment or two when a man in a dark jacket approached, the soles of his shoes scraping along the grit-littered sidewalk.

She'd gotten more than the usual tips today, so she placed her purse on her lap, wrapped her arms around it, and drew it close. But then she noticed the telltale shuffle in his walk, the life's-a-drag slump in his shoulders.

His hair was shaggy, his beard, too. It was easy to surmise he was homeless.

A lot of people might have blown him off, but Kristy wouldn't. She'd been in a similar situation for too long to be as callous as others could be. And while some of the homeless had addiction problems or mental health issues, she knew many had just been the victims of rotten luck.

"Excuse me," he said, his voice much softer and gentler than his appearance. "I don't suppose you can spare a dollar or two for a man in need of bus fare. I'm not sure when I can pay you back, but I will."

She would have given him ten or twenty dollars, if she had it to spare, but, thanks to Jason's last bout of strep throat, which had required two visits to the pediatrician and an expensive antibiotic, she'd been alternating utility bills this month, paying one and letting the others ride. And if she didn't come up with a hundred and twenty-six dollars by Monday, the city water department would be shutting off the meter.

"Actually," she said, "I'm pretty stretched right now."

His eyes were an intense shade of blue, something that didn't escape notice, even in the muted light from the streetlamp, and he slipped her a wistful smile. "I understand."

As he turned to walk away, she grabbed his forearm, pulling him back. "That's not what I meant. I'd like to do more, but I can certainly spot you bus fare." She reached into her purse and pulled out the only cash she could spare, which was four dollars. "I'm sorry it's not much, but it's all I've got."

"I hate to leave you with nothing," he said.

"I'll be all right."

His smile had a way of reaching something deep inside of

her, and she wondered what his story was. How he'd come to lose it all.

"Thanks," he said. "And for what it's worth, I meant what I said about paying you back."

"I know you will." She smiled, playing the game, even though she didn't expect to ever see him again.

She hoped he didn't use the money to buy drugs or booze, but she'd always been a sucker for the downtrodden, in part because she and her mom had often found themselves in a similar state.

Even though it had been years since they'd had to beg on street corners, she would never forget what it felt like to be seen as only an apparition instead of a real person.

But we're here, she'd wanted to shout. *And we're hungry. Don't pretend you can't see us.*

Something inside told her to keep to herself, to let him be. But she knew what it was like to feel like a second-class citizen.

"My name's Kristy," she said. "What's yours?"

"Jesse." He took a seat next to her, keeping a respectful distance.

See? she told herself, some people might be forced to beg and to sleep outdoors, but there was always a bit of pride and humanity left—if one was willing to look for it.

She glanced down the street to see if the bus was coming and, convinced that it wasn't, she turned back to the homeless guy. "Do you live around here?"

"Temporarily. I'm just passing through."

The conversation lulled, which was to be expected. He probably wasn't comfortable sharing too many details with a stranger, and she could understand that. She had a few things in her past she'd like to keep under mental lock and key, even though it seemed that the whole world already knew.

"Tough day at work?" he asked.

"Not any worse than most." She tossed him a weary smile. No need to complain about her job, when she at least had one.

"It'll get better," he told her.

What would? Her job? Her life? Her prospects for the future?

Assuming he was just making small talk, she played along by broadening her smile and nodding her agreement. "Yeah, I know. It always does."

"Life's a journey, Kristy. And yours has been an especially difficult trek so far. There've been twists and turns and potholes, most of which haven't been of your own making."

Why was it that so many of the homeless she'd known seemed to think that they had cornered the market on wisdom and common sense and became roadside philosophers?

"Things are going to start looking up," he added.

She wanted to chuff and say, "A lot you know." Instead, she said, "I'm sure they will."

"You've been toting a heavy load, but it's about to get easier."

The roar of a diesel engine sounded, and she pointed to the south, glad to have an interruption. "Here comes the bus."

He stood, and she followed suit.

As the city bus slowed to a stop, he placed a hand on her shoulder and said, "Your mother didn't abandon you."

Her gaze slammed into his. "How do you . . . ?"

He shrugged. "I can't explain how I know, but she didn't leave that night because she didn't love you. You were right about that."

"What are you?" she asked. "A psychic?"

"Not exactly."

"Then did you know my mom?"

Before he could respond, the bus driver opened the door.

Jesse swept his arm toward the waiting vehicle, indicating that she should get on first. She couldn't very well dawdle, so she took a step, then stalled, half in and half out. "I asked how you knew my mom."

He blessed her with a gentle smile. "Let's just say that I have . . . a gift."

"Hey!" the driver called out. "I've got a schedule to keep. Are you getting on or not?"

Kristy climbed onto the bus with Jesse on her heels. She took the first empty seat, and he took the one across from her.

As the transmission ground and the engine roared, the bus lumbered back onto the road.

Kristy tried to make sense of what Jesse had said. He hadn't mentioned her mom by name. And he hadn't admitted to having ever met her.

So how could he have known that her mother had left one night without leaving word of where she was going or when she'd be back?

He could have picked up on rumors and gossip easily enough, she supposed—if he'd asked around town.

As the bus approached the next stop, which was on Applewood Drive, Jesse stood to leave.

Unable to help herself, Kristy tugged on the sleeve of his jacket. When he glanced down, she asked again, "How did you know that?"

"I can't explain it."

"*Are* you psychic?" she asked again, this time shedding all signs of sarcasm.

"Not a garden-variety kind, if that's what you mean." He left her with a smile and a parting word. "Your mother had a lot of problems, Kristy, but she loved you as much as she possibly could."

Then he shuffled down the aisle and disembarked.

As the bus roared off down the street, Kristy sat back in her seat. She hoped that Jesse had some kind of psychic gift and that what he'd said about her mom was true.

But she was afraid he was just a garden-variety nutcase.

Craig had gotten the directions to Lorraine Smith's house on MapQuest, so it had been easy enough to find. He turned left onto Sugar Plum Lane, a street of old Victorian houses, each one quaint in its own right, and drove slowly, scanning the numbers until he found 162.

There were two cars in the driveway, which made him think Mrs. Smith already had company. If so, he'd just say hello and come back another time.

He parked his car at the curb, closer to the neighbor's house, then strode up the walk and knocked at the door.

Moments later, a forty-something brunette answered. She cocked her head slightly and eyed him closely. "Yes? Can I help you?"

"I'm Craig Houston, the new associate minister at Parkside Community Church. I stopped by to see Lorraine Smith. Is she home?"

"Yes, she is." The woman introduced herself as Barbara Crenshaw, then stepped aside and allowed him in.

As he entered the living room, the woman suggested he take a seat while she told Lorraine that he was here.

"Thank you." He checked out his options, a brown tweed sofa with an autumn-colored afghan draped over the back and one of two green vinyl recliners. He chose the sofa, but before he could settle into his seat, a barefoot kid wearing Spider-Man pajamas padded into the room.

The brown-haired little boy looked him up and down. "Who are you?"

"I'm Pastor Craig."

"How come Pastor George didn't come?"

The truth? Because George had passed this chore on to Craig. But he wouldn't tell the kid that. "Pastor George is at home, I believe. This time, it's my turn to visit your grandmother." Then, on second thought, he asked, "She is your grandmother, isn't she?"

The boy nodded.

"What's your name?" Craig asked.

"Jason."

The boy was a bit young—first grade, maybe—but since Craig was going to be in charge of the youth ministry at

Parkside Community, he thought it might be a good idea to get a child's opinion of the classes and programs currently in place.

"Say, Jason. Can I ask you something?"

"Sure." The boy drew closer to the sofa.

"How do you like Sunday School?"

"I don't know. I never go."

Some kids preferred to sit in the service with their parents. And there were different reasons for that. Craig wondered if Jason's had anything to do with the teacher, the structure, or the curriculum. "Don't you like Sunday School?"

He shrugged, and his face scrunched up in a cute, *Leave It to Beaver* way. "It's okay, I guess. I only went there once, when I stayed all night at Danny's house and his mom made us go."

"Your mother doesn't take you?"

"No, because she works."

"On Sundays?"

"Yeah, sometimes."

Apparently, even though Mrs. Smith had once been a church regular, Kristy wasn't anywhere near as devout.

Well, so much for an attempt to strike up a conversation with the boy. Maybe Craig should have asked him about sports. Or, better yet, Spider-Man might have been a better choice.

"Pastor?" Barbara asked from the doorway.

"Yes?"

"I'll take you back to her room."

Craig got to his feet, but before she led him down the hall, she cupped her hand over her mouth and whispered, "I'd probably better warn you. She's not at all happy that Pastor George has passed her on to someone else."

Great. Craig supposed he couldn't blame her for being hurt, but from what he'd gathered from Lorena, George was probably only too happy to pass the shut-ins, especially this one, off to someone else.

"Lorraine," Barbara said, as she led Craig into a small bedroom that smelled a bit musty and medicinal. "This is Pastor Craig."

The elderly woman, her gray curls mussed from resting in bed, turned to face him, a scowl upon her craggy face. "This really isn't necessary."

"What isn't?"

"Your visit."

Okay, now what? Seminary hadn't prepared him for this. Or if it had, he'd been daydreaming through that particular class.

Craig neared the hospital bed where she lay. "George told me to be sure to introduce myself. He said that you were once very involved in the church. And a lady everyone loved."

"Once was a long time ago."

Silence filled the room, and he tried to come up with something to say. But the struggle for the right words felt about as effective as a drowning man grasping for air bubbles.

"I've been staying at the Delacourts'," he said. "And Cassandra spoke highly of you."

Lorraine arched a gray brow, but she didn't speak.

"I saw the portrait you painted of Shana. It's hanging in their living room, and I was taken by it. I've never seen their daughter, but you captured something in her expression. Something . . ."

"Haunting?" Lorraine asked.

"I guess. It was as though she had something on her mind. Something only she knew."

"All I did was paint what I saw."

"Well, your talent is incredible."

She humphed. "A lot of good that does me now."

"We don't know why things happen the way they do," Craig began.

Lorraine didn't let him finish. "Now, listen here, young man. Look at you—all full of life and spunk. You're no different than George Rawlings. You want to spout off about how happy

I ought to be stuck in this bed, unable to walk, to paint, to babysit my great-grandson so that his mother doesn't have to pay for a sitter. And if you think I ought to enjoy what little time I have left on this earth, you'll have to try and sell that pretty little cottage on the swamp to someone else."

Okay, so he'd been prepared for a little negativity, but that didn't mean he had any ready words to say, any lofty scripture verses that would right her world.

"I'm sorry, Mrs. Smith."

"You ought to be. You don't have any idea what it's like to have everything taken away from you, everything you love."

Didn't he?

But somehow, a baseball career couldn't seem to compete with health and the ability to walk.

Oh, God. What am I doing here? I'm so out of my league.

He glanced at the clock on the bureau, wondering how much longer he'd have to stay.

Well, he'd better come up with something to say or some kind of game plan quickly, or else word would get out that Mrs. Smith had run off the new minister within sixty seconds of his arrival.

And then Craig wouldn't be the only one questioning his call.

Kristy got off the bus nearly two blocks away from home. She was eager to kick off her shoes, soak in the tub, and get some sleep, so even though her feet hurt, she picked up her pace.

When she reached Sugar Plum Lane, she turned down the street. At the curve in the road, she looked ahead and saw two cars parked along the curb in front of her house. One belonged to Barbara, the vocational nurse.

She'd never seen the Ford Taurus before and suspected it belonged to a guest of one of the neighbors. She didn't give it any more thought as she strode up to the front door and let herself in.

The television was on, and Barbara was seated on the sofa, the afghan draped over her lap. Jason sat next to her, sharing the cover and gaping at the screen as he watched a Disney movie.

"Hey," Kristy said, her thoughts brightening at the sight of her son. "Where's the best kid in the whole wide world?"

"Here I am!" Jason jumped up and ran to her, giving her a quick hug before rushing back to his seat, diving back under the covers, and returning his full attention to the animated movie.

She hung her jacket on the coatrack near the door, but didn't feel the comforting warmth of the heater, as she'd expected.

Was the thermostat on the blink again? She hoped not. She really couldn't spare the money to replace it now. The small savings Gram had accrued over the years was taking a hard hit from the salary they paid Barbara. But there was no way around the expense of a repair. They had too many cold nights left this spring.

"How'd it go today?" she asked the nurse.

"All right."

Kristy couldn't ask for more than that, she supposed. "Do you know whose car is parked out front?"

"It probably belongs to the new minister. He's in the bedroom, talking to your grandmother."

Uh-oh. Last week, Pastor George had mentioned that they were bringing on someone new, that the man would be staying temporarily with the Delacourts. He'd hinted that the new minister would be handling visitation. Then, after he'd left, Gram had grumbled and said, "I guess George thinks he's too important to bother with me, so he's dumping me off on someone else."

Kristy had thought about calling the church and warning them, but she figured they were probably trained to deal with that sort of thing.

She couldn't hear any noise or yelling down the hall, so maybe the new pastor was having better luck with Gram than she'd expected.

Barbara removed the afghan, then after getting to her feet, made sure it covered Jason.

"Lorraine didn't complain too much today," she said. "But I still think the doctor ought to prescribe a stronger antidepressant."

"I'll have to discuss it with him at her next appointment." Kristy rubbed her arms to ward off a chill. The old house, as quaint and homey as it was, didn't have adequate insulation, so it could get drafty, especially near the doors and windows.

"Well," Barb said, "I'd better hurry home. Harry gets into the ice cream before bedtime if I'm not there to scold him. And his cholesterol is entirely too high."

Sometimes Kristy wondered what it would be like to have a husband to worry about, a man with whom she could share the load of daily life. But then again, it would be unfair to burden a man with a crippled grandmother who wanted to die, a fatherless boy, a dilapidated old house, and more money going out than coming in.

"I may not get in until late again tomorrow," she told the nurse. "I need to help cover someone else's shift."

"No problem. Will you be home by seven? Harry and I are planning to watch 'The Cowboy Jamboree.' It's a television special they've been advertising all week."

If the car weren't on the blink and she didn't need to rely on public transportation, it wouldn't be a problem. "I'll try my best to catch a ride with someone. That way, I'll be able to get home in time."

Barbara grabbed her purse from the hutch, where she always left it, and headed for the door. As she reached for the knob, she looked over her shoulder. "You know, I probably ought to mention something. Harry put in for a promotion, and there's a possibility that he might get it. If so, we'll have to move to the L.A. area."

Kristy's heart thudded to a near halt. What would she do if she lost Barbara?

She'd have to find someone else, she supposed. But it

wouldn't be easy to replace the woman who loved her son as though he were her own little boy. Still, she managed to smile. "I guess we'll have to play it by ear."

Barbara opened the door and stepped onto the porch, then added, "There's another guy at the company who has more seniority, so it's really just a possibility at this point. But I didn't want to spring anything on you."

"Thanks, I appreciate that."

As Barbara shut the door behind her, Kristy took the seat next to her son and slipped an arm around him.

"This looks like a cool movie," she said.

His eyes remained glued to the screen. "It is. And some parts are really funny."

Footsteps sounded in the hall, and Kristy glanced to the doorway. When her gaze landed on the new minister, her breath caught.

She didn't know what she'd been expecting—a young, nerdy type, she supposed. So needless to say, when she spotted the tall, broad-shouldered hunk, whose blond hair was as sun-streaked as a surfer's and whose coloring was that of an outdoorsman, she was caught by complete surprise.

Wanting to be polite, she quickly got to her feet, and he closed the gap between them.

He reached out his arm in greeting. "I'm Craig Houston."

"I . . . uh . . . I'm Kristy Smith. Lorraine is my grandmother." She couldn't remember taking the hand he offered, but she found her fingers enveloped in his warm, steady grip.

"It's nice to meet you," he said, letting go of her hand.

Her fingers curled into a useless fist, and she dropped her arm to her side. "I hope my grandmother wasn't rude to you. She's not easy to talk to sometimes."

He shrugged in a way that seemed almost boyish. "I have to admit, I did get off on the wrong foot. But I stuck it out. She's one of the parishioners, and she has needs the church would like to meet."

A slow but wry grin stretched across Kristy's face. "Yeah,

well good luck. I've been trying to meet her needs for the past seven years, and it hasn't been easy."

"I can only imagine." His expression matured, then grew boyish again. "I'm sorry. I guess I shouldn't admit to understanding your frustration. My inexperience must be showing, huh?"

Her grin developed into a full-blown smile. "To be honest, I still feel pretty green in dealing with her crotchety attitude, which isn't at all like the woman she used to be. So I certainly can relate."

"Thanks." He nodded toward the door. "Well, I guess I'd better go. But I'll be back next week."

"Apparently that means she didn't chase you away."

"She sure gave it her best shot."

Kristy laughed, and the lighthearted tone almost stopped her dead. Her moments of laugher, with anyone other than Jason or Shana, had been rare. And this was the first time she'd found someone safe to commiserate with.

Pastors did abide by the client-patient privilege thing, didn't they?

She sure hoped so, because she didn't want news of her own frustration with Gram to get out.

When Craig reached the door, he turned, his gaze sweeping over her in a way that made her heart stumble and fumble in her chest. If she didn't know better, she'd think that he was . . . checking her out.

"Goodnight," he said.

"Thanks for stopping by."

"No problem."

Even though there was no need for it, she followed him out to the porch and pulled the door closed behind her.

She told herself that she'd escorted him out to be polite, and that she'd shut the door to block the chilly night air from going into the house.

Craig didn't head right for his car. Instead, he hung around, too.

A mannerly gesture, she decided.

Okay, now what?

"You know," he said, "I can ask one of the women from the Ladies Aid to come and sit with Lorraine on Sunday morning. That way, if you'd like to bring Jason to Sunday School, you can."

Kristy didn't care how handsome the man was. He was still a minister. And she wasn't the churchgoing type. "Thanks, but that's not necessary."

"Why not?"

She hadn't been to church since before Gram's stroke, and it wasn't because there was no one to look after her grandmother. As much as she wanted to slam him with an it's-none-of-your-business line or to conjure some kind of generic response, she figured it was best to level with him. That way, if he actually had been checking her out earlier and found himself even the least bit interested in her, she'd do them both a favor and put an end to things before they got started.

"God and I aren't exactly on speaking terms," she admitted.

"I'm sorry to hear that."

She could let it go at that, but she decided to take it one step further, to let him know that any interest he might have in her was off limits, especially for a pastor. "I made a big mistake several years ago, and I'm still dealing with the repercussions."

"You don't think God can help?"

"I don't even want to approach Him about it."

His gaze locked on hers, and she sensed a dose of compassion flowing through.

"Church is a good place to get a second chance and to make a fresh start," he said.

"Maybe so, but I still wouldn't feel comfortable showing up there."

"Why not?"

"Because I'm one of the black sheep in this community."

She'd meant to chuff and laugh off the truth of her comment, but something in his eyes stunned her into silence.

For a moment, she sensed that he was looking beyond the emotional armor she wore. If he had been, that was a first.

Most people never even bothered to try.

Chapter 7

Late yesterday afternoon, the boys had brought Renee a pillow and an old comforter, so she'd slept better on her second night in the tree than she had the first. Still, she'd stayed up late and had woken up several times, which was why she'd decided to take a nap before heading to the soup kitchen for lunch.

She'd no sooner than stretched out to rest when a boy hollered, "Hey, Renee! Are you up there?"

"Yes, I'm here." She got to her knees, poked her head out the tree house door, and spotted her pint-sized landlords, their arms loaded with more supplies.

But this time, they'd brought a younger boy with them.

"We got some more junk for you," Danny said.

"Thanks." Her gaze drifted to the new kid, then back to Danny. "I thought this was going to be our secret."

"I know, but this is Jason. He's the one who found the fort in the first place, so we had to tell him."

She hadn't wanted her secret to get out, and with each new person who knew she was here, the odds were in favor of a citywide news flash.

They'd probably put it on the front page of the newspaper:

Pregnant Teenager Living In Tree. Social Workers Decide She's Crazy and Not Fit To Be a Mother.

"Jason won't tell anyone," Tommy said. "He's pretty cool for a little kid."

Yeah, well, she didn't know how cool he could be if he was just five or six.

He was kind of cute, though.

Jason tugged on Danny's shirt. "I gotta get home before my mom gets back, and she's been gone awhile already."

"It's okay. We'll just be here a minute." Danny put down his load. Using his hand to shield his eyes from the sun, he looked up at Renee. "His mom had to take his grandma to the doctor, so he's staying at our house for a while."

Tommy scanned the brushy area that surrounded the path to the tree. "I don't know why, but she doesn't like him on the Bushman Trail, even though we told her we'd watch him."

"The Bushman Trail?"

"Yeah, that's what we call the path that cuts through the canyon. Sometimes we're explorers. And sometimes we're on safari. You know how it is."

She supposed she did.

"Jason's mom is pretty fussy," Danny added. "Mine is, too, in some ways, but she used to let me come down here when I was his age, and I didn't even have big kids to watch out for me."

Renee was going to be one of those kinds of moms—strict. She wasn't going to let her kid eat junk food or stay up late. And she'd make sure they did their homework. She'd even read the notices they brought home from school and go to programs and stuff like that.

Some of her friends used to say she was lucky because she could come and go as she pleased and never got in trouble. But she hadn't felt lucky. It would have been nice to have someone care enough to get mad at her. Like Jason's mom probably did.

She looked at the little guy. He was pretty young. Or maybe he was just small for his age.

Still, something didn't seem right. "I thought you said that he found the tree house. How'd he do that if he's not allowed to come out here?"

"He gets to do a lot more stuff when he stays at Danny's house." Tommy turned to Jason and, using his finger, pushed his glasses back up his nose. "Sorry, Jay. Your mom's nice and all, but she does treat you like a little kid."

She ought to, Renee thought. He *was* a little kid.

"Where do you want us to put this stuff?" Danny asked.

"I'll take it." Renee climbed down to get it.

She'd no more than touched one foot on the ground when a woman's voice echoed through the canyon. "Jason! Danny! Where are you, boys?"

"Uh-oh." Tommy handed the small, wooden stepstool he'd been holding to Renee. "Jason's mom got home. And now he's going to get his butt kicked."

"No, I'm not," the smaller boy objected. "My mom doesn't believe in spanking. But I better go anyway. She believes in yelling and in time outs and in not letting me watch TV or eat dessert for a whole week."

"Then you'd better go," Renee said.

Danny nodded down the path. "I'd better go, too. I need to make sure he gets home all right, or else I'll really be in trouble. I'll have to come back later for the rent."

"Okay. But I might not be here until about four." She hadn't found a job yet, so she was going to have to start looking extra hard today. But she still wanted to be home before dark. The canyon started getting spooky at twilight.

The boys took off, and Renee had to make a couple of trips into the tree to take her new things inside. When she finished, she put everything away. Then, while kneeling, she sat back on her heels and surveyed her temporary home.

Hey, she even owned art. A small, framed picture of a fox hunt would soon adorn a wooden wall, once she found a nail and hammer.

She was also the proud owner of a battery-operated hand-held fan, which was going to come in handy if it ever got hot.

"Oh, God," she muttered. "Please let me get into a real house before summer."

She checked out the Mickey Mouse alarm clock they'd brought, guessing it to be about ten. She set it, then wound it up. But she didn't hear any ticking sound. Maybe it was the silent kind.

Next, she glanced at the three-legged footrest. She wasn't sure what she would do with that. Use it as a chair, she guessed.

All in all, the tree house was beginning to feel like home, although she wasn't sure if that was a good thing or not. She sure didn't want it to get too comfy.

As she folded up her bedding and set it aside, she thought about the boys who knew her secret. She sure hoped she could trust them.

She also hoped Jason didn't get in too much trouble with his mom, especially since he might decide to trade news about her for leniency. Kids did that sometimes.

But at least his mother wouldn't spank him. That was good to know.

Renee had gotten a few good licks in her life—some of them were real humdingers. But that was a long time ago, back when she stayed with the Haydens.

Now *there* was a woman who believed in spanking, whether it was her kid or someone else's. But it wouldn't do Renee any good to stew on the past. Not when she was trying hard to start over and create a decent future.

She glanced at the clock, wishing it was more accurate. If she found someone who was wearing a watch before she came home, she'd reset it.

Still, she didn't think it was eleven yet. But maybe it wouldn't hurt to go to the church early. If she showed up before the others did, she could always volunteer her time to help. At least until she got a job, of course. That way, she wouldn't feel like a freeloader and would be making some kind of contribution, especially if she kept sneaking extra buns and things.

She had a feeling that guy, Pastor Greg or whoever he was, saw her take those rolls yesterday. She'd almost pulled them out from under her shirt, apologized, and given them back. But her granola bars were gone, and the bread had made an okay breakfast this morning.

So she climbed out of the tree house, wishing she had a way to lock it up, now that she was acquiring some household belongings, and headed toward the church.

When she reached the soup kitchen, she noticed the door was open. So she eased inside. "Hello? Is anybody here?"

A woman with curly brown hair, the one who'd been wearing a red apron and serving food yesterday, poked her head out of the kitchen doorway. "Oh, hello there." She wore a friendly smile as she strode toward Renee. "It's a bit early, but you're welcome to come in and wait."

Renee shoved her hands in the pockets of her jeans. "Well, actually, I thought if you needed some help, I could do some chores. You know, to pay you back for the meal I ate yesterday?"

"Well, that's really nice of you." The woman wiped her hands on her apron. "My name is Dawn. And if you're willing, I'd be happy to put you to work."

"Cool."

The aroma of tomato sauce, garlic and basil filled the air, and Renee's stomach growled in response, as she followed Dawn back to the kitchen. "What are you serving today?"

"Spaghetti."

"Oh, yum. My favorite."

"Mine, too," Dawn said. "We're also having salad, garlic bread, and vanilla ice cream for dessert. So this is your lucky day."

Renee sure hoped so. She hadn't had much luck in the past, and it seemed as though she might be due for a break.

*   *   *

On Sunday morning, as a favor, Barbara came by for a couple of hours to sit with Gram so Kristy could run some errands. She'd also offered the use of her car, since Gram's sedan was still on the blink.

"Be sure to pack a lunch while you're at it," Barbara had said. "That way you can spend an hour or so at the park. I'll bet Jason would like that."

With her schedule, Kristy didn't get as much quality time with her son as she'd like, so she gave the woman an appreciative hug.

Barbara had been a blessing, and Kristy wished her and her husband all the best. Harry was still in contention for that promotion, although a decision hadn't been made yet.

"This is really just a long shot," Barb had said. But sometimes those paid off.

Kristy wouldn't stress about that now, though. She needed to focus on her driving.

As she turned onto Bedford Parkway, she spotted a group of teenagers huddled together. She figured it was just a bunch of kids messing around and didn't think anything of it—until she noticed Jesse in the middle of them.

One boy, a tall, shaggy-haired blond, gave the homeless man a shove that nearly knocked him off his feet.

She reached for the prepaid cell phone she carried in her purse, a luxury item she only intended to use in case of emergency. If she didn't have Jason in the car, if she . . .

Oh, for goodness sake. Who knew when the police would arrive? And she couldn't just sit by and let them harass the poor guy like that.

She set the phone in the console, laid on the horn, and pulled over to the curb.

As the boys turned toward the noise, she rolled the window down far enough for her voice to be heard. "What in the world are you guys doing?"

The blond teen, his baggy pants riding low on his hips,

turned to her and crossed his arms. "We're telling this guy that he needs to go somewhere else to live."

"Why? What did he ever do to hurt you?"

"He's homeless," another kid said. "And it's all because of that dumb soup kitchen. It's drawing them all into Fairbrook."

"If you don't leave him alone . . ." Kristy picked up her cell phone and flashed it at them. "I'll call the police."

"Yeah, well he's a transient, and there's vagrancy laws, you know. And these lazy guys ought to all be rounded up and locked away until they clean up their acts and get a job."

"Jesse," Kristy said, much the way she spoke to Jason when her temper was wearing thin. "Get in the car."

"Yeah, he needs a ride to the city limits," the big-mouthed kid said.

Shifting their stances in a cocky manner, the other boys chuffed, as Jesse strode toward the car.

Kristy unlocked the door for him, and he climbed into the passenger seat.

She hit the lock button, then blew out a breath she hadn't realized she'd been holding. She shifted the automatic transmission into drive and pulled back into the street.

Once they were on their way, she nodded toward the rear of the car. "What was that all about?"

"I was just heading toward the church when that mouthy kid took it upon himself to discourage me from settling in Fairbrook."

"I'm sorry they gave you trouble."

"It's not your fault. You can't do anything about someone else's attitude. You can only change your own." Jesse looked over his shoulder at Jason and offered him a smile. "Hey, there. How're you doing?"

"I'm okay."

Kristy wasn't sure if it was a good thing Jason had been in the car or not. But she'd definitely talk to him about the situation later. She certainly didn't want him to grow up to be as heartless as those teenage boys had been.

As she proceeded down the road, she glanced across the console at Jesse. "Is the soup kitchen open on Sundays?"

"Yes, but not until one o'clock, and then they just pass out boxed lunches. But that's okay. A sandwich and a cookie will hit the spot."

She supposed it would.

The church parking lot was nearly empty when she turned into the drive. Apparently, services were over for today, which was probably why the soup kitchen didn't open until one.

"You're going to be a bit early," she said.

"That's okay." Jesse pointed toward a man striding across the parking lot and heading for his car. "I'll just hang out and talk to Pastor Craig."

The sun glistened off the golden strands of the young minister's hair, and Kristy was struck by his sturdy build and his all-American good looks. But she turned her head before anyone realized her gaze had lingered a bit too long on him.

She wasn't ready to get involved with another guy. And while she planned to find someone decent the next time around, someone who would be a good father and husband, she knew better than to set her sights on the cream of the crop. To her, that's exactly what a preacher was.

How was that for setting her sights over the top?

Even if she was open to dating a guy like him—and she certainly *wasn't*—he'd never be interested in used goods.

Jesse reached for the doorknob. "Thanks a lot. And not just for the ride."

"No problem. I'm glad I came by when I did."

Jesse, who stood before the open passenger door, leaned his head back into the car. "Before I go, do you mind if I share a story with your son?"

Kristy had no idea what he was going to say, but she figured it wouldn't hurt. "Sure, go ahead."

Jesse dropped to one knee. "Once upon a time, there was a widowed king who had it all—land, gold, power. But the love

of his life was his daughter, a baby girl who was just a tod-
dler. He spent every moment of his free time with her—until
war was declared upon his kingdom.

"The king knew the only way his soldiers would win is if
he rode with them, but that meant leaving his beloved daughter in the care of three others—a nursemaid, his highest ranking political advisor, and a priest who planned to build a new
chapel in the kingdom.

"The nursemaid was an attractive woman, and he hoped
that she would not only love and care for his child in his absence, but also teach her how to be a lady of the finest measure. The advisor was one of the wisest men in the kingdom, so
the king instructed him to teach the girl all she would ever
need to know, since she would one day take the throne.

"But the king wanted his daughter to be more than wise
and beautiful, which is why he chose the priest. He hoped the
holy man would guide her heart in all that was pure and just
and true."

Kristy glanced at Jason, saw him listening intently, his eyes
wide with concentration. And she pondered the possible reasons Jesse had wanted to share this particular story.

To entertain her son as a repayment of her kindness?

Jesse clicked his tongue and slowly shook his head. "But
unfortunately, the nurse was so pretty, she spent enormous
amounts of time in front of her looking glass, admiring herself. And the advisor grew busy, running the kingdom in the
king's absence. The job was important and demanding, and
he decided he couldn't spare the time for one small child,
when so many important men needed his attention.

"Even the priest got caught up building the chapel, using
the daylight hours to construct the building and his nighttime
hours working on sermons that would reach the heart of
every person in the kingdom and fill the pews each Sunday.
So the little girl was left to herself much of the time."

Jesse glanced at Kristy—to check and see if she was listening to the fairy tale, she assumed. And she had been. Yet the

intensity in his gaze suggested there was far more to the story than its entertainment value.

A beat later, he resumed the tale. "It wouldn't have been so bad, had the king returned when he'd hoped he would. But the war was long and brutal, and the king had to stay away from the palace for years on end. Still he believed—and trusted—that he'd left his daughter in the best of hands."

"But he didn't," Jason said. "The people he left her with didn't do their jobs."

"You're right. They were each given an assignment, but they failed the king. And before you know it, the child grew up. Time took a toll on the nurse, and her skin began to sag, her hair turned gray. Yet she focused even more on her appearance, bemoaning what she once had been. The advisor thrived on running the kingdom and forgot there'd ever been a real king. And the priest, who'd built a beautiful chapel and had amassed a large congregation, was amazed at all he'd accomplished in his life, and he soon grew busy counting the gold coins that poured into the offering box each week."

"What happened to the girl?" Jason asked.

"She grew to believe that she was unimportant and had very little value."

"That's sad," Jason said. "Nobody taught her the stuff they were supposed to."

"That's true, and for a while, she let others steal her sense of worth."

"What do you mean?" Jason asked.

"The girl didn't know anything about fashion or how to fix her hair, but when she took a close look in the mirror, studying her features rather than admiring herself as the nursemaid had done, she realized she was pleasing to the eye. And even though she didn't have an education, she'd learned something important already, just by growing up the way she did. She'd come to see that an overabundance of vanity, pride, and greed could twist a person's soul and make them forget their true purpose in life.

"Then, as she began to search her heart, she became aware of something staggering, something eye-opening. Something she should have known all along and had nearly forgotten."

"What was that?" Jason asked.

"That she was a princess, the child of a king, a young woman whose father loved her beyond measure. Yet for a while, she'd let others assign her value. And it wasn't until she stood tall and demanded her place in the kingdom that she received all that was her due." Jesse straightened and got to his feet, his hand still on the edge of the car door.

"That was kind of a weird Once-upon-a-time story," Jason said. "It wasn't like the other ones."

"I think it is." Jesse smiled and turned to Kristy. "You've got a lot going for you, Princess. Don't ever sell yourself short." Then he closed the door and turned toward the church, leaving her to wallow through all he'd said.

And all he hadn't.

As she finally began to pull away from the curb, she glanced through the passenger window and saw Jesse heading toward Craig.

She wondered what kind of a story he had for the preacher.

Chapter 8

Craig removed a box of paper plates and napkins from the trunk of his car and snapped the lid shut. He'd just started toward the soup kitchen when he heard footsteps approaching. He turned toward the sound and spotted Jesse coming his way.

The man still hadn't shaved, and he wore the same dark jacket, even though today wasn't as cool as it had been recently. It seemed safe to assume he didn't have a closet in which to keep his clothes.

Craig noted that his smile appeared forced, but he returned it just the same. "Hey, Jesse. How's it going?"

"Not too bad. How about you?"

"I'm settling in." Craig nodded toward the modular building at the back of the property. "I was just heading to the soup kitchen. Come on, I'll walk with you."

Jesse fell in step beside Craig, a bit of a shuffle to his stride. "You working in the kitchen today?"

"I'm supposed to be off this afternoon, but I still want to check in with Dawn and make sure everything's okay."

"Folks sure appreciate having the opportunity to eat here," Jesse said.

"The church saw a need and stepped up to the plate. Sometimes people just need a little assistance until they can get back on their feet again."

"You know," Jesse said, "speaking about those needing help, I talked to a guy the other day. And he's trying to organize a group of disadvantaged kids into a baseball team."

Craig transferred the box to his left arm so he could reach for the door knob. "That's good."

"Yeah, that's what I thought. So if you're free next Saturday afternoon, you might stop by the ball fields and see what he's doing with those kids. I bet he'd appreciate any help you could give him."

Craig had never mentioned his baseball days to anyone in Fairbrook and didn't intend to. "I'm not much of a coach."

"Aren't you?" Jesse asked, as he followed Craig into the soup kitchen.

"You mean because I'm a pastor? I guess, in a way, I am." Yet, in all honesty, Craig felt more like a batboy. He slowed beside one row of tables. "Why don't you have a seat. I'll see if I can rustle up a lunch for you now. There's no point in making you wait if the food is ready."

"Thanks." The shaggy, bearded man pulled out a chair and sat.

"I'll be right back." Craig took the box into the kitchen, where Dawn and a blonde teenager were packing up disposable lunch boxes. It was the same girl who'd eaten here yesterday.

"Hey," he said, placing the cardboard box on the counter. "We've got some help today."

"Isn't that great?" Dawn smiled at the teen. "Thanks to Renee, we've got most of the work done already."

"That's good because we've got our first guest. I didn't see any reason to make him hang around outside." Especially with some of the locals complaining about the "bad element." But Craig let that go unsaid while Renee was within earshot.

Dawn reached for one of the small boxes they'd packed with a sandwich, an apple, and a chocolate chip cookie. She tucked in the tabs, closing it, and handed it to Renee. "Would you mind taking this out to our guest?"

"Not at all." Renee reached for one of the plastic bottles of water. "Should I take him one of these, too?"

"Yes, would you please?"

When the girl disappeared, Craig eased closer to Dawn. "How'd you manage to snag a helper?"

"She volunteered, so I put her to work. I think it makes her feel better about eating here."

"I wish we had the money to actually hire her." Craig peered through the open doorway and saw Renee talking to Jesse. "She took a couple of extra corn bread muffins home yesterday, so I have a feeling she's not getting enough to eat."

"That's too bad. I'll give her ten dollars for helping me today. And I'll have her take an extra lunch home with her."

"Good idea. And if she shows up tomorrow, I'll chip in another ten." Of course, Craig wouldn't be able to keep that up for very long. Maybe he'd just have to help her find a real job, although he wasn't sure what.

"How old do you think she is?" Dawn asked.

"It's hard to say. My guess is about fifteen. Maybe even sixteen."

"That's what I was thinking." Dawn tucked a brown lock of hair behind her ear. "But she told me she's twenty-one."

"It's possible I guess. Sometimes it's hard to tell."

"I know, but I'm still skeptical."

"Eighteen would make her an adult," Craig said, "if that's what you're concerned about."

"You're right. I guess there's an old mother hen inside of me."

Their voices stilled when Renee came back to the kitchen.

"Where's Joe?" Craig asked Dawn. "I saw him in church this morning."

"He ran Mrs. Rogers home. She's not able to drive anymore."

"How far away does she live?" Craig glanced at the clock on the side wall, thinking he should have been back by now, unless Mrs. Rogers lived in another city.

Dawn laughed. "He usually drives through McDonald's and buys her a milkshake as a treat, but I have a feeling he's been getting one for himself, too. That man loves sweets."

"So you expect him soon?" Craig asked, hating to leave Dawn on her own.

"Any minute now."

"Well then," Craig said, "it looks as though you two have everything under control, so if you don't mind, I'll head back to the Delacourts' house. Cassandra made Sunday dinner, and I hate to come dragging in late."

"I've been to a few dinner parties at Cassandra's house," Dawn said. "She's our resident Martha Stewart, so you'd better get out of here. I'll see you tomorrow."

Craig nodded, then left the kitchen. On his way out, he stopped by the table where Jesse sat and patted the homeless man on the back, his fingers grazing the frayed shoulder seam of the old jacket. "I hope to see you again tomorrow."

"I expect that you will."

Craig left the building and went to his car. As he stuck the key in the driver's door, he glanced across the street to the playground. It was fairly empty today. A family of four ate under the shade of a large Mulberry in the center of the park. And two boys played Frisbee with a dog on the grass. But his gaze was drawn to a woman and a child swinging side by side.

As he recognized the redhead, his hand movements froze, and he took a moment to watch Kristy Smith with her son.

For some reason, he found himself withdrawing the key and slipping it back in his pocket. There were a hundred reasons for him to walk over to the park and say hello to her— all of them church related.

First of all, she was the granddaughter of a parishioner. And secondly, as a pastor, it was his job to invite her to Sunday services and make sure that she felt comfortable attending.

She was also going to be the maid of honor in Shana Delacourt's wedding, unless something blew sky-high, which he sensed was a possibility, albeit slight. And just in case he was called upon to soothe ruffled feathers, it wouldn't hurt to get to know her better.

So he strode across the street, studying her as he approached the playground.

She'd called herself a black sheep last Wednesday night. Yet, as he saw her swinging next to her little boy, carefree and laughing, her long red curls blowing in the light ocean breeze, she didn't seem the least bit rebellious.

On the other hand, the word "responsible" came to mind. He suspected that a lot of people might have found it easier to place a bitter disabled woman in a convalescent hospital, yet Kristy had kept her at home for the past seven years.

As he crossed the lawn and toward the swings, he realized Kristy hadn't been anything like he'd expected. Sure, she was tall and had red hair, just as the Delacourts had implied. But the oversized top and baggy jeans she wore made her look plain and not at all like the leggy, boy-crazy wild-child Cassandra had suggested she'd once been.

When he reached the edge of the sand, he smiled and said, "It's a nice day to play in the sun."

She looked up, and surprise splashed across her face. "Oh, hi."

"Do you come to the park very often?"

"Not often enough." She stopped pumping, and the swing began to slow. "Barbara, the woman you met the other night, is watching Gram while I run a few errands."

Craig thought it was nice that she'd scheduled time for her son. His mom used to do the same thing. "I suppose playing at the park is one of them?"

"Actually, it is." Kristy's feet skimmed the sand, slowing her momentum even more. "But to be honest, this was supposed to be our last stop, not our first."

"So, you're a bit of a free spirit and had a change of plans?" That was more in line with the image he'd had of her.

"I'm afraid my free-spirit days have been over for a long time." She offered him the ghost of a smile. "Actually, I was on the way to the grocery store and caught some teenagers harassing a homeless guy. So I chased them off and gave him a ride to the soup kitchen. So since we were across the street from the park, I decided to stop here first."

"That must have been Jesse," Craig said.

"It was. Do you know him, too?"

"I met him my first day in town." Craig slid his hands in the pockets of his slacks and felt the keys that rested there. He let them stay put. "Why were the kids giving him a hard time?"

"They'd hoped to send him packing, although I suspect he wouldn't need a suitcase."

"I was afraid something like that might happen. We've had some complaints in the community. They don't like seeing the homeless in town and want us to move the kitchen far away from the park."

"Out of sight, out of mind?" The breeze whipped a red curl across her cheek, and she brushed it aside. "That's really too bad."

Jason, who was swinging beside his mother, leaped from his seat and landed in the sand with both feet. He tottered a moment before falling on his rump, then jumped right up and ran to the slide.

"He's a cute kid," Craig said.

"Yes, he is. A truly unexpected blessing." She turned and called out to her son. "Jason, we're going to have to leave in a few minutes."

"Aw, Mom." He scrunched his face. "Do we have to?"

"I'm sorry, honey. I've got a lot of errands to run, and we need to be home before two o'clock."

To relieve the nurse, Craig assumed. "How's your grandmother doing?"

"She's all right. I'm sorry she gave you a hard time the other night. She's been laid up for so long that it's done a real number on her attitude. Believe it or not, she used to have a sweet, loving spirit."

"I'd heard she was active in the church, so that doesn't surprise me."

Kristy slowed to a complete stop, then got to her feet. "Her sullen mood tends to rub off on the rest of us. But, apparently, you knew just what to say to her the other night. I didn't hear any complaints after you left, and that's not usually the case."

"Well, I was definitely at a loss at first, but then I took a different tack."

"Oh, really?" She stepped away from the swing and closer to him. "I'm always open to suggestions. What did you do that worked?"

Craig wasn't sure what Pastor George would think, or what any of his professors back at the seminary would say, but his honesty and candor had taken a bit of the edge off the elderly woman's irritable tone. "I told her that there were times when life really sucked. And that she was right. Bad things sometimes happened to good people, and it really didn't seem fair."

"You commiserated with her? And that worked?" Kristy's brow furrowed as she pondered what he'd said to her grandmother. "Everyone else has tried quoting scripture and offering upbeat platitudes, which only seems to make things worse."

"I'm not saying that the approach I used was right. Or that it would meet with the approval of other ministers. But she didn't throw anything at me."

"Well, that's always a good sign." Kristy grinned, and her eyes brightened several shades of green.

She really ought to smile more often. She was a prettier woman than he'd realized, even without makeup. Or maybe it was because she hadn't used any of the typical props. There was something wholesome about her, something appealing.

"The next time she complains," Kristy said, with a slight lilt to her tone, "I'll have to remember to agree with her."

Craig had a feeling she was teasing, but he couldn't be sure.

"I'm afraid there was a bit more to it than that. I also admitted that I could relate, at least a little, to what she was going through."

"How's that?"

He really hadn't meant to get into the whole baseball thing—and he wouldn't really go there now—but he figured he owed Kristy an explanation. "I told her that I'd wanted to play professional ball in high school, and just when the opportunity of a lifetime came up, I was injured and had to put it off." He didn't mention anything about the decision he'd been forced to make after that.

Why should he? It was no one's business but his own. Besides, he didn't want anyone in town suspecting that his heart really wasn't in the ministry. What kind of pastor would that make him then?

He glanced at his watch, realizing that he'd spent more time at the park than he should have. "I'd better get home. It would be rude to show up late for Sunday dinner."

"And foolish," Kristy said. "Mrs. Delacourt's a good cook. And she's a good hostess, too."

Craig thought about the wedding, about the elaborate plans Cassandra had mentioned over breakfast this morning, but he bit his tongue. Neither of the Delacourts were thrilled with their daughter's choice for a maid of honor, and something told him that news might not come as a surprise to Kristy.

Either way, he wasn't going to risk stirring things up. Nor did he plan to get sucked into the middle of that drama unless circumstances forced him to take a stand. So he took a step away from the playground. "I'll see you on Wednesday evening—if you're at home when I come to visit your grandmother."

"I'm not scheduled to work at all that day, so you probably will."

He meant to say, "Good," but bit back his gut response. Instead, he said, "Have fun."

Then he walked across the grass, heading for the church parking lot.

Surprisingly, he was actually looking forward to his visit with Lorraine on Wednesday night.

And church business had nothing to do with it.

Dawn stood next to Renee at the table that served as a buffet line, passing out boxed lunches to each person who showed up to eat.

Sundays were usually light at the soup kitchen, and while Charlie Ames, one member of the advisory board, had suggested that they not serve any meals at all on the Sabbath, the others had agreed that people needed to eat on Sundays, too, and that a light lunch was doable without much effort.

Dawn hadn't minded the extra work; it kept her busy and her mind off the sadness that sometimes overcame her when Joe was on duty and she was left to wander though the big, empty house alone.

So she appreciated Renee's company today, as well as her help. It was nice to have someone to talk to during the lulls. Besides, Dawn had a heart for kids—and that's exactly how she thought of Renee. There was no way that girl was twenty-one. But like Pastor Craig had said, eighteen was the magical age—no matter how old she looked.

Still, Dawn risked another sidelong glance at the petite blonde and watched her stroke her stomach for about the tenth time. Neither the baggie clothes nor the tummy bulge was what one would expect to see on a teenage girl. Not when most of them were wearing snug-fitting tops that bared teeny tiny waistlines.

Dawn had once had a shapely figure, but after fifteen years of marriage and several pregnancies, none of which went to term, she'd put on weight and was now what you'd call pleasingly plump, which sounded better than heavyset, matronly or just plain fat.

So it wasn't hard to distinguish a pregnant belly from one that had been rounded due to too many helpings of dessert.

Ever since Dawn and Joe had tried to start a family, she'd been keenly aware of expectant mothers and could spot a maternal glow or a baby bump from across a crowded room— a glow and a bump she would have gladly given anything to have at one time.

So pregnancy seemed completely plausible. And if that were the case, it didn't seem fair.

Why did some people conceive so easily, while others tried for years, crying their eyes out month after month?

Dawn and Joe had married in their late twenties, then put off having children until they could buy a house. They found the perfect place about five years ago, a sprawling, four-bedroom home with a big backyard that was located in a great, kid-friendly neighborhood.

But their plans hadn't worked out the way they'd hoped.

After several heartbreaking miscarriages and a subsequent hysterectomy, Dawn had been forced to accept the fact that she and Joe would never have a child.

They'd talked about adoption, of course. But then her mother had gotten sick, and Dawn's time had been taken up driving her mom to dialysis and doctor's appointments until she passed away last month. So she and Joe had never gotten around to filling out the paperwork. And from what she'd heard, there was a shortage of babies and an abundance of willing parents. So who knew how long they might have to wait.

She stole another peek at Renee. There she went again, caressing that rounded belly.

Dawn supposed a large stomach could be part of the girl's natural build, but that didn't seem likely. Her small, delicate hands didn't seem to fit with a large midsection.

"Your husband hasn't come back yet," Renee said, drawing Dawn from her speculation. "Do you think there's a problem? Like maybe he got a flat tire or something?"

"It's possible, but he has a cell phone, so I'm sure he would have called. I think it's more likely that he's chatting with Mrs. Rogers. She lost her husband recently, after fifty-six years of marriage, and she's been lonely. I know Joe feels sorry for her. I imagine he's running errands or fixing something for her because she doesn't have any children to look after her."

The reality of the elderly woman's plight slammed into Dawn, and she struggled not to wince at a pang of sadness.

Is that what her future held? Would she find herself alone and helpless in her twilight years, waiting for neighbors and friends to step in to drive her places and fix her clogged sink?

Renee tucked a stringy strand of hair behind her ear and smiled. "That's kind of cool, don't you think?"

"What's cool?" Dawn asked, afraid she'd missed part of the conversation while she pondered her lonely fate.

"That your husband's a guy and all, and that he's being so nice to an old lady."

"Joe's got a soft spot for the elderly."

"How come?" she asked. "Not that I think it's weird and all, but old people are kind of . . . Well, the ones who lived in the apartment building where I used to stay were kind of mean and cranky. So I avoided them whenever I could."

"Joe came from a large family, and his grandparents lived at his house while he grew up. They're both gone now, and he misses them a lot."

She seemed to think about that for a moment. "I'm glad to know there are some really nice guys out there."

Dawn suspected Renee might have gotten pregnant by a not-so-nice guy. That is, if she was really pregnant. Again she tried to shrug off the possibility by saying, "You're right about Joe. I certainly lucked out when I met him."

Gerald Martindale, a Korean War veteran, stood from where he'd been sitting with Harvey Kingman, and waved at Dawn. "See you tomorrow," he called out. "I've got to get home. The neighbors asked me to let their dog out while they're gone."

Dawn waved back. "Have a good afternoon, Gerald."

"He seems kind of nice, too," Renee said quietly.

"Remind me to introduce you to Mrs. Rogers. She's not the least bit crotchety, and I think you'll really like her."

"Okay."

Dawn couldn't help wondering about the place where Renee used to live. It was hard to imagine that *all* of the elderly tenants were mean. But it was her current situation that concerned her the most.

"Where do you live now?" she asked.

"Not too far from here."

"What street are you on?"

Renee paused for the longest minute, as though she couldn't remember the name. Then she said, "Canyon Place."

Dawn knew where Canyon Drive was, so she must be talking about one of the side streets, but she just couldn't picture it in her mind. "Are you living in a house or an apartment?"

"I guess you'd call it kind of a studio apartment. It's pretty small, but it's clean. It's also furnished and has a great view, so I can't really complain."

At least she wasn't homeless. But Dawn suspected most of her money went to rent, which was probably why she was utilizing the soup kitchen.

"Do you live with anyone?" Dawn asked, wondering if she had parents or friends.

"Just myself."

Maybe Dawn was reading more into her situation than she should, but she had a feeling that Renee hadn't had too many people in her corner over the years—no matter how many of them she'd actually lived with.

Either way, it wouldn't hurt to befriend the girl. "Pastor Craig mentioned that you were job hunting. How's the search going?"

"Not so good. I talked to the managers at a couple of shops, like The Creamery and Specks Appeal, but they're not hiring right now. And I left an application at Café Del Sol, but I didn't have a phone number to leave with them, so I'll have to check every day."

Café Del Sol was a trendy little café across from Mulberry Park. In fact, all of the shops she mentioned were near the park. Was she just looking for work in this area?

Dawn glanced at the clock, noting that it was almost one-thirty. Joe definitely must have been working on a fix-it project for Mrs. Rogers. But she was beginning to wonder why he hadn't called.

She was just about to go back to the kitchen and pull out her cell phone to see if he had, when the door opened and Helene Waverly entered. Once the office manager for a local plumbing contractor, Helene was injured in a car accident by an uninsured motorist, which had left her on disability.

"You're just in time, Helene." Dawn offered her a warm smile.

"I'm sorry I'm late," the woman said, "but I've been having this awful pain in my side."

"That's too bad." Dawn reached for one of the boxes to give to her. "Have you seen the doctor?"

"I'm afraid my health insurance ran out. And since it's the end of the month, I'm a bit short on funds. So I've been trying to hold off as long as I can."

"Why don't you try the community clinic?" Dawn asked, handing her a lunch. "I think they have a sliding scale."

"I think I just might have to do that." Helene took the box in one hand and the water Renee offered her with the other. "I've never had use for the place before. Where's it located?"

"It's on Fourth Avenue, not far from the elementary school."

As Helene carried her lunch to one of the tables, Dawn watched her limp more than usual. The poor woman was really having a time of it.

"How far away is Fourth Avenue from here?" Renee asked.

"Why? Do you need to see a doctor?"

"I . . . uh . . . probably ought to."

"Are you sick?"

Again she paused. "No, not really. I think I was supposed to get a flu shot or something."

Dawn tried not to react to her explanation, but she wasn't buying the flu shot excuse.

The girl had to be pregnant.

Chapter 9

On Monday night, Kristy called Barb from the pub to let her know she'd be working overtime again. She'd hoped to be home by seven, but one thing led to another, and she didn't even get to the bus stop until nine.

Barb had offered the use of her car, as she'd done before, but Kristy refused to take her up on it. What if there was some kind of emergency and Barb needed transportation?

Now, though, as Kristy walked along the sleepy street of her neighborhood, where only a few of the porch lights still burned bright, she slipped her hands into her jacket pockets, trying to keep them warm. She sure hoped this was her last night without wheels—and it just might be.

One of the pub regulars owned an auto repair shop, and when he'd found out she'd been taking the bus to and from work, he agreed to give her a good deal if she took the car to him tomorrow morning.

He said to have it towed if she couldn't drive it to his shop, which might sound like an easy solution. But even if she got a bargain on the repair work, she would have to figure out a way to make her monthly budget stretch. Otherwise, she'd have to get into the dwindling savings one more time, which she hated to do.

It didn't take a math whiz to figure out that, at this rate, there wouldn't be anything left in a year. And then where would she be?

If she were a religious person, she might try praying about it, but she'd done that once, and it seemed that God wasn't paying much attention to her or her needs.

Of course, He hadn't seemed to be paying much attention to Gram's needs, either, and if He didn't listen to a woman who'd devoted most of her life to the church and to others, why would he pay any attention to Kristy?

As she neared the house, she noticed that trash cans and recycling containers dotted the sidewalk, reminding her that she would have to get hers out, too.

Sadly, she'd begun to mark the passing weeks by the trash days, and every time she turned around, she was facing a Tuesday morning all over again.

She opened the front door and let herself in—quietly so as not to wake anyone.

The lights were dim, and the television was on, with its volume turned low. Barbara was dozing on the sofa, with the crocheted afghan draped over her lap and legs.

"Barb?" Kristy whispered.

The nurse jerked to a sit and blinked her eyes. "Oh, dear. I dozed off for a moment. I'm sorry. I don't like doing that."

"That's all right. I apologize for being late."

"It's not a problem. I know they've been shorthanded at the pub." Barbara got to her feet and folded the afghan. "But I'm afraid I've got good news and bad news."

"What's that?"

"Harry called. He got the job."

Kristy's heart dropped with a thud, but she did her best to provide a genuine, unaffected smile. "It'll be tough to find a replacement, but I know that the promotion and the move will be good for you."

"Thanks. To be honest, I'm really happy about this. It means that I can finally retire. But it also means we'll have to move."

"How soon?"

"That's the hard part. He's supposed to start next week. I don't know why they took so long to make a decision. And then they tell us everything needs to happen quickly. The company will buy our house in Fairbrook and help us relocate, but there's so much to do. We need to talk to a real estate agent in Costa Mesa, and . . . Well, I'm not even sure where to begin."

"I'll have to start looking for someone to take over for you," Kristy said.

"I'm really sorry to put you in that situation."

"Don't be." Kristy smiled. "That's life."

And speaking of life . . .

As luck would have it, Mrs. Delacourt had called this morning before Kristy left for work, inviting her to a meet-the-in-laws dinner on Friday night. Kristy would have loved to have told her that she couldn't make it because she had to work, which was true, but she'd promised Shana to run interference. And the first place she'd have to start speaking up for the bride-to-be was at that particular get-together. So she would have to figure out a way to pull it off, even if she'd rather schedule a root canal.

"Remember when I mentioned that I was invited to a dinner on Friday night?" Kristy asked.

"Yes, I do remember. And I told you that I was free that night, but that's no longer true. With the promotion and all, Harry wants to drive up to Irvine this weekend and start looking around. He has a meeting with his new supervisor on Friday afternoon, so he'd like for us to leave about noon. I hope that doesn't leave you in a terrible bind."

Actually, it did, but there was no need to admit it and make Barbara feel bad about something that couldn't be helped. "Don't give it another thought. I'm sure something will work out."

If worse came to worst, she'd ask Maria Rodriguez, Danny's

mother, to babysit. But Maria had her hands full with three children and a job, and Kristy hated to always be the one asking for favors.

"Will you be able to work on Wednesday evening?" Kristy asked. "I was able to swap Friday with Sandra, but that was the only other day she was able to trade."

"Wednesday isn't a problem."

Maybe not to Barbara, but it still seemed problematic to Kristy, since that meant she'd miss Craig's visit. But truly, she couldn't dwell on that. If a preacher had caught her eye, she was truly losing it—no matter how good looking he was.

She'd sensed that the attraction might be mutual, but Craig didn't know anything about her yet.

For the briefest of moments, she forgot about her track record and let Jesse's fairy-tale parable came to mind, but not for very long. Kristy wasn't a princess by any means. And she wouldn't ever date a preacher—assuming Craig went so far as to ask her out.

"Well," Barb said, as she grabbed her purse and coat, then headed toward the door, "I'd better hit the road."

"And I'd better take out the trash."

As Barb got into her car and started the engine, Kristy headed to the side of the house, unhooked the gate, and began to drag the cans to the street. The sound of plastic receptacles dragging along the concrete driveway echoed in the night air, which was crisp and cool tonight.

"Need some help?" a man asked.

Kristy jumped back at the unexpected sound, then searched to place a face with the voice.

It was Jesse.

She was surprised to see him on her street, and for a moment she felt a bit uneasy. But there was something warm and gentle in his eyes, something that belied the hopelessness of his homeless situation.

A chilly breeze kicked up, and he shivered.

She noticed that he was wearing only a threadbare long-sleeve shirt. "Where's your coat? You had one on the other night."

"It was a bit warm this afternoon, so I took it off. But apparently someone else needed it more than I did."

"Someone stole it?"

"If they meant to borrow it, they forgot to mention it. So I guess they needed it more than I do." He tossed her a wry smile.

"Wait here. I'll get you a jacket." She returned to the house and climbed the stairs to the spare bedroom where Gram kept her late husband's things. The door remained closed most of the time, and Kristy only went inside to dust.

After entering, she sought the light switch and illuminated the room. As she scanned the interior, she breathed in the musty scent of time and memories laced with a hint of the lemon oil that she'd used last week on the antique furniture.

A double bed with an old chenille bedspread took up most of the space and sat close to a window that was adorned with a lacy curtain and had a functional, pull-down shade.

A black leather Bible, its spine worn and cracked, lay on the dark oak nightstand, next to a tobacco pipe, a pair of horn-rimmed glasses, and an ornate alarm clock with gold-leaf trim.

Before the stroke, Kristy had caught Gram in here a couple of times, holding an old flannel shirt close to her nose, trying to breathe in the scent of a man who'd passed on years earlier.

Kristy had never met Stan Smith. He'd died when her mom had been in high school, but his clothes still filled the closet.

She couldn't understand why Gram had kept all of his things. A couple of times, when Kristy had been a kid, she'd come into the room to snoop around and to try and get a handle on the kind of man that Gram had once loved and lost way too soon. But she was always thwarted by this overwhelming sense that she was encroaching on a shrine, so she'd slipped out almost as quickly as she'd slipped in.

But not tonight.

She shoved through those honor-the-shrine thoughts and searched the closet, looking for a jacket to give to Jesse. There were several to choose from, but she ended up taking a blue one made of a quilted, nylon fabric. She thought it might be warmer and rain resistant.

On impulse, she checked the pockets, just to make sure they were empty.

But they weren't.

One of them had a good-size bulge in it, so she unzipped the opening and reached inside. She removed a folded white envelope and suspected, even before tearing into it, that it contained money.

She lifted the flap and peeked inside. "Oh, wow." She pulled out a stack of hundreds and counted more than five-thousand dollars, a windfall that would buy her and Gram more time before they hit rock bottom and were forced to sell the house.

Somewhat in awe of her good fortune, she carried the cash to her bedroom and hid it in a musical jewelry box that had been hand-carved out of pine. The wooden box had a false bottom, so it would make an ideal hiding place. She placed it in the top drawer of her nightstand for safe keeping.

That task done, she carried the jacket out to Jesse and handed it to him.

He carefully looked it over, caressing the quilted fabric and clutching it close to his chest before slipping his arms into the sleeves. His blue eyes, which were always striking, were especially bright now. "Thank you, Kristy. You have no idea how much I appreciate your generosity. I'll find a way to pay you back for your kindness to me. And I'll return the jacket when I no longer need it."

Kristy could start a tab, but she wouldn't bother doing so.

"You don't owe me anything. That jacket has been inside the house for years, and it wasn't doing anyone any good. So please keep it. I'm glad someone will finally get some use out of it."

"Thank you." Those compelling blue eyes searched hers. "You look tired. More so than you ought to be."

"I guess I am. But mostly it's from pedaling as fast as I can and not making much progress."

The money would help, she realized. But she still needed to find someone qualified to look after Gram and Jason while she worked. If it was just her son, she could let him go to the YMCA after school and insist upon daytime hours at work. But Gram needed in-home care.

"And to make matters worse," she added, "I lost my grandmother's caregiver, who was also my babysitter."

"Oh, yeah? That's too bad, but I know someone looking for a job like that, and I can heartily recommend her."

"Who is it?" she asked before realizing that she probably needed to find someone with better character references than a homeless man Kristy had just met.

"Her name is Renee. She's young, but she's a decent person with a good heart, and she needs the work. She'd probably do it for less than whoever you had, which would be a win/win for both of you."

"I'd have to talk to her. And the job isn't that easy. My grandmother has run off several caregivers already, so there's no telling how long anyone will last."

"You won't have your grandmother much longer," Jesse said. "So enjoy the time you have left with her."

Goose bumps chased up and down Kristy's arms, but more out of uneasiness than cold.

It sounded too much like a premonition, a prophecy, especially when Jesse had said that he had "a gift."

But she wouldn't let that get to her.

His revelation was an easy prediction to make. Gram was in her late seventies, not in the best of health, and had lived the bulk of her life already. Common sense would suggest that she might not live much longer.

So she chased off her uneasiness.

Jesse might be unique, but he was also too weird to be true.

Danny's voice rang out in the canyon. "Hey, Renee!"

Every weekday, after school let out, the boys showed up, and Renee found herself looking forward to their visit. And not because they kept bringing her more stuff. It was actually nice to have someone to talk to.

She poked her head out the door of the tree house and saw them laden with even more gifts.

This time Jason was with them again, which seemed like a bad idea, especially if his mom didn't like him being in the canyon. But Renee wouldn't harp on him about that. Instead, she climbed down and looked over the things they'd brought this time.

Danny carried a birdcage made out of wire coat hangers and adorned with a fake canary, artificial red flowers, and greenery. "I thought you might want to hang this up some-place. The bird is fake, but it's kind of pretty."

It wasn't something she would have picked out if she had a choice, but she'd find someplace for it.

Tommy lifted a silver statuette of a soldier aiming a rifle. "Cool, huh?"

Renee scrunched her face. "I guess so, if you like G.I. Joe."

He pushed his glasses back along the bridge of his nose and studied the figurine. "What's wrong with it?" he asked.

If she had a real house, she might use it as a doorstop. "I guess a boy would think it was neat."

"I told you she would have liked that picture of cupid bet-ter," Danny said.

Kristy gave all the items a once-over. "Where'd you guys get this stuff? I don't want anyone getting mad at you for tak-ing it."

"It's just junk no one wants. We found some of it in our attics, but the army man was in my garage. My mom only keeps stuff she wants inside the house. I think she was planning to give that to the Salvation Army." Tommy brightened. "Hey, that's kind of funny."

"What is?"

"You know, a metal soldier going to the Salvation Army?" He laughed, but no one else did.

Jason held another clock. It was kind of big, and bulky, but it had pretty gold trim. Renee wondered if it was an antique.

"Are you sure that's just stuff no one wants?" she asked.

"Yeah," Jason said. "I found it in the junk room in our house. It's usually all closed up, except the door was open this morning, so I went inside and looked to see if there was anything you could use. And I found this. I think it even works, but it probably needs batteries."

Renee took a better look at the clock. It had a little wind-up thingy, which was good since she didn't have electricity. So she gave it a try, and sure enough, it started ticking. "Cool. It does work. Thanks."

The clock was definitely going to go to the new place, when she got one.

She glanced at the younger boy. "Hey, aren't you going to get in trouble for being out here again?"

"Nope. I'm staying with Danny till my mom gets back from getting her car at the car place, and he's being babysat by Walter, who said I could come on the Bushman Trail. So if she gets mad, she'll have to get mad at a grownup."

"Yeah," Danny said. "Walter's cool. He's kind of old, and you'd think that he probably forgot what it was like to be a kid. But he still remembers lots of neat stuff he used to do when he was a boy. And he thinks the canyon is a good place for us to play."

As Renee started up the tree with a handful of stuff, her sandal slipped off the step. She lost both her grip on the wooden frame and her balance, then fell to the ground, landing on her butt with a thump.

Her eyes widened, and her hands immediately went to her stomach. She hoped she didn't hurt something—or jar the baby loose.

"Are you okay?" Tommy asked.

"I hope so." She was planning to go to the clinic at the end of the week or after she got a job, but maybe she'd better go sooner. Some girls her age might be happy to have something go wrong and miscarry, but Renee wasn't like the others. She'd grown to love her baby, even if it looked like some kind of alien right now. She'd even begun to think of it as the little girl Jesse had said she was having.

But that probably wasn't too smart of her. The baby could be a boy.

Dang, her butt hurt. Her stomach, too.

She must have been wincing because Danny asked, "Are you *sure* you're all right?"

"Yeah, I think so." She got up and brushed herself off. Then her stomach cramped when she bent to pick up the birdcage she'd dropped in the dirt, and she winced.

"You landed pretty hard," Tommy said. "And you're walking kind of funny. Maybe you broke your back or something."

"I'd still be on the ground if that happened. But I am worried that I might have hurt . . ."

"Hurt what?"

Aw, man. She really couldn't tell them. What if they didn't keep her secret?

But the weird thing was, these guys had kind of become friends—her only friends in Fairbrook. And they'd been nice to her.

Besides, she still had that fake ID in case anyone wanted to know if she was really twenty-one.

"Come into the tree house," she told them. "I want to tell you guys something. But you have to swear on a hundred Bibles not to tell anyone."

She started up the laddered steps—more carefully this time because her dumb shoes were so loose—and the boys followed her. Once they were all inside, they sat cross-legged, facing each other.

"What's the big secret?" Danny asked.

Renee rested her hands on her knees. "I'm pregnant."

"What's that?" Jason asked.

"It means she's going to have a baby," Tommy told him.

The smaller boy looked at her stomach. In fact, they were all looking at her stomach.

She placed her hands over the bulge, allowing them to see the bump where her baby was growing.

"Does the baby have a daddy?" Jason asked.

"Yeah, but the baby will never know who he is."

Jason studied his lap and grew pensive.

Danny elbowed him. "Hey, don't feel bad about that, Jason. I know who my dad is, and it's not that big of a deal." Danny looked at Renee. "His mom doesn't know who his dad is, and he gets sad about that sometimes. But my dad is in prison for getting in a fight with a guy who died. So having a father isn't always that great."

Renee reached over and patted Jason on the knee. "Hey, my dad hasn't been in my life for almost as long as I can remember. And the way I see it, sometimes having a dad can be more trouble than it's worth."

"Yeah," Tommy said. "And some kids get stuck with two of them, which is really weird."

"How'd you get two dads?" she asked.

Tommy adjusted his glasses again, something that seemed to be a habit. "My first dad picked another family over mine, so he and my mom got divorced. And then she got married to Mac."

"Yeah, but your dad buys you a lot of neat stuff because he feels so crappy about leaving. And Mac is really cool." Danny turned to Kristy. "His stepdad is a detective, and he's got a gun and a badge and everything."

Whoa. She hadn't realized Tommy's stepfather was a cop. That could be a problem, especially if there was a law against people living in trees. And even if there wasn't, what if he asked her age, then checked out her ID? It was a good fake, but it might not be good enough to fool a detective.

She was suddenly sorry she told the boys her secret, but it was too late now.

"That's kind of neat that you're having a baby," Tommy said.

Renee looked at the boys, all listening intently and staring at her like she was one cool kid, when she was really scared and dumb and not at all sure where to turn.

All she'd ever wanted to be was *somebody* and to belong somewhere. And here she was—almost sixteen years old, a high school dropout by default, and living in a tree.

"Don't worry about us telling," Danny said. "You're our secret. Right guys?"

They all nodded.

"Well, I've got another problem," she said. "I need to find a job, and no one seems to be hiring right now. They keep telling me to check back in the summer, but I can't wait that long."

The baby was coming in July, as best as she could guess. And even with the rent only costing a dollar-fifty each day, she'd probably be out of money by then. And she'd still be living in a tree. What kind of mother brought her baby home to live in a tree?

"Barbara isn't going to work for us anymore," Jason said, "and my mom needs someone really bad."

Renee perked up. She could clean house or iron or something. "What kind of work did Barbara do?"

"She babysits me and looks out for my grandmother."

"What's wrong with your grandmother?" she asked, thinking maybe she was going a little goofy, like some of the old people who'd lived at the Regal Arms Apartments.

"She can't walk," Jason said, "so she's stuck in bed unless

someone puts her in the wheelchair and takes her in the living room. But she kind of likes staying in her room."

"It's hard work," Danny said, " 'cause his grandma needs help to go to the bathroom. I wouldn't want to have a job like that."

"And she gets cranky sometimes," Jason added.

Right now, Renee was desperate. Besides, she was used to people being mean, especially old people. "Well, I'm definitely interested, Jason. So tell your mom that you know someone who would like to apply for the job."

"Okay." He brightened. "It'd be cool to have you as a babysitter, Renee."

Before she could respond, a woman's voice shouted into the canyon. "Jason! Jason!"

"Uh-oh. I'd better go."

The boys got up to leave, and Renee watched them go, hoping she hadn't made a big mistake in sharing too much personal information with them. She'd never actually admitted to them that she was living in the tree and not just using it sometimes. But she figured they had to know.

"Don't forget to tell your mom that I'd like the job," she called out to Jason.

"I won't!" he said, before scampering off.

Kristy stood at edge of the canyon, hands on her hips. She didn't care that Walter Kleinfelter told the boys it was okay to play on the Bushman Trail. Jason knew she didn't approve, and he should have spoken up.

She was going to have to chat with him about this as soon as they got home.

"Here, I am!" Jason called out, the other boys trailing behind him.

Maria, Danny's mother, thought the canyon was pretty safe. But Kristy worried about Jason something fierce. He was only six, and the other boys were much older. Maybe when he was their age, she wouldn't be so fussy. And then, maybe she would.

There were probably snakes in the brush, not to mention that this world just wasn't as safe as it had been when she was a kid.

As the boys approached, she assumed her best stern expression. "I've told all of you that I don't like Jason down in the canyon."

"Yeah, but Walter said—"

"I don't care what he said. You should have told him that Jason isn't allowed down there. He would have respected my wishes." At least, she hoped he would have.

She placed her hand on Jason's shoulder, then guided him toward the house.

"Hey, Mom," he said. "I forgot to tell you, but I know a nice lady who needs work. And she'd make a cool babysitter. I think Gram would like her, too."

Kristy's steps froze. "You met her in the canyon?"

Jason's eyes widened, and he seemed to consider either her question or his response. "No. I met her the other day."

"Where?"

"She was . . . She was coming out of her house."

"Is she one of our neighbors?"

"Yeah, she lives pretty close."

At least that was convenient. "I'd like to talk to her. Why don't you point out her house, and I'll go to see her."

"I . . . uh . . . can't do that."

"Why not?"

"Because he doesn't remember exactly where she lives," Danny interjected. "But I do. How about I go and tell her you want to talk to her about a job, and then she can come to your house and talk to you."

"Well, that would be better for me. Thanks, Danny. I'd appreciate that. I have to work this afternoon, but if she has time to talk to me this morning—"

"I'm sure she does." The bigger boy took off like a shot, taking the path down to the canyon.

"Where's he going?" she asked Tommy.

"To the lady's house. She lives kind of by the park, and he's taking a shortcut through the Bushman Trail."

Twenty minutes later, while Kristy was doing the dishes and Jason was hanging out in the living room, peering out the window and waiting for the lady to show up, the doorbell rang.

"She's here, Mom!"

Kristy dried her hands on the dish towel, then strode into the living room, where Jason had already let the "lady" inside. She studied the young blond teenager with long, stringy hair.

"Hi," the girl said. "I'm Renee."

Was she the one Jesse had mentioned?

Kristy introduced herself and reached out a hand in greeting. "It's nice to meet you."

Renee tucked a stringy piece of hair behind her ear and smiled. "Danny said that you needed a babysitter."

"Actually, I need a nurse, too."

Her expression drooped. "Well, I don't have that kind of experience, but I can cook and clean. And I'm willing to do whatever it takes. Except maybe give shots or something."

"How old are you?" Kristy asked.

"Twenty-one." The girl, who was wearing a pale pink sweat shirt and a pair of jeans, reached into her pocket. "I've got an ID, if you want to see it."

Kristy was used to carding people at Paddy's, not when it came to hiring someone, but she found it hard to believe that Renee was that old. She glanced at the ID, saw the photo. But she didn't study it too long.

"I've got references, too," the girl added.

"Where did you work last?"

"Actually, I've been volunteering my time at the soup kitchen with Dawn Randolph and her husband, Joe. I've also worked with Pastor Craig. I don't know if you know him or not, since he's kind of new."

"Actually, I *do* know him."

Renee smiled, her blue eyes glimmering with hope. "I've

been helping out at the church in my free time, but I really need a job that pays. So maybe I could work for you for minimum wage or whatever to start. And then, if you like me, you could pay me more."

Well, she was definitely cheaper than Barbara. And if she was volunteering down at the church, that was a good sign. Kristy didn't know Dawn Randolph, but she would talk to Pastor Craig, of course. But without a dependable and responsible sitter and caretaker, she wouldn't be able to work, and even though she'd found the money, it wouldn't last long. So she was a bit more desperate than she wanted to be.

"I'll tell you what," Kristy said. "If you're available on Friday night, I'll try you out. And we'll take it from there."

"Cool." Renee brightened. "What time do you want me?"

Mrs. Delacourt had said dinner was at six. So Kristy figured she'd want Renee here a lot sooner than that so she could show her around and get to know her better. "How about five o'clock?"

"No problem. I'll see you then."

Renee let herself out the door, but Kristy could have sworn she saw her wink at Jason.

Chapter 10

On the night of the Delacourts' dinner party, Kristy stood before the bathroom mirror, struggling to get a faux diamond stud into her right earlobe and wondering if the set of pearls Gram had given her for her sixteenth birthday might be a better choice.

At the time she'd unwrapped Gram's gift, she'd thought the earrings and necklace were too sophisticated for a teenager. She'd planned to exchange them for something a little more trendy, but one thing had led to another—that stupid party, Gram's stroke, pregnancy—and she'd never gotten around to it.

Fortunately, they just might do the trick now. So she returned to her bedroom and rummaged through the chest of drawers, hoping she remembered where she'd stashed them.

The doorbell rang, and she quit searching long enough to glance at the clock on the bureau. 4:43.

"She's here!" Jason called out from the living room, where he'd been awaiting the new sitter.

Renee had agreed to be here at 5:00, so the fact that she'd arrived a few minutes early was a good indication that she was responsible.

Kristy left the drawer open and went into the living room to see that Jason had already invited Renee inside.

She wore a pair of jeans and a large tie-dyed T-shirt, and

her shoulder-length hair had been pulled into a ponytail, which made her look especially young this evening.

"That's a great dress," she said. "You look really nice. Where are you going?"

"To a dinner party. And thanks."

Renee had no idea how many outfits Kristy had already pulled out from the closet and tried on, even though the black dress that Shana had given her for Christmas last year had been her first choice all along.

You need to start going out, Shana had said, as they'd sat around a twinkling Charlie Brown tree in Kristy's living room last December.

Yeah, right. I have enough trouble getting a sitter for work. Besides, there's no place to go by myself.

I was talking about dating.

Deep inside, Kristy had known exactly what her friend had been hinting at. But she didn't have any interest in men. At least, she hadn't until now, but Craig Houston didn't count.

"Thanks for coming," Kristy said. "I don't have to go yet, but I thought it would be best if you came early. I'll pay you for the entire time."

"That's okay. I didn't have anything else to do."

Kristy was a bit uneasy about leaving Gram and Jason with a girl she really didn't know, but she'd been comforted by Renee's connection to the church. She'd also been desperate.

"You sure have a nice house," Renee said, taking in the cream-colored walls that needed a new coat of paint and the dark wood beams that could stand to be sanded and refinished.

"Thanks."

A lot of people liked the old Victorian-style homes and were drawn to Sugar Plum Lane, where some of the houses had been renovated better than others. And a few, like this one, needed a lot of work.

Even the décor, with its drab curtains and shabby furniture, left a lot to be desired, so Kristy figured Renee was commenting about the overall appeal of the place.

"I'll leave you a number where I can be reached," she told Renee. "I also baked some chicken and potatoes. I'm not sure if you've eaten yet, but there's plenty if you'd like to join Gram and Jason for dinner."

"Sounds good. Thanks."

"Gram will be coming out into the living room to watch television with you this evening. So I'll help you get her into the wheelchair before I leave." Kristy had already talked to her grandmother about Renee coming to work, and Gram, of course, wasn't all that keen on having anyone new. But Kristy had insisted she'd feel better if Gram would come out into the living room in her wheelchair and keep an eye on things.

She also planned to give Gram the portable phone that was programmed for a one-touch dial to either 9-1-1 or Kristy's cell.

Interestingly enough, when she'd explained the situation and the game plan to Gram, she'd only met with an initial grumble but no further complaints.

This was, Kristy realized, the first time in seven years that Gram had been given a chore to do, other than the rehab she'd had during the first year. Not that Kristy hadn't tried to encourage Gram to cultivate new interests, but Gram had refused until Kristy had just given up.

So, taking a lesson from Pastor Craig, she made a mental note: *Admit to Gram that life indeed sucks and then give her a job to do anyway.*

Something told Kristy it wouldn't be that simple, though.

"Is there anything I should know?" Renee asked. "Like does anyone have allergies or anything like that?"

"No. Jason isn't allowed to go outside tonight. I also monitor the television he watches. No violence, no bad language. Just G-rated shows, if you know what I mean."

"Yeah, I totally get it." Renee smiled, and her eyes, an

ocean-blue shade, glimmered. "Those rules will be easy to follow."

Kristy hoped so. "Would you mind helping me get my grandmother out of bed now?"

"No, not at all."

Another good sign. If Renee had any qualms about working with Gram, the chance of any long-term employment was out of the question.

"Just tell me what you need me to do," the girl added, as she followed Kristy down the hall. "I'm a fast learner."

Kristy entered her grandmother's bedroom, the one she'd had to fix for her downstairs. The footsteps behind her seemed to freeze at the entrance, but just briefly. She wasn't sure if Renee had paused out of respect or because the hospital bed was a bit daunting. But she guessed it didn't matter; she was beside her now.

"Gram, this is Renee."

"It's nice to meet you," the girl said, as Gram gave her a once over.

"You're not a nurse," Gram said.

"No. But I can call the paramedics if you need medical help."

Gram gave a little humph, then said, "I doubt that'll be necessary."

"Me, too," Kristy said, hoping to put Renee at ease. "Come on. I'll show you how to get her in the chair. She can help a little."

Moving Gram was a bit awkward at first, but Kristy had to give Renee credit. She jumped right in and gave it her best shot.

Once they had Gram set up in the living room and turned on the television, Kristy returned to her room to fix her hair.

She could hardly remember the last time she'd done anything more than pull it back in a ponytail or let it hang loose. So it took her a while to get her fingers and the curls to comply.

Ten minutes later, she returned to the living room, her hair swept up into a twist, the pearls adorning her ears and throat.

"Oh, wow," Renee said. "You look super."

"Yeah, Mom." Jason beamed. "If you had a crown, you'd look just like a princess."

"Thanks, honey."

For a moment, Jesse's comment about being a child of the king came to mind. Kristy still struggled with the whole concept, but she decided that, when she went to the Delacourts' house tonight, she was going to try to carry herself with the grace and dignity of a woman born to nobility.

The trouble was, she was afraid she'd feel more like a duck sitting on a pond—calm and serene on top of the water while paddling like crazy underneath.

Renee was glad to have paid employment, even if this particular job wasn't exactly what she'd planned on landing.

There was an upside, though. She was getting dinner out of it—a hot meal for a change.

And she'd also get to watch a little television—a luxury she hadn't had in a long time, since Mary Ellen had never hooked up the cable at her apartment and without it, the reception was awful.

There was a downside, too. While Renee wanted to do an exceptional job so that she'd be asked to come back and work again, she wasn't exactly sure what Jason's mom expected from her.

And then there was Mrs. Smith to deal with. She had a mean expression glued on her face and refused to return a smile, which wouldn't have hurt her to do.

She also smelled funny, although it wasn't stale sweat, tobacco or booze, which is what some of the people who had lived in Mary Ellen's apartment building used to smell like.

This was more like medicine, Renee decided.

It would be nice if Mrs. Smith gave Jason's mom a thumbs

up about Renee, but that wasn't likely. She just hoped she didn't give her a thumbs down.

She tried one last time to connect with her by saying, "You have a nice house." And she did; Renee wasn't just blowing smoke about that.

"It's not so nice when you know you'll be cooped up in it for the rest of your life," Mrs. Smith said.

Oh, yeah? Renee wanted to snap back. *How would you like living in a tree?*

But she didn't respond because, to be honest, Renee would much rather live in a tree house than be stuck in a hospital bed.

So she asked, "Are you guys hungry? I could put dinner on the table."

"I want to eat," Jason said.

Good. She had an excuse to get out of the living room and away from Mrs. Smith's evil eye.

When Renee had finished setting out the food, she wheeled Mrs. Smith into the dining room and made a place for her so the chair would fit.

They pretty much ate in silence, other than Jason's happy chatter about "the cool go-cart" Tommy's stepdad was helping him build "with a real engine and everything."

But to his credit, Jason never once mentioned the Bushman Trail or the tree house, which was a huge relief.

After dinner, Renee took Mrs. Smith back into the living room and turned on the television for her.

Renee expected her to be super fussy about the station they watched, but she wasn't. She let Jason have his choice, which was good.

In fact, she was pretty nice to him, so Renee had to give her credit for that. She didn't like to see kids yelled at or mistreated.

Eager to put some space between her and the crotchety woman, Renee said, "If you don't need anything from me, I'll go into the kitchen and do the dishes."

"Go ahead and do that. We're fine."

"Yeah," Jason added. "But hurry back so you can watch SpongeBob."

Cartoons weren't all that appealing anymore, so she was glad she wouldn't miss out on something good. "Start it without me, okay? You can tell me about the parts I missed during the commercials."

Renee not only did the dishes, but she cleaned the stove, too, making sure that the kitchen was cleaner than she'd found it. She also took out the trash and mopped the floor.

All the while, she kept poking her head into the living room to check on Jason and his grandmother. She hated to admit it, but she was kind of avoiding Mrs. Smith.

No matter what Dawn had said the other day about old people, the only ones Renee had ever run into had been grumpy and mean.

And Mrs. Smith was no different.

But Renee wouldn't complain. She needed this job. Maybe, if Jason's mom came home and saw that Renee hadn't just eaten up all her food and watched television all night, she'd hire her permanently.

If she did, Renee planned to make the best of it—even if she half-expected Mrs. Smith to jump out of that chair with a wild-eyed cackle, grab a broomstick, and fly through the house.

Craig had volunteered to be away from the house while the Delacourts hosted the dinner party for the Rensfields, but Cassandra wouldn't hear of it.

"Don't be silly, Craig. We'd love to have you with us tonight."

He had no choice but to believe her. "All right. Is there anything I can help you with?"

"Not really. I have all the food prepared and the table set. I've also hired someone to serve the meal and clean up. So there's nothing to do other than to welcome our guests."

At five-thirty, Cassandra's parents, Carlton and Shirley Price arrived. Daniel greeted his father-in-law with a firm handshake and his mother-in-law with a stiff-armed hug before introducing the couple to Craig.

Dressed in an expensive gray suit, Carlton was a dapper gent in his late sixties. His yellow shirt and striped tie coordinated nicely with the silk dress his wife, Shirley, wore. Together they made a sharp-looking pair.

"I hope you don't mind us coming early," Carlton said. "We've been looking forward to this get-together and to meeting the Rensfields."

"It's an exciting night," Cassandra said. "You have no idea how pleased we are that Shana and Brad have finally made a match. When they were in high school, I thought they'd make a perfect couple someday. It's almost as though I had a premonition about it."

Carlton leaned toward his daughter as though sharing a confidence, yet not lowering his voice enough to keep his words a secret. "From what I've heard, the Rensfields made a killing in stocks a while back, selling at just the right time. So Shana made a great catch."

Daniel's smile faded. "I'd like to think that Brad is the one who lucked out."

Cassandra placed a hand on her husband's forearm. "Sweetheart, will you please pour Mother a glass of wine and get Daddy his bourbon and water?"

"Certainly." Daniel drew away from his wife and addressed Craig, his grin only a shadow of what it had been earlier. "Can I get you something, Pastor?"

"Not right now. Thanks."

As Daniel left the room, Craig turned to Carlton, only to find the man was making his way toward a built-in bookshelf that boasted fancy knickknacks as well as leather-bound volumes of the classics.

Somewhat at a social loss, Craig was left to eavesdrop on the women's conversation.

"Who will be coming tonight?" Shirley asked her daughter.

"The Rensfields, of course—Eric and Darla. I'm sure you'll like them. Eric has been very generous with his financial support of the hospital, as well as the Boys and Girls Club. And Darla volunteers a lot of time to various charitable organizations."

"Will Brad be here?"

"He's going to drop by for a while, but I'm afraid he'll have to leave early."

Shirley smiled. "I'm glad I'll get a chance to meet him."

"You're going to love him, Mom. He's the nicest young man. Not what you'd call handsome, but he certainly carries himself well." Cassandra waited a beat before adding, "I've also invited Kristy, the maid of honor."

Shirley's brow lifted. "Was that necessary?"

Cassandra cleared her throat, then dropped her voice. "Shana insisted."

"Well, then. You didn't have much choice. I'm not at all sure why she insisted upon—"

Cassandra slid an arm around her mother's waist, as though roping her in—or perhaps joining forces. "I know, but there isn't much that can be done about that."

"No, I suppose there isn't."

A knot formed in Craig's gut, and he clenched his hands at his sides. For some reason, he had the urge to go to bat for a woman he hardly knew. But he kept his mouth shut. He really didn't have a dog in this fight, and he ought to be glad that he didn't.

Daniel reentered the room and served drinks to his in-laws, providing them with linen cocktail napkins. "We've hired a waiter for this evening, so he'll be taking care of refills and passing out hors d'oeuvres."

The doorbell rang, and Daniel excused himself. When he returned, he escorted the Rensfields into the living room and made introductions.

Eric Rensfield, a short, heavyset man in his late sixties, wore a dark blue suit and a predominantly yellow tie, the only thing about him that seemed noteworthy. With sparse gray hair, hazel eyes, and thin lips, the man seemed almost nondescript.

On the other hand, his wife, Darla, was a shapely and attractive brunette who wore a red knit dress and appeared to be about twenty years younger than her husband.

Again the doorbell rang, and this time Daniel brought Brad into the fold. The fair-haired young man resembled his father more than his mother, and Craig couldn't help wondering if he and Shana, whose portrait suggested she was a striking young woman, would seem just as mismatched as his parents.

Probably not.

"Thank you for inviting us to dinner," Brad said. "My parents and I have been looking forward to this evening. My only regret is that Shana can't be here."

"I'm sorry about that, too, Brad." Daniel placed a hand on his future son-in-law's shoulder and grinned. "How's school?"

"It's going very well. I'm prepping for the bar and looking for a law clerk position this summer." Brad chuckled and leaned his head toward Daniel. "Of course, I haven't settled on one yet, so if you hear of an opening . . . maybe at your firm?"

"I'm afraid all of our positions have been taken," Daniel said.

Shana's grandfather, who'd been looking on, eased into the conversation. "Surely, you can find a place for him, Daniel. It's usually just a matter of pulling in a favor or two."

Daniel seemed to stand taller, straighter. "I'll certainly let you know if I hear of any openings, Brad."

Tension rolled into the room like fog over the Pacific coast. Craig wasn't sure if the women had picked up on it, but he had.

And the maid of honor hadn't even arrived yet.

The waiter, a tall, lanky gentleman dressed in a crisp white shirt and black slacks, carried a silver tray with a variety of appetizers. He stopped and offered Craig his choice.

Craig took a crab-stuffed pastry puff and a napkin. "Thank you."

The doorbell gonged again, and this time Craig volunteered to answer, hoping for a reprieve but not expecting one. On the way to the entry, he glanced at his watch and wondered how long this evening would last. Too long, he suspected.

When he swung open the door, he was expecting to see Kristy, but his jaw nearly dropped to the ground at the sight of a stunning, red-haired beauty standing before him in a classic black dress and pearls, her curls swept up in a stylish swirl.

"There were several cars already parked out front," she said, "so I hope I'm not late."

Even her voice held an elegant lilt tonight, and he struggled to shake off the pulse-skittering effect by stepping aside to allow her in.

"Actually," he said, "you're right on time."

Her heels clicked on the travertine flooring in the foyer, while her perfume—an exotic, tropical scent—followed her into the house. As they walked to the living room, where the others waited, he couldn't help casting another glance her way.

He hoped she didn't think he was ogling her, but he couldn't seem to get over her metamorphosis from the tired waitress he'd met two Wednesdays ago or the single mother he'd run into at the park.

Would it be appropriate for him, as a minister and practically a stranger, to tell her how pretty she looked?

He suspected it would be, but he was afraid he'd stumble over the words like an adolescent on hormone overload. And, strangely enough, as they reached the others, he felt remiss for not complimenting her when he had the chance.

The conversations hushed at her entrance, while drinks and hors d'oeuvres stalled in mid-sip or mid-bite.

Daniel was the first to recover and greet her. And once the formalities were out of the way, he asked, "Can I get you a drink?"

"Yes, please. Diet soda if you have it."

"I'm sure we do."

As Daniel excused himself, Brad approached Kristy, a grin stretched across his face. "Hey, it's good to see you. How long has it been?"

"Five or six years, I suppose."

Brad's smile bore a hearty sign of male appreciation. "They were certainly good to you."

Her brow furrowed. "Excuse me?"

"The years," he said. "They've been good to you."

She seemed to stiffen.

"You've always been hot," he explained, "but now you're almost breathtaking."

She thanked him, but the words fell flat.

Craig could see why they would, though. A guy who was engaged to be married shouldn't tell another woman she was hot and breathtaking, even if she was.

It was weird, but Craig had this odd compulsion to take Kristy by the hand and lead her away from the Rensfield heir.

And away from this dinner party.

"Congratulations on your engagement," Kristy said to Brad. "You certainly scored when Shana agreed to marry you."

"I know."

While Craig tried to connect the dots between the words spoken and those omitted, Brad's mother called her son to her side.

He shrugged and threw up his hands in a Hey-what's-a-guy-supposed-to-do? manner. "If you'll excuse me . . . ?"

"Of course." Kristy turned to Craig, and her gaze seemed to latch on to his as though she was trying to stay afloat.

He wished that he could somehow help, but he didn't know how or even why he should. So he filled the silence by asking, "How's your grandmother?"

"She's doing all right. I hired a new sitter tonight, so I can't stay long."

"I was hoping for an early evening myself." He didn't explain, didn't think he had to.

"You know," she said, "I meant to call you today."

She did? His pulse rate spiked. "Why?"

"The new sitter's name is Renee, and she said you knew her and would be a reference. From what I understand, she's a volunteer at the soup kitchen."

Before he could ponder a truthful response that wouldn't hurt Renee's chance of employment, Daniel returned with Kristy's diet soda and announced that dinner was ready.

"After you." Daniel motioned for Kristy to lead the way to the dining room, where the table had been artistically set with fine china, crystal, and silver.

A vase of tropical flowers served as a centerpiece and was flanked by white tapered candles, each flame flickering and adding an elegance and warmth to the formal occasion.

"Pastor?" Daniel asked. "Would you say grace?"

Craig nodded, then bowed his head, making the prayer both short and sweet. When he finished, the waiter served Caesar salad and the meal began.

The conversation was a little too polite and stiff for Craig's taste, but he figured it was par for the course for everyone else.

As the waiter removed the dinner plates, Brad scooted back his seat and asked to be excused. "As much as I'd like to stay, I need to get home and prepare for a moot trial tomorrow."

"Of course," Cassandra said, "but I was hoping we could discuss the wedding plans over dessert. Apparently we should have done that over dinner instead."

Brad placed his napkin on his plate and stood. "I'm sure you don't need me here for that. I'm going to be busy until after I take the bar, so I'll go along with anything Shana wants."

As Daniel walked Brad to the door, Darla Rensfield turned to Cassandra and said, "We can still discuss the wedding plans. Have you checked with the country club yet?"

"Yes, I have." Cassandra smiled and settled back in her seat. "I've locked in the twenty-fourth of August. It's a Saturday evening. Shana and Brad can have the ceremony outdoors. There's a pond on number ten with a pair of weeping willows that would make a lovely backdrop."

"How many guests can the club hold?" Darla asked.

"Four hundred." Cassandra bit her bottom lip, then glanced across the table at Darla. "Do you think they will be able to accommodate everyone?"

"I hope so."

Kristy lifted her linen napkin and dabbed her lips before laying it next to her plate. "Shana wants a small, intimate wedding, so there won't be a seating problem."

"Shana mentioned that, but we have a lot of friends and associates who must be invited." Cassandra turned to Brad's mother. "Don't worry, Darla. I've always been able to get my daughter to see reason. The Rensfield-Delacourt wedding will be talked about for years."

"I'm sorry to object," Kristy said, her voice stern yet maternal. "But this is Shana's day, and her wishes need to be honored. If Brad were here, I'm sure he'd agree."

Silence hovered over the table, and Craig wanted to say something, to nod in agreement. But who was he to get involved? George had been the Delacourts' pastor for years and would undoubtedly be performing the ceremony. Craig merely a houseguest and one who really shouldn't even be at this dinner tonight.

Cassandra cleared her throat. "Like I said, Darla, I'll be talking to Shana. She's a reasonable young woman, so I'm sure she'll concede."

"She won't give in on this," Kristy said.

The silence was almost crippling, and the conversation didn't start up again until the waiter began serving individual chocolate soufflés. And at that point, the wedding discussion ended completely.

When the dessert plates were being picked up and the waiter was asking if anyone wanted more coffee, Kristy said, "I hate to be rude, but I really need to get home and relieve my sitter. Thank you so much for a lovely dinner, Mrs. Delacourt. It was delicious."

"You're welcome." Cassandra prepared to stand. "I'm sorry you have to go, Kristy, but I understand. You have a lot of responsibility for a woman your age. Let me walk you to the door."

"That's not necessary, Cassandra." Craig pushed back his chair and got to his feet. "I'll do it so you can stay with your other guests."

"Thank you, Pastor." Cassandra settled back into her seat.

Still, the conversation remained mute until Craig and Kristy left the room.

He escorted her to the door, but rather than stand on the porch and watch her go, he followed her out to her car. "I admired you for making a point and standing your ground. I imagine those women can be formidable in an argument."

Polite but venomous, he thought.

"I had no choice. It's what Shana asked me to do. And that's the only reason I agreed to come here tonight."

"You're a good friend."

"So is she."

They stood beside Kristy's car, yet neither of them made a move.

The stars overhead seemed especially bright, but even the magic of the night didn't hold a candle to the beautiful woman standing next to him.

"I really do have to go," she said.

He knew she did. And he needed to let her. But he couldn't seem to say goodnight until she finally did.

"Drive carefully," he added.

"I will." She opened the driver's door, and as she slid behind the wheel, the hem of her dress lifted and provided him a shadowed glimpse of a shapely thigh.

A glimpse he had no business taking.

As he watched her start the car and drive away, he made no attempt to return to the house.

Things aren't always what they seem around here, Jesse had told him on his first night in Fairbrook.

He suspected the man had been right.

So who was Kristy Smith?

Who was she *really*?

Chapter 11

On Saturday evening, at the end of her shift, Kristy changed out of her Irish work garb and removed her purse from the locker. Then she headed for the kitchen and the pub's rear exit.

She'd left her son and grandmother with Renee again, and even though she'd called a couple of times to check on them, she was still eager to get home.

Apparently, while she'd been at the Delacourts' for dinner last night, things had gone well. Jason had sung Renee's praises, and while Gram had more or less humphed and shrugged about the girl, she hadn't actually complained. So after Kristy had paid Renee, she asked her to return the next day.

A smile had lit the girl's face and put a spark in her eyes that made her almost look pretty. Kristy suspected that a professional haircut, a splash of makeup, and a new outfit would make a world of difference in her waiflike appearance.

After Renee had left, and while Kristy was putting Gram to bed, she'd asked, "So what did you think of her? Will she work out for us when Barbara moves?"

"She was all right, I suppose. But I didn't see much of her until right before you got home."

When Kristy went to get a glass of water before bed, she'd realized why. Renee had scrubbed the kitchen from top to bottom, something Kristy hadn't found the time or the energy to do lately, especially on nights she got home late and wanted to spend some time with Jason before bedtime.

As she exited the pub, she had to make her way around Bart Osgood, the dishwasher, who was sitting on the back steps, taking a smoke break.

A cigarette that was more ash than tobacco bobbled in the lanky, long-haired man's mouth when he spoke. "You headin' home now?"

"Finally." She unzipped her purse to remove the car keys. "I would have been out of here fifteen minutes earlier, but Sandra was late again. They keep giving her a split shift, which gives her an opportunity to be late twice in one day."

Kristy scanned the rear parking lot where she'd left her vehicle, relieved to see that it was still there, although she doubted anyone would ever steal it.

But a few years ago, she'd had a recurring dream in which Gram had gifted her with a shiny red sports car that had not only been her pride and joy, but had made her the envy of the town. She'd taken it to the mall one day, and while she was inside shopping, a guy hot-wired the engine and took it for a joy ride. She came out just in time to see him speed away.

She'd opened her mouth to yell for him to stop, but no sound came out. And as she tried to give chase, her legs wouldn't cooperate.

On the walk home, she'd spotted the car smashed against a tree, the thief nowhere in sight.

"At least the insurance will take care of the damage or replace your vehicle," a bystander had said. But she soon learned that Gram had forgotten to send in the payment and the policy had been canceled.

For a dream that hadn't been scary, Kristy found it freaky and unsettling, especially because she'd had it over and over. She'd tried to laugh it off when she'd told Shana about it later, but Shana had recently had a lecture in a psych class on dream analysis and had given Kristy her interpretation of what that dream had meant.

"That car represents the future you'd mapped out for yourself, and someone stole it from you."

That made sense, Kristy had supposed, but she didn't buy into psychobabble. If you asked her, dreams were the result of an imagination at play while the body slept. Besides, she had to take some personal responsibility for messing up her life.

Yet she still felt compelled to worry that someone might steal the only wheels she had available to her now.

She'd no more than grabbed the handrail and taken a step around Bart when someone or something moaned.

"Oh, for crying out loud. Would you look at that?" Bart lifted his index finger, the tip of which was missing, and pointed toward the Dumpster. "There's a drunk sleeping it off over there."

Kristy glanced in that direction, squinting to get a better look. It was difficult to see at night, especially with that flickering bulb in the streetlight, but she spotted the man, and he was wearing a royal blue jacket that looked a lot like the one she'd given Jesse.

Bart stood, dropped his cigarette butt onto the concrete step, and ground it out with the sole of his shoe. "Hey, you! Get on out of here or I'll call the cops."

The homeless man lifted his head slightly, then slumped back against the dark green trash receptacle.

Was he drunk?

Or was he *sick*?

Kristy placed her hand on Bart's shoulder. "It's okay. I'll take care of this. You go on in and get back to work."

"I'm not going to leave you out here alone."

"It's okay. I'm sure he's harmless." Kristy made her way to the Dumpster. As she got close enough to make out the man's features, she realized it was Jesse all right. At least, she thought it was. One eye was swollen shut, and the blood that was smeared on his face had matted his hair and beard. "What happened to you?"

"A couple of guys down by the bowling alley were giving me a hard time."

She furrowed her brow, wondering why he was downplaying what "the guys" had done to him. "'Giving you a hard time' sounds as though they were only razzing you, but it was more than that. You were in a fight."

"That's not exactly true. Those two fellows wanted a fight, that's for sure. But I wouldn't swing back, and I think that only made them angrier."

"They hit you, and you didn't fight back?"

He shrugged. "I don't believe in it. Never have."

Kristy dropped to one knee and reached for his wrist, checking his pulse. She'd taken a first aid class at the YMCA after Jason was born, but a sudden lack of confidence made her realize she was due for a refresher course.

His pulse rate was slow—too slow, she guessed.

"Come on. I'll drive you to the hospital." She would call the house along the way and tell Renee that she was going to be later than she'd thought.

But when she reached out to help Jesse up, he slowly shook his head. "I don't want to go to the hospital."

"Why not?"

"No money. No insurance. No need." He offered her a wistful grin. "I'll heal in a day or so."

"I can't leave you like this."

"Don't worry about me."

She doubted that anyone had worried about him in a long time, and she couldn't help doing so now. Jesse was too kind and too gentle for his own good. "I'm sorry, but I'm a mother, so worrying has become ingrained in me."

He didn't answer, leaving them at a bit of an impasse.

"Okay," she said, "I won't force you to go to the ER, even though I think that's where you need to go. But come home with me. I've got a spare bed you can sleep in tonight. Then we'll talk about whether you need to see a doctor tomorrow."

He seemed to ponder her words for a moment before slowly

getting to his feet by using the side of the Dumpster to steady himself. She helped him to the car, then got in herself and started the engine.

She hoped she wasn't making a mistake by taking him with her to spend the night. To be honest, while she truly believed Jesse was harmless, she was a bit uneasy about bringing a stranger into the house.

The only way for her to reconcile her action with common sense would be to put on a pot of coffee and stay up all night to keep an eye on things. So she made a decision to do just that.

She parked the car in the driveway, then helped him into the house.

Renee, who was sitting on the sofa watching television, gasped when they entered. "Oh, my gosh. What happened to you?"

"A couple of guys beat him up," Kristy whispered. "Where's Jason?"

"He's in bed. I checked him a few minutes ago, and he's asleep."

Good. Kristy didn't want to have to explain all of this to her son now, although she certainly would have, if he'd been awake. But then again, maybe there was a lesson here, a lesson that would help him to grow up compassionate and able to sympathize with the downtrodden.

"And what about Gram?" she asked Renee. "Is she asleep, too?"

"I helped her get into bed about an hour ago. Her back was aching, and she wanted some ibuprofen. I hope it was okay for me to let her have some."

"Of course, that's fine. Thanks."

Kristy led Jesse to the guest bathroom and gave him a towel. Then she went upstairs to her grandfather's old bedroom and grabbed a change of clothes for him.

Leaving Jesse to shower, she returned to the living room to pay Renee and to ask how the evening had gone.

"It was all right. I don't think Mrs. Smith likes me too much, but I'm okay with that."

"She doesn't seem to like anyone these days." Kristy reached into her purse and pulled out her tip money, counting out forty dollars.

"Do you need me again tomorrow?" Renee asked.

"No, I'm off." Kristy wasn't sure what Barbara's week would look like, whether she'd be available or not. And she didn't want to completely cut the woman out if she needed the work. "Why don't you give me your telephone number, Renee. That way I can call you and let you know when I need you again."

"I don't actually have a telephone right now, but I'm planning to get one soon."

"How can I get ahold of you?"

"You could, uh . . . leave a message for me at the soup kitchen, I guess. I'm there every day—except if you need me to work for you. Then I can come here instead."

"All right." Kristy walked Renee to the door, and when she'd left, she locked up the house. Then she went into the kitchen to open a can of soup and fix a sandwich for Jesse to eat. She waited there until the old pipes rumbled in the walls, letting her know the water had been shut off.

She gave him a few more minutes, then met him in the hallway and invited him into the kitchen.

"Bless your heart," he said, as he limped to the table and took a seat before a bowl of chicken noodle soup and a bologna sandwich. "This looks wonderful."

The food might, but Jesse was still a mess. His hair was wet, but clean. And the wounds on his face had stopped bleeding. But that eye looked nasty.

"You're going to have a shiner," she told him.

"It could have been worse." Jesse pointed to his good eye and attempted a smile. "At least I can still see out of this one."

She crossed her arms and leaned against the kitchen counter. "Apparently, you're an optimist."

"An eternal one." He smiled again, this one more successful than the last. "And you're a natural born healer. You'll make a great doctor."

Kristy's heart tightened. For a moment, she wondered if he'd talked to someone, if he'd known she'd once harbored thoughts of attending medical school. But she shrugged off his comment as a coincidence.

"What was it you told me about going to the hospital?" She tossed him a wry grin. "No money, no insurance, no need? Well, the same can be said about me going to college."

And like him, she was healing, too, although not nearly as quickly as he would.

"It's not too late," he said, taking a bite of the bologna sandwich.

"Too late for what?"

"A medical degree."

Yeah, right. She took a seat across from him. "When I was in high school and my grandmother was still able to paint and had a regular income, I had plans to apply for scholarships and attend one of the state universities, but I made a huge mistake one day. And here I am." She tried to smile, but her lips failed to fully comply.

"Dreams aren't lost, Kristy. Sometimes they're merely postponed. Or they take another direction."

He *was* an eternal optimist, she realized. And a pacifist who'd rather take a beating than stand up for himself. He was also homeless and unable to even provide himself with the basic necessities.

She ought to tell him he was full of crap, but before she could open her mouth, her eyes began to sting, and a tear slipped down her cheek. She swiped it away with the back of her hand, only to find another one taking its place.

"Can I tell you something?" he asked.

Emotion clogged her throat, and she feared the words wouldn't form, so she nodded.

"God doesn't give a person a dream without also giving the power to make it come true. But that doesn't mean it won't take a great deal of work on your part. The determination and follow-through has to come from the heart and the gut."

She'd known med school would be tough, both to get accepted and to maintain a scholarship. At one time, she thought she'd had the heart and guts to pull it off, but that was before she'd ended up as sole support of the family.

He ate in silence for a bit, then looked up, his face marred by the brutality of the men who'd repeatedly struck a man who'd refused to fight back. "You know, sometimes the unexpected happens. Dreams get dashed. But in those cases, it's best to have a backup plan."

"A backup plan?" she asked.

"A wise man once told me that the essence of mental health is knowing that you have options. And you have several, Kristy."

"Like what?" She couldn't see many. "Like whether I want a sandwich made out of white or whole wheat or rye? I'm afraid my life is mapped out, and there aren't many alternatives that I can see."

"The trees often block you from seeing the vastness of a forest."

"That's not the exact quote," she said, "but I know what you mean."

"Well, then how's this for another analogy? Your life was once mapped out for you, and you'd planned to hit the road at a good clip, sailing along in a little red sports car. But you blew a tire. Hit a tree. Fortunately, you survived, a bit battered by the blow. And you brush yourself off and head home."

The little red sports car reference caused goose bumps to skitter along her arms, but she shook them off and continued to listen, unsure of where he was going with his pep talk.

"But you didn't lose the map, Kristy. You merely lost your mode of transportation."

"Okay. But now I've got some extra travelers."

He nodded. "So maybe a solid, dependable minivan might be more appropriate."

She chuffed. "Maybe so. But no money, no insurance, no need. Remember?"

"Are you sure about that?"

Yeah. Unfortunately, she was absolutely convinced.

When he finished eating, she took him upstairs to her grandfather's room and told him to "sleep tight." Then she returned to the kitchen, put on a pot of coffee and waited for it to brew. She poured herself a mug and carried it into the living room, where she sat on the recliner, determined to settle in for the night.

As sometimes happened in this particular room and in this particular seat, her gaze was drawn to the picture over the mantel, to the little red-haired girl who sat in a field of dandelions, her wishes and possibilities legion.

Kristy would have loved to claim Jesse's optimism, but she'd blown her chance to ever see her dream come true.

And even if she hadn't, even if there were options and opportunities she hadn't yet realized, she was afraid she no longer had the heart or the guts to make the dream come true.

It was getting late—well after nine o'clock—and Craig was seriously thinking about turning in for the night. He and Daniel had been sitting in the family room, kicking back and watching a pay-per-view movie, a thriller that was actually pretty good, but Craig hadn't been able to keep his thoughts from straying away from an all-star cast and a complicated plot.

Instead, he'd been thinking about how badly he'd like to move out of the Delacourts' house, in spite of how hard they'd tried to make him feel welcome.

The church had promised to provide him with a small, two-bedroom house on Bayside Terrace, but the place was being remodeled by one of the congregants, a busy contractor who'd only been able to work on that particular project in the evenings and on weekends.

It wouldn't be right to press either the guy volunteering or the church, but Craig certainly could offer to help the contractor get it done. He hadn't done much construction work, but he was a fast learner, strong, and dependable.

He was also extremely motivated.

Outside, the engine of a car sounded, followed by the raising of the automatic garage door.

Apparently, Cassandra was finally home. She'd put dinner on the table earlier, then had gone to meet Darla Rensfield at a bridal boutique in San Diego.

When Daniel had questioned her about it, offering some cautionary advice about putting the cart before the horse, she'd disagreed. "Darla and I are just going to look at bridal dresses and get to know each other a little better. We'll both report back to Shana. The store has a Web site, so she can look at some of the gowns we like, then she can make the final decision."

Daniel's only response had been a slight roll of the eyes that he probably didn't realize Craig had noticed.

Now, as Cassandra entered the house, her hair a bit windblown and her expression a bit harried, Craig instantly sensed that something was wrong.

The woman who was usually well-groomed and in control blurted out, "My purse was stolen."

"Did you call the police?" Daniel asked.

"Yes, I did."

Her husband returned his focus to the movie, since the big chase was on and the climax was in full swing.

"Daniel!" Her voice came out as a shrill. "Did you even hear me?"

The man tore his gaze from the screen. "Yes, I heard you, Cassie. Your purse was stolen, and you made a police report. There's not much more you can do now, other than cancel your credit cards."

Her pinched expression suggested that he'd failed to give her the response she'd wanted. And when it became apparent that the movie held more interest for him than her dilemma, she blew out a frenzied sigh and plopped down in an over-stuffed chair. "Thank goodness Daddy insisted we use that magnetic hide-a-key. Otherwise, Darla would have had to bring me home, and we would have had to go back for the car later."

"Did you have any credit cards in your purse?" Craig asked.

"Fortunately, only one. I'd better call now and cancel it." She reached for the telephone that sat on the lamp table beside her, then slowly returned the receiver to its cradle. "Oh, dear. This is so unsettling, I can't even think straight. I need to go upstairs and get my list of important numbers."

Craig decided now was the time to excuse himself, but before he could open his mouth, the movie credits began to roll, and Daniel said, "Oh, Cassie. I almost forgot. While you were gone, Claire Dawson called. She'd like you to give her a call tomorrow. She and Sam are having a couple of the attorneys in our firm over for dinner next week, and they'd like us to join them."

"All right." Cassandra turned to Craig. "Sam Dawson and his wife, Claire, are also new members of the church. I'm not sure if you've had a chance to meet them yet."

"I'm afraid I haven't." If they didn't have a teenager in the youth group or weren't housebound or regulars at the soup kitchen, it wasn't likely that he'd be meeting them anytime soon.

"Is Claire feeling any better?" Cassandra asked Daniel. "The last I heard, morning sickness was slowing her down."

"She didn't say."

Cassandra faced Craig and explained, "Sam is raising his orphaned niece, a sweet little girl who reminds me a lot of Shana when she was that age. In fact, Analisa is so happy about the new baby that it makes me wish we'd had another child."

When Cassandra returned her focus to her husband, as though hoping for some kind of reaction from him, he failed to take the cue.

Another awkward stretch nearly sucked the air from the

room, but before Craig could fake a yawn and get to his feet, the phone rang.

Cassandra answered almost immediately, and her expression softened a moment later. "Hi, honey. I'm so glad you called. You'll never guess what Darla Rensfield and I did this evening."

She sobered. "You've moved up the wedding date? Oh, no, we aren't going to have enough time to do things up right as it is."

Cassandra listened a moment longer, then placed her hand over the receiver. "Daniel, Shana is coming home early. She wants you to pick her up at the airport tomorrow afternoon at four."

"What's all this about?" Now it was Daniel's turn for a revolving set of expressions as he mouthed, "Is she . . . *pregnant?*"

Cassandra shrugged, then returned to the telephone conversation. "You're talking about coming home in mid-semester. And your last one at that. Are you okay, honey? I mean, if you're pregnant, we can work this out. No one needs to know, so it won't ruin the wedding."

As Cassandra's gaze met Craig's, a sense of "oops" crossed her face. Had she and Daniel forgotten he was in the room? That he didn't need to be involved in this?

Again, he wished he'd gone to bed when the idea had first crossed his mind.

Cassandra glanced at her husband and shook her head, mouthing the words, "No, she's not."

"Okay," Cassandra said into the receiver. "I understand. At least, I think I do. You can talk to us about it more when you get home. I just hope this doesn't jeopardize your graduation requirements."

A frown furrowed her brow. "Okay, I'll trust you on that. And I'll see you tomorrow."

Cassandra hung up the telephone, ending the conversation.

Still, the silence was deafening. And the walls and ceiling seemed to bow from the heavy tension.

Craig snatched his chance for escape. "If you'll excuse me, I really need to go to bed. One of the shut-ins, Harry Stevens, is going in for a triple bypass at seven in the morning, and I promised his wife I'd sit with her during the surgery."

"Goodnight," Daniel said. "We'll see you in the morning."

Not if Craig could help it. He planned on getting up at five so he could slip out of the house and have coffee and breakfast at the all-night diner.

Moments later, as he closed himself into his room in the den, he felt a sense of escape. But it didn't last long. Muffled voices from the living room seemed to murmur through the walls.

"I'm not happy about Shana leaving school," Daniel said.

"Neither am I, but she says that she has everything under control."

A testosterone-laced grumble erupted.

"We need to support her in this," Cassandra said. "Besides, she said that Brad needs her. That it has something to do with all of his classmates getting law clerk positions and him being nervous about not having one."

"Those with the highest grades tend to find positions the easiest."

"Are you suggesting he's not a good student?"

No response.

"Daniel? Is that what you're suggesting?"

"I'm not suggesting anything, Cassie. Just let it go."

"You didn't have a position for him, remember? He certainly hinted at it during dinner."

A stretch of silence was followed by, "I'm not going to bat for him, Cassie."

"Why not? Daddy went out of his way to find a position for you."

"That's exactly why I won't do it."

"You, of all people, should be grateful."

"Why? So that Brad can get stuck in a position that will make him miserable one day?"

"Stuck? *Stuck?* For goodness sake, Daniel. You're a partner in one of the most prestigious firms in the county, if not the state. Are you suggesting that you're stuck and miserable?"

"You know I never wanted to be a defense attorney. That I wanted to be a prosecutor."

"We discussed that. And we decided that there was no money to be made as a prosecuting attorney."

"No, Cassie. Actually, it was you and your father who had that discussion and came to that conclusion. And like a fool, I agreed. And even though I've tried to make the best of it, I still don't measure up."

"Daddy's so proud of you. How can you say that you don't measure up?"

"Did you ever stop to think that I don't measure up in my own eyes, either?"

Craig stepped into the bathroom and closed the door, finally stilling the voices he didn't want to hear. After a hot shower, he brushed his teeth, then returned to the den, where he was met with peace and quiet.

That is, until he glanced at all the baseball memorabilia on the bookshelf.

Would he end up as miserable as Daniel Delacourt one day?

"Mom?"

After a poke on the arm and a second "Mom," Kristy shot out of the recliner with a start.

Jason, who was wearing his SpongeBob pajamas, stood at her side. "Sorry, Mom. Don't wake up, but can I have some Lucky Charms for breakfast?"

She searched the dawn-lit living room, trying to get her bearings. She'd meant to stay awake all night, but obviously hadn't. Raking a hand through her hair, she blinked her eyes a couple of times. "Sure, honey. I'll get it for you, but I need to check on something first. It'll just take a minute."

"Okay." He grabbed the television remote from the coffee table, then climbed onto the sofa and pushed on the power button.

"Turn the volume down, please. People are sleeping."

"What people?" he asked, his focus clearly glued to the TV screen.

Since he didn't have a follow-up question, she let the subject drop and tiptoed up the stairs, avoiding the squeaky step. She made her way to her grandfather's old bedroom, only to find the door open and the bed stripped, the dirty linen folded neatly on the mattress.

Jesse was up already?

A check of the bathrooms, as well as the rest of the house—both upstairs and down—convinced her that he was not only awake, but gone.

As she neared Gram's room, her grandmother called out, "Kristy? Is that you?"

She slowed her steps and peered into the open doorway. "Yes. I'm sorry if I woke you."

"That's okay. What time is it?"

Kristy glanced at her wristwatch, which she'd been wearing since yesterday. "Six-fifteen. Do you want me to help you to the bathroom?"

"If you don't mind."

"Let me fix a bowl of cereal for Jason first. And I'll be right back."

Moments later, Kristy returned and helped Gram out of bed and into the portable commode.

"How'd you sleep?" she asked, as she pushed Gram to the bathroom.

"Better than usual, although I had the *strangest* dream last night."

Once Gram was inside, Kristy stepped back into the hall

and pulled the door shut to provide the elderly woman with privacy.

"That dream was so real," Gram said, "but I know it wasn't since I wasn't the least bit afraid about having a bearded stranger in the house."

Kristy, who was leaning against the wall while she waited for Gram to finish, straightened.

"There was something very gentle and kind about him," Gram added. "And his eyes were the prettiest shade of blue I'd ever seen."

Eyes? Plural? Last night, one of them had been swollen shut. Had the swelling gone down with a shower and a rest?

"It's amazing how the mind plays tricks on us, but the man was dressed in your grandfather's clothes. In fact, he was even wearing the royal blue jacket that I'd given Stan on our last Christmas."

Kristy hadn't realized that particular jacket had any significance. If she had, she would have chosen another one from the closet.

"He said some of the weirdest things," Gram said.

"Like what?"

"For one thing, it seemed as though he had some kind of divine message."

The sci-fi tones of *The Twilight Zone* theme song seemed to play in Kristy's mind. "Did he tell you he was a messenger?"

Gram chuckled. "No. In fact, he seemed too real for that. I'd expect a heavenly being to be . . . well, ghostlike, I suppose."

"What did he say to you?"

Gram cleared her throat. "I'm finished."

Like in finished living in this world? Kristy scrunched her face. "Excuse me? I'm not sure I know what you mean."

"I'm finished using the bathroom," Gram said. "You can come in and help me back to bed now."

Kristy released the breath she hadn't realized she'd been holding, then went inside.

"He asked me how I was doing," Gram said, "and I told him exactly how I felt—useless, a burden, and ready to die."

Kristy emptied and rinsed the pot, washed her hands, then pushed Gram back into the hall.

"He told me I still had unfinished business on earth."

"Well, I imagine that's probably true." Although Kristy knew there wasn't much the woman was capable of doing anymore.

"He mentioned you, too."

"*Me?*" Kristy cocked her head. "What did he say about me?"

"That my attitude is weighing down on you. That you need my full support right now, and not my complaints."

What had Kristy said to Jesse? She couldn't remember venting or discussing her grandmother.

Gram turned her head, glanced over her shoulder. "I'm sorry, honey."

"About what?" The lack of support? The complaints?

"The more I thought about what the man had said, the more I realized he was right. I didn't mean to make things any more difficult for you. And I can't promise that I won't be a burden in the days to come, but I'll try not to be."

"Thanks, Gram. Your apology is accepted." Kristy thought about what Craig had told her, and tried using an honest approach. "He was right, Gram. As much as I sympathize with you and realize how tough your lot in life is, there's not much I can do to make it better. And that frustrates me."

"See? There's one more reason it would be best if God took me home."

"It's obviously not time."

"I suppose you're right." Gram blew out a weary sigh. "I'll try to focus on what the man in my dream said."

Did Kristy dare tell her that she hadn't been dreaming? That the man who'd talked to her had been made of flesh and bone? That he was a vagabond, a pacifist, and possibly a psychic?

Maybe not. The message he'd given her had been clearly true—and maybe even divinely inspired.

"Jesse was right," Kristy said. "You still have an earthly job to do."

"Jesse?" Gram said. "Who's Jesse?"

Truthfully?

Kristy wasn't sure.

Chapter 12

On the way home from the airport, Shana Delacourt sat in the passenger's seat of her father's black Mercedes and gazed out the window at the scenery along northbound Interstate 5.

It had been a long, tiring flight from Australia, and while she'd told her parents and Brad that filing an incomplete on her courses at the university in Sydney wouldn't have any adverse effects, she was actually uneasy about the decision she'd made.

Her father turned on the blinker, then looked over his shoulder before changing lanes. "I still don't understand why you came home without finishing that last term, Shana. Of course, your mother and I are happy to see you, but it's not like you to leave something undone or to quit in midstream."

Wasn't it? There were things her parents didn't know about her, things they'd failed to observe.

She shook off the heaviness that had dogged her from Sydney. "Don't worry, Dad. I have enough credits to graduate."

"That's not my point."

Maybe not, but that was about all she was going to admit to. Her loyalty ran deep, but so did her need for privacy, and she found it easier to offer her parents—and others—very little information. That way, it left no room for questions she didn't want to answer.

"So why did you really decide to come home?" her father asked. "Was it just to plan the wedding?"

"Don't you remember what it was like to be in love?"

He didn't comment.

"Besides," she added, "Brad misses me." He also needed her, and since there'd been a time when he'd stepped in and had taken charge when she'd been scared senseless and had nowhere else to turn, it was only fair that she return the favor now.

"And you miss him?" her father asked.

There was more to it than that, but she sidestepped the question. "Brad's concerned about our future, and I'm worried that he's getting depressed. Some of the third-year law students already have clerk positions, and he hasn't found one yet."

"What's his class rank?"

"I'm not sure." She didn't know the actual number, just that it was low.

And that didn't surprise her. Brad had been footloose during high school and college, and his work habits had followed him to Cal Western School of Law. So now, as he faced the bar exam and the promise of a successful career lay just beyond reach, his irresponsibility had come back to haunt him. He needed to secure a law clerk position for the summer, and due to his low ranking, his options were limited.

Her dad reached for his Starbucks cup, which had been sitting in the holder, and took a drink. "The cherry positions go to those who are at the top of the class."

Obviously, her father had come to a clear conclusion about Brad's ranking.

"Which positions are those?" she asked.

"Clerkships with judges for one. Prestigious firms are another. In fact, when I was in law school, the district attorney's office only interviewed people who were in the top ten percent."

"You were in that group, weren't you?"

Her dad smiled and nodded. "I was number three."

"But you didn't want a position with the DA's office because you earn more as a defense attorney."

He was silent for a moment, introspective. Then he cleared his throat. "Your grandfather advised me to take a position with a criminal defense firm, and so did your mother."

"But that wasn't your first choice?"

"No." He seemed to ponder his answer, and she stole another sidelong glance at him. He wore a frown and held the steering wheel as though he was afraid he'd eject from the sunroof if he didn't. "To be honest, I would have rather worked for the DA's office."

His admission took her aback, and she struggled with the perception she'd always had of him—the champion of the underdog and the downtrodden.

"You mean you actually considered being a prosecutor?" she asked.

He shrugged, then his stoic expression morphed into a wistful grin. "I watched too many John Wayne movies growing up."

She'd never realized that he might have a few regrets of his own. That he'd been urged and guided to make the right choices, choices that might not have been in his best interest.

"For what it's worth," she said, "you've always been one of the good guys to me."

"Thanks, honey." He reached across the seat and patted the top of her knee. "How many men have their own private cheerleader?"

Shana risked another peek at her father's profile and studied him in a way she'd never done before.

He'd always been a handsome man, but in the past year his hair had grayed more at the temples and the laugh lines had deepened around his eyes.

But now, on the drive home, she couldn't help noting how his thoughts had created a V-shaped line that marred his brow.

"Are you sorry?" she asked.

"About what?"

"Not working for the DA."

"Hey." He tore his gaze from the road and tossed her a smile. "It's no big deal. Years ago, I made a decision that was best for the family."

"So you're not bogged down in regret?"

He glanced back out the windshield, and she wasn't sure if it was for safety reasons or to wait a beat before answering.

Finally, he said, "It's only natural to look back and wonder what life would have been like if you'd chosen another road, but that doesn't necessarily mean you regret the one you took."

Shana had done a lot of that, imagining what her life would have been like if she'd stood up to her mother years ago. If she hadn't taken the easy way out each time she'd been presented with a dilemma.

She supposed that, over the course of her college years, she'd imagined every possible alternate scenario in her mind, and not too many of them had ended up with her being happy, so it wouldn't have really mattered if she'd chosen another option or not. She'd come to learn that life wasn't an Etch A Sketch; one couldn't shake things up and start over.

As her father turned on the blinker, signaling his intent to exit the freeway, she had second thoughts about going straight home, about facing her mother and talking about the wedding details and the guest list.

Or her decision to come home.

"Would you mind dropping me off at Kristy's? I need to talk to her about a few things. She's not working today, so she'll be home."

"Your mother will be disappointed that you didn't stop to see her first."

"I'll make it up to her somehow."

Minutes later, the Mercedes pulled along the curb in front of Kristy's house.

"Thanks for picking me up. I'll see you at the house this evening." She tossed him a love-you-Daddy smile, then grabbed her purse, shut the passenger door, and strode up the walk.

Before she even reached the door, Kristy stepped out on the porch and greeted her with a warm hug. "It's good to have you back, Shana."

"I'm glad to be home."

Okay, that wasn't completely true. But there were things even her best friend didn't know, things Shana didn't want to share. Things that, even though she'd tamped them down so far and so deep, she still feared would rise to the surface if she wasn't careful.

"Come on inside," Kristy said, leading her into the living room of the old Victorian that had always felt more loving, more welcoming than Shana's own house.

As she scanned the worn interior, she was actually glad to see that nothing had changed while she'd been gone.

"Where's Jason?" she asked.

"He's playing at Tommy's house and will be home shortly."

The two friends chatted for a while, playing catch-up, until Kristy said, "Ramon came by Paddy's Pub the other day and asked about you."

Shana's heart nearly imploded at the news, yet she scurried to appear only slightly curious. "What did he say?"

"Just that he was surprised to hear you were marrying Brad, that he thought you could do better."

Could she?

She had her doubts.

But as her thoughts were prone to do whenever they went unchecked, they drifted to Ramon, the boy she'd once loved with all her heart.

The relationship had been short-lived and star-crossed from day one.

When her mother had learned that Shana had been seeing Ramon on the sly, she'd been shocked.

"What are you thinking?" she'd asked. "He's an immigrant,

the son of a groundskeeper. You can—and you *will*—do better than that."

But had she?

Shana shook off the memory and managed a smile. "I haven't seen Ramon since high school graduation. How's he doing?"

"Good. *Great*, actually. He's started his own business and it seems to be taking off nicely."

"I'd heard he'd started up a mobile lawn-mowing business."

"That might be how it started out," Kristy said. "But next time you go to Mulberry Park, check out the flower garden he created and maintains. The city took proposals and then chose his plan over quite a few others."

"He always did have an eye for color." Shana's thoughts again drifted to the boy she'd once loved, to what they'd had, to what might have been.

It's only natural to look back and wonder what life would have been like if you'd chosen another road, but that doesn't necessarily mean you regret the one you took, her father had said earlier.

Maybe not, but the sadness that had begun to darken her mood, the heaviness she'd managed to shake on the drive to Sugar Plum Lane, came back in full force.

On Monday afternoon, Renee sat in the waiting room at the free clinic, where she thumbed through a shabby issue of *Better Homes and Gardens* while waiting for her name to be called.

She paused when she spotted an article about decorating the home on a shoestring budget by shopping at garage sales, studying each photo, all of which were unique and interesting. It was amazing what a person could do with junk no one else wanted.

A smile pulled at her lips as she thought about the boys who kept bringing her things for the tree house—stuff that could be found at yard and garage sales. If they kept it up, she would have to build a second floor to extend her space.

Of course, now that she was working and earning money rather than just spending it, things had begun to look up. In a few weeks, she hoped to be able to rent a room from someone who wouldn't mind having a baby in the house.

Mary Ellen certainly hadn't been okay with it.

Renee glanced at the backpack that sat next to her. The zipper was partially open, and a little stuffed teddy bear that had been made by someone who knew how to knit or crochet poked its head out, its pink string mouth stitched into a grin.

"This is for the baby," Danny had said yesterday when he'd given it to her. "A lady at the soup kitchen gave these to us kids when my mom took us there to eat once."

Renee assumed Dawn Randolph was the woman who'd given it to him since she was the one who made those little stuffed animals and passed them out to the kids.

Dawn really liked children; it was obvious. She reminded Renee of Mrs. Wolfe, her first grade teacher.

Mrs. Wolfe had been super nice, too. She used to keep a hair brush and comb in her desk drawer, along with ribbons and barrettes. And she would call Renee in each morning before school started and fix her hair. Back then, Renee always thought it was because Mrs. Wolfe didn't have kids of her own and kind of liked fussing over a girl's hair.

Looking back, though, Renee suspected she'd done it because she'd felt sorry for the only girl in class who hadn't had anyone to help her get ready for school in the mornings.

Mrs. Wolfe also used to keep snacks and goodies in her desk drawer, like granola bars. So when it was snack time, Renee always had something to eat, like the other kids.

At the soup kitchen, Dawn was concerned about Renee having plenty to eat, too, and always sent extra food home with her.

Yesterday, while they were fixing lunch, Dawn mentioned

that she and Joe would like to adopt a baby since they couldn't have kids. The comment had kind of come out of the blue, since Renee hadn't been expecting it. And for a moment—a very brief one—Renee had thought that Dawn would make a better mother for the baby than she would.

But then the baby started kicking, reminding Renee that there was a real kid inside her stomach who had rights and feelings that shouldn't be ignored. So she'd let the idea pass as quickly as it had come to her.

There was no way she would ditch her baby, the way her mom had ditched her. Not even if the baby went to someone like Dawn.

"Renee Delaney?"

"Yes?" She spotted a woman holding a medical chart while waiting in the open doorway. So she put the magazine on the table in front of her, stood, grabbed her backpack—taking care not to jostle the little bear loose—and headed toward the door that led to the exam rooms.

"How are you doing?" the nurse asked.

"Okay, I guess."

First stop was the scale. After getting Renee's weight, the nurse took her to a room, where she laid out one of those open-in-back gowns and a sheet on the small exam table. "If you'll get undressed, I'll be back to check your blood pressure."

Renee nodded, then waited for her to shut the door before putting on the gown and climbing onto the table. Before long, the nurse returned to check her blood pressure, as well as her pulse.

"Dr. Purvis will be in shortly," she said.

Ten minutes later, a stocky, gray-haired man who was wearing a white lab coat and half-lens reading glasses that rode low on his nose, entered the room and introduced himself as the doctor. He wasn't happy that Renee had waited so long to come in to see him.

She had a hundred excuses she could have made, but they

would only make her sound young and dumb and in dire straits, so she kept quiet.

He didn't continue to give her a hard time about it, so that was good. He asked her quite a few questions, and she answered them the best she could.

"The chart says you're twenty-one," he said.

Did her real age matter? Doctors were supposed to turn people in who abused kids. She knew that for a fact because one of her foster moms, Darlene Griffin, got mad once and twisted Renee's arm until it snapped. The doctor at the ER reported Darlene to child protective services, and they removed Renee and another foster kid from the home.

There was no way Renee would ever hurt her child, but what if Dr. Purvis thought she wouldn't take good care of it? Or what if he thought the baby would be better off with someone older? Someone who had a house or a yard?

"Yes," she said, hoping a breezy smile would put his concerns to rest. "I'm twenty-one. But don't worry. I've got an ID if you want to check it."

Paternal eyes swept over her, almost like he'd learned how to tell a person's real age by looking, but he didn't challenge her. Instead, he asked her to lie down. When she did, resting her head on the pillow, he proceeded to poke and push on her stomach.

Then, after he called the nurse back into the room, he did a pelvic exam. When he was finished, he asked the nurse to set up for an ultrasound.

"What's that?" Renee asked.

"It's a scan that will show us what's going on inside your uterus," Dr. Purvis said. "It's routine at this point. I want to make sure everything is proceeding and developing the way it's supposed to."

That made sense.

"In your case," he said, "I'll be watching you closely since you're a high-risk pregnancy."

"Why?" she asked, wondering if he'd found something wrong.

"Your age for one thing."

She wouldn't cop to lying about it unless he started yelling at her. But he didn't.

"I want you to start on prenatal vitamins right away," he added. "And we'll need you to have blood drawn before you leave the office. I also want a urine sample. If I find anything we need to be concerned about, I'll give you a call."

"Would it be okay if I called you? I don't have a phone."

His glasses slid to the tip of his nose, and he looked at her over the top of them. "Okay."

For some reason, she felt busted again.

The nurse wheeled in a machine, and as she set it up, the doctor smeared a cold gel on Renee's belly. Moments later, she was instructed to look at the screen. Her first thought was that it had bad reception like a TV on the blink.

"There's your baby," Dr. Purvis said.

"Where?" Renee studied the black and gray images on the screen, trying to spot something baby-like swimming around.

Dr. Purvis pointed out the head and the spine, which he said looked good. He also showed her the arms and hands, as well as the legs and feet.

A fist went up and seemed to disappear into the baby's head.

"See that?" Dr. Purvis asked. "The baby's sucking its thumb."

"Really?" Renee's lips parted, and her eyes widened, as she looked at the doctor to see if he was messing with her. But he didn't seem to be.

He fiddled with a couple of buttons and typed in some numbers, then he made the screen freeze. "You're about twenty-two weeks along. Do you want to know if you're having a girl or a boy?"

"No kidding? Can you really tell?" Renee tore her gaze away from the screen long enough to check out the doctor's face.

Again, his expression was serious. "If the baby will cooperate, I can tell."

"Then, yes. Absolutely. I want to know what it's going to be."

He went back to work, pushing the camera-thingy against her belly. "Aw, there we go. I've got a clear view. And . . . it's a little girl."

Renee hadn't given the baby's sex any thought until Jesse had said it would be a girl. And from that day on, she'd begun to imagine herself with a daughter.

Weird that Jesse would know that.

She bit down on her bottom lip, then asked, "Can you tell if she has dark curly hair?"

Dr. Purvis chuckled. "I'm afraid our technology isn't that good yet."

Her head sunk back on the pillow. "It doesn't really matter. I was just wondering, that's all."

Jesse had probably been blowing smoke when he'd made his prediction, which really wasn't that big of a stretch. There'd been a fifty-fifty chance that he would guess right.

But none of that really mattered.

The baby had become real today, and for the very first time, Renee was looking forward to holding her daughter in her arms.

Shana had stayed at Kristy's until six last night, catching up with her friend and getting a chance to play with Jason and visit with Mrs. Smith.

It had been sad seeing the once warm and vibrant woman bedridden and so clearly miserable. As a child and a teen, Shana had gravitated toward Kristy's grandma, a woman who hadn't minded when the girls made cookies in her spic-and-span kitchen or stayed up all night yakking and giggling. And she'd never fussed about social pretenses, something her own grandmother always did.

So, when it neared the dinner hour, Kristy had asked a neighbor to sit with her grandma and had driven Shana home.

Upon entering the house for the first time in months, Shana had found her mother in the kitchen, peeling potatoes. She greeted her with a hug, and they went through the usual I-missed-you motions.

"I'll have dinner on the table shortly," her mother said.

"I'm really sorry, but I'm going to pass. I'm exhausted after that flight. All I want to do is sleep."

Her mother had undoubtedly gone above and beyond by fixing all of her favorite food, but she put on a good-little-soldier smile. "I understand."

Shana had then gone to her bedroom, sequestering herself inside, where nothing had changed while she'd been gone. The bed was still covered with that blue comforter with white trim, the walls bore the same matching wallpaper. Even her Fairbrook High pom-poms and megaphone remained in the corner where she'd left them, a memorial to a carefree teenage girl who'd ceased to exist.

Today she'd let her mom talk her into going to San Diego to shop for wedding dresses, but she'd tried on so many white gowns that her head was spinning and she couldn't make a decision.

At least, that's the excuse she'd used when her mom had asked which one she liked best.

Now, after ending the shopping trip, she and her mother pulled into the driveway.

"I'll have dinner on the table in less than an hour," her mom said.

"Please don't rush for me. I'm going to Mulberry Park to run, and I won't be back for at least that long."

Her mom's expression faltered before offering Shana one of her please-be-my-friend-again smiles, but Shana couldn't bring herself to fully return it.

"How does spaghetti sound?" her mother asked.

"Great." Shana wasn't consciously trying to maintain a cold war, but she didn't have the energy to fix the unfixable. Their mother-daughter relationship had been irrevocably damaged, a fact that they both knew.

The only trouble was, her mother wasn't sure why.

To Cassandra's credit, she tried to do everything in her power to make things right, but hadn't been able to. Everything she said or did rubbed Shana the wrong way, even though she'd rarely confronted her about it.

"I'll wait to serve dinner until you get home," her mom said, handing over the car keys. "I can't wait for you to meet Pastor Craig. You'll like him. In fact, if you hadn't decided to marry Brad, I would have played matchmaker."

That's all Shana needed. To hook up with a minister, of all people. A man who strove for perfection when she'd fallen so short of the mark.

Ten minutes later, after changing into her running clothes, she'd driven to Mulberry Park and parked in the shade.

She'd told her mother that she was going to run along the jogging paths, but her first stop was the new fountain and the flower garden that surrounded it.

Call her crazy or stuck on the past or whatever, but she didn't care.

She needed to see what Ramon had done.

As she neared the drinking fountain, her gaze was drawn to a colorful display of flowers—the zinnias, the asters, the morning glories.

She stood there, immersed in the floral beauty and remembering the young man who'd turned her heart on end. She tried to imagine him as an artist—because that floral masterpiece proved that he was.

The scent of spring laced the cool sea breeze, and she closed her eyes, willing herself to forget all the reasons she'd left town. All the reasons she'd dreaded her return.

She took a drink of water and relished the cool liquid as it trickled down her throat before she headed toward the concrete paths that started near the baseball fields.

A couple of years ago, the city had created the trail, which was now used by bikers, joggers, dog-walkers, and nature lovers who enjoyed the canyon views.

Shana had no more than reached the fence near the third-base line when a late-model Jeep Wrangler drove up and parked. She merely gave the driver a cursory glance, but as he did a double take of her, she was forced to do the same thing.

Recognition dawned, and she froze in her steps, watching Ramon get out of his vehicle.

He wore faded jeans, a white T-shirt, and a red baseball cap, but his casual clothing was the only reminder of the boy he'd once been.

"Hey," he said. "How's it going?"

Emotion clogged her throat, and she had to clear her voice in an attempt to speak at all. "Fine. How about you?"

"Not bad."

He'd always been tall, six foot or so. But he'd grown another inch or two since she'd seen him last. He'd also bulked up now that he was a man.

"I . . . uh . . ." She gave a nod toward the drinking fountain. "I saw the garden you created. It's beautiful."

"Thanks." He seemed to be taking her in, checking out the changes seven years had made in her appearance, too.

She couldn't help wishing she'd chosen running shorts instead of sweats, a new tank top rather than the oversize shirt. That she'd left her hair down instead of pulling it back in a ponytail.

"I heard you're getting married," he said. "Congratulations."

"Thanks." She managed a half-smile, which was about all she was good for these days. Truthfully, though? She hadn't been happy about anything in a long, long time.

He nodded toward the ball fields. "I'm coaching a kids' baseball team."

Before she could respond, a blond boy near the dugouts yelled, "Hey, Ramon!"

The kid jogged toward his coach, his shaggy hair flopping up and down with each stride. As he neared Ramon, a grin burst across his freckled face. "Want some help?"

"Yeah, sure." Ramon addressed the boy, yet his gaze remained on Shana a bit longer. Finally, he ended the tentative connection and turned toward the Jeep. He opened the back end, pulled out a black canvas duffel bag full of gear, and handed it to the boy.

"Thanks, Matt. Why don't you take this to the dugout, and I'll be there in a minute."

As the boy did as he was instructed, Ramon turned back to Shana. "My team has started to arrive, so I'd better go."

She nodded. "Yeah, me, too. I'm trying to sneak in a run before dinner."

"If you're bored after you finish," he said, "feel free to stop by and watch for a while. We don't get many cheerleaders."

"Maybe I will."

He didn't make a move to walk away, so neither did she.

"It's good to see you," he added.

"Same here."

But it was actually bittersweet because it reminded her of how painful their breakup had been. How she'd wanted to curl up and die in the months that followed.

How a part of her actually had.

Chapter 13

Craig entered the Delacourts' house at five-thirty on Monday evening, expecting to smell the hearty aroma of dinner cooking. Instead, he was met with the faint scent of lemon oil and cleaning products.

He couldn't help thinking it was odd, since Cassandra routinely went out of her way to plan and prepare exceptional meals.

"Is anyone here?" he called out, not wanting to surprise his hosts, especially since Shana had come home.

"I'm in the family room," Daniel said.

Craig dropped his keys into his pocket and joined Daniel, who was watching ESPN on the plasma TV.

"The girls are out shopping again," Daniel said. "So we're on our own for dinner. What do you say we call out for pizza?"

"Sounds good to me."

"Me, too. Cassie's a great cook, but I'm a junk-food lover at heart. And every now and then I miss having take-out or drive-through." Daniel reached for the telephone. "Do you have a problem with pepperoni and sausage?"

"None at all."

Thirty minutes later, the Leaning Tower of Pizza delivery driver had brought their order, which Craig placed on the glass-topped table in the family room.

"How about a Miller Lite?" Daniel asked.

"You know," Craig said, "I'd rather have a Coke."

A sheepish expression crossed Daniel's face. "I'm sorry for offering you a beer, Pastor. I should have realized you don't drink alcohol."

"Don't apologize. It really has nothing to do with me being a minister. I just never acquired a taste for beer."

Daniel went after their beverages and a couple of napkins. When he returned, he took a seat beside Craig on the sofa. "In my defense, you really don't look like a minister. And you don't act like one, either. So I tend to forget."

Craig wasn't sure what a minister was supposed to look like—or act like for that matter. If he hadn't already felt as though he was wearing a borrowed suit that belonged to a much bigger man, he might have had some kind of retort.

"Did you always want to be a minister?" Daniel asked.

Craig wasn't sure how much he wanted to divulge, but he liked Daniel. Maybe it was the fact that they'd had baseball in common. Or that he'd always admired men who clearly loved their children.

Yeah, yeah. He knew the psychology behind that. His dad had been bigger than life when he'd been alive. And even more so after death. So his loss had left a big hole in Craig's life.

"Being a minister was never part of my game plan." Craig reached for a slice of pizza, the melted mozzarella stretching until it threatened to slide right off the top of the piece he'd chosen. He used his finger to pull the cheese free and to keep it where it belonged. "I'd wanted to play professional baseball."

"Interesting." Daniel shot him a grin. "When I was a kid, I had the same dream, but I never had what it took to play at that caliber."

Truthfully, Craig wasn't sure he'd had the skills needed to be more than a second-string pitcher, but he'd wanted to give it his best shot. "When I was a senior in high school, I was drafted by the Dodgers and was sitting on top of the world."

Daniel popped open his beer. "I can only imagine how that must have felt."

"I also had a full-ride scholarship to Arizona State, which my family encouraged me to accept. But I was giving some serious thought to forgoing my education and playing pro ball." Craig popped another bite of pizza in his mouth, then picked up the napkin and wiped his hands and mouth.

There'd been no guarantee that he'd make it past the farm team, but he'd wanted to try. It might have been his only chance for a bit of fame and glory.

"Your parents must have been proud," Daniel said.

"My mom and grandparents were, although sports never did hold that much importance in their lives. I suspect my dad would have felt differently, but he died during Operation Desert Storm when I was just a kid."

"I'm sorry to hear that."

Craig shrugged. "It was tough. He was in special ops and died a hero."

"So what happened?" Daniel asked. "Why'd you give it up?"

"During the last game of the season, I tore my rotator cuff, so the decision to play pro ball or go to college was taken from me."

"That sounds like a serious injury, but I wouldn't think it would have sidelined you permanently."

"I couldn't play for at least a year." The memories, the disappointment, barged into the room—front and center. And while he wanted to take his pain and run from Daniel's intense gaze, he decided to level with the man instead, to make the admission out loud. "I thought life couldn't get any worse than that, but I was wrong. Two weeks later, my granddad was diagnosed with liver disease, and I realized just how bad it could get."

"You two must have been close."

"We were. My granddad was a missionary, and when my

dad died, he gave it all up and came home to be with my mom and me. So, yeah, we were very close. He stepped up to the plate and became the father I'd been missing."

"So you decided to follow in your grandfather's footsteps?"

Craig studied the half-eaten pizza on his plate, but was no longer the least bit hungry. "I promised God that if Granddad was spared, I would forget about baseball and go to the seminary."

"So I assume your grandfather pulled through."

Craig nodded. "They found a liver donor just in time. During surgery, they lost him but managed to bring him back. The doctors called the whole thing a miracle."

"Which left you with a promise to keep."

A big one.

Daniel grew momentarily silent, pensive.

For two guys who'd been hungry and looking forward to wolfing down an extra-large pizza, Craig noted that neither of them seemed to be focused on food.

"Can I ask you something, Pastor?"

There went the P-word again, scratching against him like an umpire's whisk broom on home plate. Craig hadn't gotten used to the title yet, and it felt especially rough coming from a man with whom he'd just opened up and spilled out his heart. Okay, so he hadn't actually spilled anything, he'd just oozed a little.

"Sure," Craig said. "Shoot."

"Maybe I ought to explain something first." Daniel glanced down at his pizza, then back again. "I've loved criminal law since my very first class at Cal Western, and I'd planned to work for the district attorney, prosecuting criminals rather than defending them. I'd wanted to make a difference in this world, or at least in the community."

Craig didn't respond, didn't need to.

"I'm one of the top defense lawyers in the state. And one thing that makes me so successful is that I prepare a mental prosecution of the case before I tackle the defense strategy. There have been times when I won a case that I should have lost. Times when I knew exactly why the prosecuting attorney lost the case and where they went wrong. And each time that happened, I'd tell myself that I was just doing my job— and doing it well. That everyone deserves the right to a fair trial, and that someone had to make sure those rights were protected. But the truth is that I'm working for the wrong side. You know what I mean? Some people were born to be defense attorneys, but I don't believe I was one of them."

Craig nodded. It didn't take much of an imagination to know exactly how Daniel felt about playing for the wrong team.

"Did you ever let someone else make a decision for you?" Daniel asked. "One that affected the rest of your life?"

"No, not in that sense." But Fate or God had thrown Craig a curve, and he'd found himself sitting on the bench and hoping he'd get a chance to show his stuff while wondering if he'd be able to pull it off when push came to shove.

"You know," Daniel said, "when you were telling me about your father's death, I was able to relate. I lost both of my parents in a boating accident when I was a freshman in high school. And I had to live in foster care for a while, which was fine. I had a good home and was encouraged to go to college. But I missed my parents, especially my father. I can't explain the hole his death left in my life or the need I had to fill it."

He didn't have to. Craig knew the hole he was talking about, yet couldn't explain it, either.

"When I married Cassandra, there was a part of me that yearned for a father figure. And I thought I found one in her dad."

"Did you?"

"I thought so. And I sold out."

"What do you mean?"

"Prosecuting attorneys don't make the same kind of money as good defense lawyers make. And Cassandra was used to having the finest things, a nice house, stylish clothes . . . I loved her, and I wanted to be able to provide everything she'd been used to, all she deserved. But I wasn't bringing a whole lot to the table, other than a law degree and a slew of student loans. And now, after more than a quarter century of marriage, my job is really grinding on me."

Craig had no idea how he'd feel about his life in twenty-five years. Better? Resigned?

Happy didn't seem possible.

"Here's where my question comes in," Daniel said.

Craig's gaze met the older man's, and he realized the attorney was looking at him as though he held the keys to the universe and beyond. It was all he could do to hope and pray that he wouldn't fail the first congregant to actually come to him with a dilemma.

"I've had some troubling cases in the past," Daniel said, "but I'm working on one now that's bothering me more than the others ever did, and I'm really struggling with it."

Craig understood attorney-client privilege and knew Daniel couldn't—and wouldn't—say more. But if this case was different from the others he'd had to defend and causing him to struggle, Craig wondered if it was the one he'd heard about on the news the other night, one that was ugly—and very high profile. A wealthy man was accused of murdering a child. It was the kind of case that made a person, particularly a parent, challenge everything that was good and right in the world.

Daniel bowed his head, the weight of his dilemma apparent. Then he looked up, his gaze snagging Craig's as though he had the answer. "You have no idea how badly I'd like to recuse myself from this case."

"You probably ought to follow your heart."

"Is that what you'd do?"

In Daniel's case?

"I think I'd have to."

But in his own?

The answer wasn't so easy. Craig would love to pursue a different career.

One that didn't break a promise to God.

Late Wednesday afternoon, Kristy stood at the kitchen counter, preparing meatloaf, baked potatoes, and green beans for dinner.

She glanced at the clock on the oven, realizing she would have to call the Maguires soon and ask them to send Jason home.

Kristy liked Jillian Maguire, Tommy's mother, although they didn't get a chance to actually chat very often. Jillian and her kids moved into the neighborhood last Christmas. At the time, she'd been newly divorced and, according to her, things had looked pretty bleak until Mac came along. The couple fell in love and were married shortly thereafter.

There were times when Kristy wished someone would sweep into her life and help her put the pieces back together again. But she'd never been a dreamer.

The doorbell sounded, and she quickly rinsed her hands, then dried them on the dish towel that lay on the counter. Gram hadn't slept very well last night and was napping—something she seemed to do a lot lately. And so Kristy didn't want to wake her.

She swung open the door only to find Pastor Craig standing on the stoop.

He wore a navy blue sports jacket, a cream-colored dress shirt, and a conservative tie. Yet his hair was stylishly mussed, making the man appear to be a bit of a contradiction.

And an appealing one at that.

"I'm early today. There's a special service at the church tonight and since . . ." His voice trailed and lowered. "Well, your grandmother is sensitive about some things, and I don't want her to think I've forgotten about her. Is this a bad time for me to stop in?"

"No, not at all." She stepped aside, letting him in.

A wisp of bay and musk followed him into the living room, and she had to make a conscious effort not to inhale his scent until it seeped into every pore of her body.

She wasn't comfortable with her misplaced attraction to Craig Houston, a man who was far too wholesome for a woman like her.

"You know," she said, suddenly realizing she'd answered the door and welcomed him in while on auto pilot, "Gram might be napping. At least, she was the last time I looked in on her. I'll check again."

"Don't disturb her if she's sleeping."

"I won't, but dinner will be ready soon."

"If you find that she's still asleep, and it's all right with you, I could wait a few minutes to see if she wakes up on her own."

"Sure." Kristy pointed toward the sofa. "Have a seat while I take a peek."

As Craig settled on the cushion nearest the arm rest, Kristy went to Gram's room, only to see that her eyes were closed and her chest was rising and falling in slumber.

So she returned to the living room and sat on the edge of the recliner, feeling a bit stiff and awkward. "She's still resting. Can I get you something to drink? Juice maybe? Coffee?"

"No, thank you." He placed his left hand on the armrest. It was a well-formed hand. Solid, strong and masculine.

"So how did the great American shopping expedition go?" he asked.

She arched a brow. "Excuse me?"

"For wedding dresses. I heard you and Shana went out again yesterday."

"Oh, yes." Kristy had asked Renee to babysit a couple of hours while the two friends went to the mall. "We found the perfect dress. Didn't she mention anything?"

"No. She's not home very often, and neither am I. So our paths don't cross very often. And when they do, I've noticed that she's pretty quiet."

"She wasn't always like that," Kristy said. "She used to be a lot more talkative. And she had a great sense of humor."

"What caused the change?"

"I'm not sure. She became a lot more introspective during our last year in high school."

Just days before Brad's party, which had become one of three significant markers along Kristy's internal timeline, Kristy had first noted Shana's introspection and commented. But her friend had clammed up, refusing to discuss it. Then came the night of the party and Gram's first of several strokes, and Kristy's life became pretty complicated for a while.

A long while.

"Daniel mentioned that Shana had leukemia. Could that have contributed to her personality change?"

"No, she seemed to pull through that without any adverse effects, physically or emotionally."

"The Delacourts said you were very supportive of their daughter during that time."

"I owed her that much. When I first moved in with my grandmother, I found it hard to find acceptance with my classmates. Kids can be cruel, and sometimes their parents can be worse. But Shana reached out to me when the others didn't, and I appreciated her kindness. So when she got sick, it seemed only fair to reciprocate." Kristy glanced at the handsome minister, saw him listening intently, felt something in his gaze. Something warm and heart-spinning.

"I can see how your bond would run deep."

"Shana became an even better friend after her illness, and there's nothing I wouldn't do for her."

"I guess it's really none of my business, but there's an aura of . . . I don't know . . . sadness about her. I first noticed it in the expression she wore in that portrait that hangs in the Delacourts' living room. After she came home from Australia and I met her in person, it struck me even harder."

Kristy sat back in the chair, relaxing a bit. Letting down

her guard. Studying the minister in much the same way he'd been studying her. "I didn't realize you were so observant."

"I didn't used to be, but someone once told me that things weren't always what they appeared. And that if I wanted to make a difference, I would need to look close and to dig deep."

"And you want to make a difference in Shana's life?"

Craig shrugged. "Not on a conscious level. I can't really explain it. But I sense there's trouble between her and her mother, and I feel sorry for them both."

"There's definitely some tension there, but I'm not sure that I can help you figure it out. Shana's my best friend, although she's not as open with me as she once was."

"Why is that?"

"I suppose there are two possible reasons."

"What are they?"

"She grew up and became more independent while she's been away at college."

"I'm sure that's true. What's the second reason?"

"The Delacourts have always tried to provide Shana with a picture-perfect life, but it's not easy living on a glass shelf in a glass house. And sometimes there are just as many consequences to being submissive as there are to being rebellious."

Craig seemed to ponder her answer.

"Why the interest in Shana?" she asked.

"It's not just her, per se. It's her parents, too. They've been nice to me, and I sense that I might be able to help. But if you think I'm being too inquisitive and butting into something that's none of my business, I'll back off."

He was asking her opinion?

Her guard slipped another notch. "The Delacourts have been good to me over the years, too, even though I've always had a strong feeling that they would have preferred having Shana choose a different best friend."

"I'm sorry to hear that. You got that vibe from them? Even as a child?"

Kristy shrugged. "I'm used to being different."

"How so?"

"Even as a kid, I was considered a wild-child. A bad seed. And as hard as I strived to be like the kids with two parents, I just wasn't."

"Why not?"

She shrugged. "I guess you could say that my zest for fun and acceptance led to a reputation as a boy-crazy party girl, which probably made parents leery of me. But I wasn't that bad."

"I'm sure you weren't."

She caught a hint of something in his eyes. Compassion? Sympathy? She couldn't be sure.

Maybe it was something he'd learned in divinity school, something that made him good at his job as a counselor of wounded souls.

The guidance counselor at school had wanted Kristy to talk to a shrink, but she never had. She'd thought about it on several occasions, but her life had been so caught up with Gram and a newborn that one day had blurred into the next.

So what would it hurt to be candid with Craig? It's not like this foolish attraction was going anywhere.

"School came incredibly easy," she admitted, "and I was often bored. But I was smart enough to know a college degree was the way to go. But then I went to an unchaperoned party, had too much to drink, and made a stupid mistake. So, long story short, my college aspirations bit the dust."

Ironically, after getting pregnant, she'd found herself shunned by the very people she'd wanted to accept her.

"You can always go back to school," he said.

Yeah, right. She wanted to make some kind of snappy retort, but the gentleness in his eyes threatened to steal the bark out of her bite.

"Maybe I will someday," she said.

When Gram could take care of herself.

When Jason no longer needed a sitter.

And when money grew on trees.

She did, of course, have that cash tucked away in the wooden jewelry box in her drawer. She could always use that to help fund her college, if she were to go back to school. That is, if she didn't spend it in the meantime on something far more important, like food, utilities, medical bills . . .

"Well," Craig said, glancing at his watch. "As much as I'd like to stay, I can't be late to that meeting. Will you let Lorraine know I stopped by and that I'll try to come back later in the week?"

"Of course."

Kristy stood to walk him to the door, and they came together in the middle of the room. Yet instead of pushing through, they slowed to a stop, and their gazes locked.

Craig placed a hand on her shoulder and gave it a warm, gentle squeeze. "I really admire you, Kristy."

His touch, the intensity of his gaze, set off a surge in her bloodstream until she could hear her pulse thundering in her ears.

She could really trip up here. Really make a crazy mistake.

"I'm not sure why." She tore her gaze away from his, daring him to give her something around which she could wrap her hope. Something she could believe.

"Because you're a bright, beautiful young woman. You're also devoted and loving. You've put your own life on hold and are doing your best to take care of your son and a disabled woman who someone else might have put in a convalescent home by now."

"I couldn't do that."

"Obviously not." His hand slid over the edge of her shoulder and along her upper arm, until he let it drop slowly to his side, leaving her to grieve a connection she didn't deserve.

Before she could say something she would probably regret, the front door swung open, and Jason stepped into the house, announcing he was home and hungry.

The interruption saved her from venturing into a conver-

sation that was jury-rigged with possibilities that were doomed
to fail.

A sea of hopeless possibilities in which her thoughts had
already drifted.

Before dinner, Shana returned to the park for another run.
At least, that's the excuse she'd given her mother.

She placed her iPod in the holder on her upper arm, tucked
the hem of her tank top into the waistband of her running
shorts, then tucked the strands of her hair out of the way as
she adjusted the earphones.

But truthfully? She really wasn't in the mood for music.

Or for exercise.

On her way to the jogging paths, as she neared the cinder-
block restrooms in the middle of the park, a man with long,
shaggy hair and a beard walked toward her.

"Good afternoon," he said.

She nodded to acknowledge his greeting.

"Going for another run?" he asked.

Again, she merely nodded, trying to be polite yet not wanting to chitchat with a stranger, particularly one who appeared
to be homeless.

"Some things can't be escaped," he said.

She wanted to turn her back to him and pick up her pace,
but something gentle in his expression, in those pristine blue
eyes, gave her pause.

What was it? Compassion? Understanding? Wisdom?

"Sometimes," he said, "confrontations are the only way
out."

She was going to write him off as a nutcase, yet for some
crazy reason, she couldn't bring herself to walk away.

"That's sometimes easier said than done," she said.

Why in the world had she even talked to someone like him?
He could be having some kind of psychotic episode, and she
was setting herself up to be sucked into it.

So who was the real Looney Tune here?

She turned to her left, toward the baseball fields.

"You've got to do the right thing," he said to her back, "even when it's the hardest thing in the world to do."

Her steps slowed, her lips parted, and she wanted to both laugh at the absurdity of his words and cry at their truth.

In spite of knowing better, she turned toward him as though facing her accuser.

"You've had a lousy childhood," he said.

He was wrong there. She'd had a perfect childhood.

"On the outside, everything looked wonderful, but it wasn't. And you're doomed to make the same mistakes that your parents made if you don't make some changes, mistakes that will make you unhappy for a very long time. You have a choice to make. Make it with honesty, self-confidence, and strength."

He seemed to know what she struggled with, and while she wanted to write him off, she couldn't help responding as though she'd been the one to seek him out and ask for his advice. "That's tough to do when I've always chosen the easiest way out."

"Things happen, people change. And you're a lot stronger and braver than you think." Then he doffed an imaginary hat, turned and walked away.

She stood in the center of the park for the longest time, stunned by what the man had said, by what he'd seemed to know.

When she finally glanced over her shoulder to take another gander at him, he was gone.

It was almost as if he'd never been there at all.

Surely her imagination was playing tricks on her. So, shaking off his words, she continued toward the ball fields.

The sun had lowered in the western sky. If she wanted to finish her run before dark, she'd need to get started.

Again, she realized it wasn't an endorphin fix that she was seeking.

Just as she'd hoped, a Jeep Wrangler was parked in the lot nearest the third-base line. And a group of boys huddled around their handsome Latino coach.

Her feet slowed as though trudging through a slough, and her heart skittered across her chest.

"Matt," Ramon said, "you take first base."

The kid dashed off to do as he was told.

Shana stood silently, watching Ramon make his assignments. When all nine positions had been filled, he gave the remaining boys a task.

She watched them for a while, long enough to see that he was good to the kids, that they obviously respected him.

When he glanced up and spotted her, he smiled. Then, after instructing one of the boys to hit balls to the others, he cut across the field, as though planning to meet her at the fence.

No invitation was necessary, and she soon found herself within arm's length of him. But it was more than a stretch of chain link separating them.

"I'm glad you stopped by," he said.

Was he?

How glad?

Before she could respond, a small, dark-haired boy ran up to him. "Coach, you forgot about me. What do you want me to do?"

A grin stretched across Ramon's face, and he tousled the boy's shaggy hair. "I was just going to give you a job when I spotted an old friend."

The boy glanced at Shana, as though assessing her and determining her to be a suitable distraction. "She doesn't look so old to me."

Ramon laughed, then turned to Shana. "This is Carlitos, our pitcher's brother. He wanted to play on the intercity team with us, which would have been fine with me. He's one heck of a shortstop and one of the best batters. But the league rules are strict. Only kids between the ages of ten and twelve can play on the team. So we made him our bat boy and the junior coach."

"Yeah," the boy said, grinning from ear to ear. "I tell them when they're messing up."

Ramon placed his hand on the boy's shoulder and gave him an affectionate squeeze.

He'd make a great father, she realized, her heart crumpling into a shell of its former self.

Unable to speak, she tried to feign a smile.

"Tell David to practice pitching just outside the dugout," Ramon instructed. "Then I'd like you to catch for him. Try to help him stay in the strike zone, okay?"

"You got it, coach." The boy took off at a run, calling for David.

Ramon returned his attention to Shana, his full attention. His gaze caressed the length of her.

"Running again?" he asked.

She nodded.

Some things can't be escaped.

She shook off the homeless man's words and offered Ramon a wobbly smile.

"It's good to see you again," he said.

She gave a little half-shrug, hoping the meeting seemed co-incidental. "I saw your car, so I thought I'd stop by and say hello."

"I'm glad you did."

Sometimes confrontations are necessary and the only way out.

But not today.

And maybe not ever.

Because some conversations, like some memories, were too painful to have, too heartbreaking to resurrect.

Chapter 14

Craig was just leaving the church on Friday morning when he glanced across the street and noticed Kristy's car at Mulberry Park. He'd had a meeting with the board of elders earlier, and now that he had a break, he planned to spring a surprise visit on the contractor who was working at the house into which he would soon be moving.

Yet as much as he wanted to get out of the Delacourts' den and into his own place, he couldn't help taking the time to cross the street and talk to Kristy again. There was something about the single mother that appealed to him, and whatever it was increased each time he saw her.

Since that day he'd spotted her and Jason at the playground, he'd gotten in the habit of searching for her car whenever he stepped onto the church property.

He couldn't explain it. She wasn't anything like the other young women he'd dated in the past.

Today she was sitting at one of the picnic tables, watching her son play on the teeter-totter with another boy, but she seemed to sense his approach before he got within fifty yards of her and looked up.

"Tired of swinging already?" he asked.

Her breezy smile nearly knocked the wind out of him. "We brought Tommy with us today. I only play with Jason when he doesn't have a friend with him."

"Mind if I join you?" he asked, nodding at the space beside her.

"No, not at all."

He sat quietly awhile, pretending to watch the kids on the playground, yet his thoughts were on the woman sitting next to him. "Who's with your grandmother?"

"Charlie Iverson," she said. "One of our neighbors. His late wife was Gram's friend."

"That's nice of him."

"Yes, it is. Most of the neighbors, at least the ones who've lived on Sugar Plum Lane for any period of time, offer to help out once in a while. They remember the old Gram, the one who used to used to make chicken soup for them when they were sick or bring in the mail and newspaper when they went out of town."

"It's good that you can get out once in a while without having to pay someone to sit with her."

"You're right, but I try not to take advantage of their kindness by asking too much or too often."

The sun glistened off strands of gold highlights in her auburn hair, and he was again caught up in his attraction, in her beauty.

"Do you think you can find someone to sit with her and Jason tomorrow night?" he asked.

"I can try. Why?"

"Because I'd like to take you to dinner."

Her eyes widened, and her lips parted. Apparently, she was nearly as surprised by his question as he was.

"Are you kidding?"

Actually, the more he thought about it, the more he liked the idea. "No, I'm not."

She paused for a beat, as though pondering her response. "I'll admit to a bit of attraction on my part, but I'm really not the kind of woman a minister should date."

He sensed that she might have a point, although it didn't seem to matter right now.

"Why is that?" he asked.

"For one thing, I'm a single mother and know very little about the guy who fathered my son. Not that I wouldn't recognize him if I saw him, but he disappeared from the planet after it happened." A strand of hair whipped across her cheek, and she brushed it aside.

He hated to see her beat herself up over something that couldn't be undone. "You have nothing to feel guilty about, Kristy. The way I see it, you were blessed with a beautiful son."

"That's true." Her gaze drifted to the playground, where Jason played with his friend, oblivious to their discussion. "He was born on Valentine's Day, nearly six weeks early. But he was a fighter, like I used to be, and I fell in love with him the moment I saw him."

"So why be so hard on yourself for a teenage mistake? How old were you?"

"Sixteen."

"You were just a kid. I can't imagine anyone holding that against you. And neither should you."

"It's not that so much. I've learned to accept being a single mom and I'm making the best of things."

For a moment, he leaned toward pursuing a relationship with her, and two beats later, he leaned the other way.

He'd spent the bulk of his life trying to live up to a certain standard—his father's, his grandfather's. His own.

The Parkside Community Church congregation had certain expectations of their minister, too. And he doubted the Delacourts were the only ones who might question his involvement with Kristy.

So why complicate things?

He'd never be able to make a difference in this community if he knowingly set himself up for conflict.

Jesse's words came to mind. *You'll need to look beyond the obvious and dig deep within yourself if you want to make a difference.*

The man might have been right, but Craig wasn't too good

at digging within himself. Maybe because he'd been too afraid of what he'd find. Afraid that he wouldn't measure up.

He stole a glance at Kristy.

What was with this growing attraction he had to her? Was it some kind of subconscious effort to sabotage his job, his position, his career?

Or was it more than that?

Was he reaching out to someone who had imperfections, too? A woman who might understand the internal struggles he faced?

It was too much to think about right now.

So why couldn't he seem to drop it? Why did he still want to ask her out?

Again, he couldn't explain any of it. Nor could he understand why he felt an almost overwhelming need to make a difference in her life.

Craig never had been one to pry, yet he wasn't sure if she'd share any more with him if he didn't. "So what's the problem? Where does the guilt come from?"

She studied him for the longest moment. "I haven't shared this with anyone before, and I really shouldn't now, but maybe it's for the best."

How so? he wanted to ask. Instead, he waited for her to explain.

She turned in her seat, her knee brushing against his thigh and sending his pulse out of whack. "I guess this will be like speed dating."

"I'm not sure I'm following you. Are you saying that after sharing your guilt you won't want to have dinner with me?"

"Or vice versa." She took a deep breath, then slowly blew it out. "After that party I told you about, I snuck back into the house, hoping not to wake Gram. When I locked the door behind me and found the house dark and still, I thought I'd pulled it off. But once inside the living room, I found her collapsed on the floor. She'd suffered a stroke while I'd been gone."

"You can't blame yourself for her medical problems and her disability."

"Oh, no? The sooner a stroke victim gets treatment, the better their chances of recovery. So I was to blame. There's no telling how long she lay on that floor, unable to move, unable to call for help. The guilt was staggering. In fact, at times, it still is. I've tried my best to make it up to her, but I just can't seem to do it."

"Have you told her how you feel? Have you asked her to forgive you?"

"When it first happened, I apologized each time I saw her lying in bed. But not lately."

"What did she say when you told her you were sorry?"

"She forgave me, I guess. But I haven't been able to forgive myself." Her gaze reached deep into his heart, threatening to unseat everything he'd locked inside—the broken dreams, the insecurities. "Did you ever feel as though you did something so wrong that you would never be able to make things right again? That you could try your best to make up for it, but that you'd always fall short—"

"Hey, Mom!"

Kristy immediately turned to her son, who was running up to her. "Yes, honey?"

"Some guys are playing baseball on the ball fields," he told her. "Can Tommy and I go watch them? *Please?*"

She seemed to ponder their request. "You can watch for a few minutes, but we can't stay at the park much longer. We're going to have to leave soon."

As the boys ran off, Kristy turned to Craig. "I don't want them to go off by themselves, so I'm going to follow them. Do you mind?"

Mind joining her? Or mind if she called an end to their time together?

"Not at all." He got to his feet, but instead of heading back to his car in the church parking lot, like he probably ought to, he found himself walking beside her.

"It's getting cold," she said.

He glanced at the sky, noting there were more clouds than when he'd left the house. And they appeared much darker. "Looks like rain."

"I hope not. Our furnace quit working during the middle of the night, and I called a repairman. But I'm not sure if he can fix it again, or if it will need to be replaced."

The conversation they'd been having appeared to be over, present-day concerns chasing off past troubles, and his dinner invitation disappeared into the rising humidity.

Kristy craned her neck, looking near the dugout where a young Latino male stood, talking to a couple of boys.

Craig suspected he was a Little League coach.

"I know that guy," Kristy said, lifting her hand in a wave.

Suddenly feeling like a tag-along, Craig wished he would have left when Jason first interrupted them, asking to watch the kids play ball.

Still, he couldn't help checking out the guy and wondering how Kristy knew him.

As they approached the third-base line, the man sent the boys into the dugout for batting helmets, then made his way toward Kristy.

"How's it going?" he asked her.

"It's all right." She offered him a warm smile. "Ramon, this is Craig Houston, a friend of mine."

Craig reached out a hand to the man, thinking he'd just been promoted from pastor to friend and wondering if it had anything to do with the pseudo speed dating technique of spilling one's heart and facing reality.

"Aren't you the new pastor at Parkside Community Church?" Ramon asked.

Craig just couldn't seem to ditch the title. "Yes, I am. How did you know?"

"A guy named Jesse mentioned your name. He said you might be interested in helping me with the team."

"I'm not a coach," Craig said, repeating what he'd told the homeless man.

"Jesse seemed to think you were. And he suggested I press you a bit, saying you'd give in and be glad that you had."

What was Craig going to do about Jesse?

"I've got plenty of baseball skill," Ramon added. "So if you don't feel as though you have the experience to coach the boys, it's not a problem. What they really need are some solid male role models and encouragement."

Yeah, well Craig had plenty of skill and experience, but he didn't think it was wise to mention that. "I don't have a whole lot of time to coach Little League."

"This isn't Little League." Ramon turned toward the boys on the field, crossed his arms, and leaned against the chain link. "It's a special intercity team made up of disadvantaged kids who are at risk. Each of them has at least one parent who is incarcerated. And we're using sports to give them something to focus on."

Craig glanced at the ragtag group of boys on the field, taking a closer look at them. For the most part, their clothing was worn and faded. Some shirts were too big, while others were too long.

His gaze was drawn to the pitcher, a tall, lanky kid who had one heck of an arm. "Is the rest of the team as good as the boy on the mound?"

"Actually, his brother is even better than he is, but he's too young to compete in our league." Ramon turned to the side, watching the boys on the field. "The pitcher's name is Luis. His dad is serving a life term for a gang-related shooting."

Craig knew what it was like to grow up without a dad, but he'd at least been able to think of his father as a hero. And oddly enough, it made him feel fortunate.

"Luis and his younger brother have been living with their grandmother, but she was recently diagnosed with terminal lung cancer and is in hospice care right now."

"That's too bad."

Ramon nodded. "I'm thinking about taking them in myself. They're good kids, and I don't want to see them turn to gangs or drugs, which is almost a given with their background and their neighborhood."

Luis wound up and pitched—low and inside. Yet the batter swung, tipping the ball and sending it sailing hard and fast into foul territory. As a blur of white approached the fence where they stood, hurtling toward Kristy, Craig stepped in front of her and snatched it with his bare hand.

It had been a long time since he'd heard the crack of a bat and felt the rush of going in for a catch. Even the burn of the hardball on his bare palm felt good.

Craig threw the ball back to Luis.

"Nice catch," Ramon said. "And you've got a good arm."

Craig shrugged. "I used to. It's been awhile since I played."

A long while.

Before Ramon could respond, Kristy glanced at her watch. "I really need to go. The repairman is coming between twelve and three." She glanced at the sky, which had grown heavy with gray clouds. "I hope he can get the furnace working before tonight."

Craig shoved his hands into his pockets. It was definitely getting colder. From what he'd been told, it had been an unusually brisk spring.

Kristy called to Jason and his friend Tommy. "I'm afraid we need to go now, boys."

"Aw, Mom," Jason complained. "Do we have to?"

"I'm afraid so." She turned first to Ramon, then to Craig. "I'll talk to you later."

Craig hoped so.

She hadn't answered his question about having dinner with him yet. And while he could certainly call her back and ask again, he couldn't bring himself to do it.

*   *   *

A couple of drops of water hit the windshield as Kristy and the boys left the park. She thought for sure it would be raining hard by the time she got home.

She should have paid more attention to the weather report this morning, although she supposed it didn't really matter. She was going straight home and would only have to leave the house once—for work at four o'clock. With the repairman coming, she'd been forced to ask for half of the day off.

Surprisingly, she was off tomorrow, too, which didn't happen often. Saturdays were usually a given at the pub, but the new manager had left Kristy off the schedule for some reason.

So, if she'd been inclined to go to dinner with Craig, she would have been able to work it out, assuming Renee could watch Gram and Jason. But Craig hadn't mentioned it again.

Her abbreviated form of speed dating had probably convinced him not to, which was for the best. If he'd asked her again, she might have weakened and agreed, and then where would that leave them?

Kristy dropped Tommy off at his house, stopping long enough to say hello to Jillian. Then she drove home to relieve Charlie.

Once they were inside the house, Jason dashed off to his room in search of his toy action figures. While in the car on the way home, the boys had been talking about making parachutes for them, and he was eager to get started.

As Kristy started toward Gram's room, Charlie met her in the hallway. She noticed that he'd yet to take off the jacket he'd been wearing when he came.

"Back so soon?" he asked.

"An hour goes by quickly, doesn't it?" She tossed him a smile. "Thanks so much for sitting with Gram."

"No problem. I'd stay here and talk to that repairman for you, but I need to go home and let the dog out before it starts to rain."

Kristy stood aside to let him pass, then followed him to the door.

As he reached for the knob, he paused and glanced over his shoulder. "I left those roses on the nightstand in your grandmother's bedroom. With it being on the east side of the house, it gets a bit dark and dreary in the afternoon, especially on a cloudy day. I figured a little color would be good for her and might liven things up some."

Kristy offered the old man a smile. "You grew those roses, didn't you?"

"They were Grace's bushes. I never could prune them right. And the stems aren't nearly as sturdy as they were when she was alive."

Grace, his late wife, had passed away more than a year ago. At that point, Kristy realized, Gram's depression had hit a low point and she'd become a lot more outspoken about wanting to die.

"Those roses used to please Grace no end," Charlie added, "so I thought Lorraine would enjoy them."

"I'm sure she will."

"By the way," he said, stepping onto the stoop, "her mood was a bit better today."

After Charlie left, Kristy went to Gram's bedroom to tell her she was home. Just as Charlie had said, thanks to the cloudy skies, the room was especially gloomy today. "Hey, Gram. I'm back."

Her grandmother, who was lying in bed with the television volume on low, turned her head to the sound of Kristy's voice. "Did Jason have a good time?"

"He loves the park."

"Most kids love being outdoors."

Jason certainly did. He especially enjoyed going down in the canyon with his friends and playing on what they called the Bushman Trail.

The other mothers felt that it was safe, but Jason was younger than either Danny or Tommy, and Kristy wasn't comfortable letting him go. Call her overprotective, but she didn't care. Jason might have been unplanned, but she loved him with all her heart and didn't know what she'd do if something happened to him.

She took a seat in the chair next to Gram's hospital bed. "It's a good thing I was able to take him today. It looks like rain, and he may not get to play outside for a while."

"I thought so. My joints ache today."

"Do you need an extra blanket?" Kristy asked. "It's a bit chilly."

"No, I'm all right for now." Gram pointed at the three roses in the bud vase on the nightstand. "Did you see the flowers Charlie brought?"

"They're pretty."

"He said the room looked too much like a hospital, which would drag anyone down. So he hoped the flowers would lift my spirits."

Kristy had noticed a bit of improvement in Gram's attitude since she'd talked to Jesse the other night, a conversation she still thought she'd dreamed. Hopefully, her mood would continue to improve.

"You know," Gram said, "I was just lying here, looking at that digital clock you put on the bureau. It's nice and all—the numbers light up and are easy to read at night. But it made me think about that antique clock that was a wedding gift from my in-laws. It's in your grandfather's room, on the nightstand. But I think I'd like to have it in here, too."

"The blue clock with the gold trim?" Kristy asked.

"Yes, that one."

Gram didn't ask for much. At one time, Kristy had tried to bring in some of her belongings, hoping to make the downstairs room feel like the one she'd once shared with her late husband. But Gram had always insisted she'd be moving back upstairs soon, that she'd get well with time.

But she never did.

"I'd be happy to get it for you," Kristy said. "And I'll bring you a picture or two, also. Something to make you feel more at home."

Moments later, after a search of her grandfather's room for the antique clock, Kristy came up empty-handed. She could have sworn it had been on the nightstand the last time she'd dusted the furniture.

Had she set it aside and forgotten to replace it?

Rather than return without anything at all, she snatched a 5 by 7 brass-framed photograph of her grandfather from the dresser and carried it downstairs.

"I couldn't find the clock," she said.

Gram wrinkled her brow. "It wasn't in the bedroom?"

"That's where I last saw it, but it's not there now."

Gram blew out a wispy little sigh. "I'd be heartsick if something happened to it."

"I'm sure it'll turn up. In the meantime, I thought you might like to have this close by." Kristy handed her grandmother the photograph.

"You know what?" Gram held the retro-style frame with both hands as she looked it over carefully. "This may sound crazy, but Jason really favors my husband."

Kristy supposed there was a slight resemblance, even though Gram and her husband had adopted Kristy's mom. She didn't dare comment, though. Her mother's teenage years hadn't been pleasant, and Gram didn't need the reminder.

Sadly, Kristy's first three years of high school hadn't been much better, and the apology she and Craig had talked about earlier seemed fitting. "I haven't mentioned this in a long time, but I feel like I need to say it again. I'm really sorry for sneaking out that night and going to that party at Brad's. You shouldn't have been home alone, and I'll never forgive myself for being gone when you needed me."

"You had no way of knowing I was going to have a stroke."

"That's true, but my mother used to give you fits, and I was aware of that." Kristy reached through the side rails and placed her hand over the top of Gram's. "I should have been more appreciative and more considerate."

Gram rolled her hand palm up and wrapped her spindly fingers around Kristy's. "You've certainly made up for a little teenage rebellion."

Kristy thought on that for a moment, savoring the pardon Gram was granting her.

"I guess life threw us both an unexpected curve," she finally said.

"Yes, it did. But we have Jason. Don't forget about that."

"I won't." Kristy was glad Gram had never held her unwed pregnancy against her. Maybe that was because Gram had tried so hard to have a child of her own when she was younger.

Kristy probably should have let it go at that, taking the forgiveness she'd been offered and running with it, but while they were having a talk from the heart, she couldn't help adding, "When I realized I was pregnant, I was pedaling as fast as I could, trying to stay afloat mentally, emotionally, and financially. I'm ashamed to admit this now, but I seriously considered having an abortion. And I would have, if Shana hadn't talked me out of it."

"I'm glad Shana was there for you. And that she was so stubborn. I can't imagine not having Jason. He's been the only bright spot of my life these past few years."

Kristy couldn't imagine not having him, either.

Gram gave Kristy's hand a gentle squeeze. "I had no idea how much you had to struggle with back then."

"You were too ill to worry about anything but getting better."

"Maybe so," Gram said, "but you shouldn't have had to go through something like that alone. I should have been there for you, but I was so . . . self-absorbed that I failed you, just like I failed your mother."

"That's not true. You're the best grandmother I could have hoped to have. And you were good to my mom, too."

"I tried, but she was never happy with me."

"She loved you," Kristy said. "One day, when she was clear-headed, she talked to me about . . . things—her life, the past. She told me that she was sorry that she gave you so much trouble. But I'm afraid her drug addiction was stronger than she was."

Gram's eyes glistened, and a smile softened the lines in her face. "When the state took you away from your mom and placed you with me, I was given a second chance to be a mother. And to be honest, there were times when I was afraid I'd botched it all up again. But you've turned into a lovely young woman, Kristy. I couldn't ask for a better grand-daughter. Nor could Jason ask for a better mom."

They sat like that for a while, silent yet bolstered by the connection that held them closer and tighter than their two clasped hands.

In spite of the chill in the room, a warmth and a sense of peace filled Kristy's heart, leaving no place for guilt to regain its hold.

When the doorbell rang, Kristy slowly released her grand-mother and stood. "I hope that's the guy who's coming to fix the furnace. I need to let him in."

As Kristy reached the doorway, Gram called her back. "Honey?"

"Yes?"

"Will you keep looking for that clock?"

"Of course." Then she went to answer the door.

Forty-five minutes later, the heater roared on. But Kristy still received the news she'd been dreading.

"I've got it jury-rigged for this evening," the repairman said. "But it'll go out again. And next time I won't be able to fix it. We've got a discontinued model back at the shop, so I can give you a deal on it."

A deal would be great, but still costly. She'd have to use the money she'd found in her grandfather's jacket.

After walking the repairman to the door and agreeing on a time for him to return and install the new furnace on Monday, she went to her room to get ready for work. Hopefully, Renee would arrive early again so Kristy would have time to stop at the bank on her way to the pub. She needed to deposit the funds into her account to cover the check she would write Monday.

She opened the drawer in her nightstand to get the money, only to find the music box in which she'd placed it gone.

A knot gripped her stomach. Where could it be? Who could have . . . ?

Renee?

It had to have been her. Who else could have taken it? Certainly not Jesse. After he'd stayed in her grandfather's room and had left without her knowledge, she'd checked the drawer for the money. And it had been a relief to find it right where she'd left it.

So the only one who could have possibly taken it was the sitter who'd had the run of the house for the past few days.

Had Renee taken Gram's antique clock, too?

Kristy didn't want to believe it. She'd come to like the girl. And so had Gram and Jason.

Heartsick, she began a careful inventory to see what else Renee might have taken.

She was going to have to confront the girl about the missing cash when she arrived. Hopefully, she would return the money, the music box, and the clock. If she refused, Kristy would have to call the police and make a report.

Then she'd have to tell her boss she wouldn't be coming in to work this evening after all.

No way could she leave Gram and Jason alone.

And no way could she let a thief back into the house.

Chapter 15

Shana stood near her closet, dressed in a pair of jeans and a white blouse. She removed a black sweater from its hanger, slipped her arms into the sleeves, then pulled it over her head, mussing her hair.

She glanced at her image in the mirrored wardrobe doors, noting a ghostlike pallor and dark circles under her eyes. The lack of sleep, she realized, was beginning to wear on her.

Ever since running into Ramon at the park, the memories she'd tried so hard to put behind her had come rushing back. And as a result, she'd spent her nights tossing and turning until the blankets had tangled at her feet.

There wasn't much she could do about that, though.

Ramon hadn't given her any reason to believe that they could ever resurrect what they'd once had. And why would he? When she'd ended things between them years ago, he'd merely shrugged and let her go. Obviously, the relationship had never meant the same to him as it had to her.

But thoughts of Ramon and what might have been weren't the only things that had disturbed her sleep.

Oddly enough, the ramblings of a homeless man had also caused some of her nocturnal distress. There'd been a whisper of truth in the statements he'd made, a whisper that had increased a couple of decibels while the house was quiet.

You're doomed to make the same mistakes that your parents made if you don't make some changes.

Now that was a scary prediction.

She raked a hand through her hair, the diamond on her finger snagging on a snarl and twisting to the left. She righted the ring, thinking it was too big and bulky for her small hand.

A lot of things no longer seemed to fit. Her college degree. Her future. Her life.

In the hours before dawn, when the house was quiet and her body refused to rest, thoughts and memories had flicked through her mind's eye like an old-style nickelodeon.

Snap.

Snap.

Snap.

Faster and faster, until they linked together in one continuous moment that finally made sense.

Her parents were miserable, a fact that had been easy for her to ignore, since they never argued or fought. If they'd even had disagreements, they'd kept them offstage.

Looking back, though, she realized there were evenings when the painful silence had become so heavy that she'd felt compelled to speak, to joke, to laugh, just to make everyone smile again. But even those smiles had been fake or short-lived.

Over the years, Shana had caught her mother crying softly. She'd found her several times in the kitchen, standing over the sink, tears streaming down her face. Once she'd been seated at the patio table, watching the hummingbirds at the feeder, eyes red-rimmed and watery.

"They're just happy tears," her mom had said each time.

Shana had believed her because she'd wanted to. Needed to. But maybe deep in her heart she'd always known that it hadn't been happiness flooding her eyes.

You have a choice to make, the homeless stranger had said.

And what decision was that? To choose tulips for the bouquets rather than roses? To insist upon keeping the guest list under one hundred?

Sometimes, confrontations are the only way out.

That might be true, but it wasn't Shana's job to fix her parents' marriage. And even if she was willing or able to get involved, she wasn't in the mood for drama today.

She went into her bathroom, grabbed the brush from the counter, and ran it through her hair. Next she uncapped a tube of lipstick and applied a light coat, hoping the sunrise-pink shade would provide some much-needed color to her face.

Then she borrowed her mother's car and drove to San Diego to visit Brad. She wouldn't stay long since he would undoubtedly be studying, but she needed to see him. Maybe being with him, even for a few minutes, would help her shake those old yearnings for Ramon that had been resurrected.

At a quarter to four, she arrived at the small house in Pacific Beach he shared with Ryan Wellborn, a third-year law student, and parked along the curb. The wind had kicked up this afternoon, and as she made her way up the walk, a light sprinkle misted her face and hair. She probably should have brought along a jacket and an umbrella.

She climbed the steps, then stood on the stoop, rang the bell, and waited.

Ryan, a tall blond in his mid-twenties, answered the door wearing a pair of gray sweat pants and a white T-shirt that sported a red and black SDSU logo.

"I'm sorry to bother you," she said, "but is Brad home?"

"No." Ryan arched his back, as though trying to work out a kink. "He took off around noon. I'm not sure where he is, but I'd guess he's at The Lamplighter. It's his favorite hangout."

Every muscle in her body tensed, and she struggled to remain calm, unaffected. Brad had told her that he intended to focus on his work, that he was serious about passing the bar and landing a position in a respectable firm. Maybe he'd just needed a break.

Or maybe he was meeting with a study group.

She thanked Ryan, then drove to The Lamplighter, a trendy bar in the middle of San Diego's Gaslamp District.

As she entered the old storefront building, with its scarred wood flooring and red brick walls, she scanned the darkened interior, which the happy hour crowd had already begun to fill.

Her vision was still adjusting to the faux-candle lighting when she heard a familiar voice ring out from the rear of the bar, above the din of the other patrons.

"Don't cut out now," Brad said. "You've only been here for an hour. Stay and have another drink."

So Ryan had been right; Brad *was* here.

Shana looked in the direction of his voice and spotted him seated in a corner booth with two other guys and an attractive brunette.

She wished she could say that he was clearly with the woman, because it would make it easy to be hurt, to get angry, and lash out. But she couldn't be sure about anything, other than the fact that Brad was clearly not studying.

"Hey, Shana. What a surprise." His grin lit his eyes and dimpled his cheeks. "Come over here and sit down, baby."

She made her way to his table, but her feet seemed to shuffle as though her ankles were shackled.

"What's going on?" she asked.

"I'm just kicking back with some friends. Let me introduce you. This is Derek, and that's Howie." He placed his hand on the woman's shoulder. "This is Kendra."

As his friends greeted her, she forced a smile, but she had no interest in remembering any of their names. No real interest in their chatter.

Brad slid further into the booth, making room so she could take a seat next to him. "Let me get you something to drink, babe. How about a green apple martini? That's what Kendra's drinking."

"I'll pass."

"Uh-oh," Derek said. Or was that Howie? Shana couldn't remember.

"I feel a definite chill in the air," the man added.

Shana hadn't meant to voice her displeasure, yet it must be apparent to those around her.

Just as her mother's often was.

"Is something wrong?" Brad asked.

Yes. No. She couldn't seem to settle on an answer. One response was a lie, and the other would unleash the drama she'd wanted to avoid.

The homeless man's words settled over her, insisting that confrontations were sometimes the only way out.

"You know," Brad said, "maybe Shana and I ought to talk in private."

He asked his friends to excuse them, then nodded toward the edge of the booth, which Shana now blocked.

She slid out, and he followed, stopping long enough to snatch his drink and bring it with him.

"So what's up?" he asked, as he led Shana to a table for two near a window that faced the street.

She wasn't sure. She wanted to laugh it all off and say, "Nothing. Everything's just fine. I have no reason to be upset."

In a sense that was true. Brad had been glad to see her. He'd also picked up on her uneasiness and had cared enough to ask what was bothering her. Then he'd been considerate enough to talk to her alone about it, rather than force her to open up her heart in front of a group of strangers.

So what did she have to complain about? Brad was a nice guy, and he cared about her.

Still, the uneasiness that had been hovering over her all day sank lower, draping her like a wet blanket until her shoulders slumped under the weight.

"I thought you wanted to turn over a new leaf," she said.

"I do. I *have*." He smiled and gave a little shrug. "I was studying all morning and needed a break. You have no idea how tough law school is."

Shana had no doubt that it was tough, but Brad wasn't taking it seriously. And he expected her to laugh it off, to pretend that he was giving it his best shot.

Just as everyone in her life had tried to make the best of things.

As she thought about what lay beneath the mask of happiness she'd lived with for the past twenty-some years, a knot formed in her stomach, squeezing out a burst of bile.

Was she doomed to make the same mistakes her parents had made? To play the same games?

Her heart thumped out an SOS beat, but there was no one who could rescue her but herself. Finally, she said, "This isn't going to work, Brad."

"What isn't?"

"A marriage of convenience." The minute the words rolled off her tongue she realized that's exactly what it was. A ploy to make Brad look solid and respectable. And a vehicle to take her safely from college to adulthood.

"Wait a second," Brad said. "You're not breaking up with me, are you?"

Her mother would be upset—embarrassed. But Shana couldn't marry a man for all the wrong reasons.

She slipped the diamond from her finger and handed it to him. "I'm sorry. I can't marry you."

"You're getting weird about nothing. Are you upset that Kendra is here with me? She's just a friend."

So they *had* been together.

Oddly enough, it didn't seem to matter one way or the other. And if she really loved Brad, if their marriage had any real potential, it ought to be rubbing her the wrong way.

"No," she said. "I don't care who you're with."

"Are you angry about me being here? Having a drink with my friends?"

She doubted that he'd only had one. "It's not that, either. It's the fact that I don't want to play games any more. I want my life back."

"You're making a big mistake," he said.

He might be right, but she feared she would be making a bigger one by following through with things.

"I need you," he added. "We need each other."

He'd used that excuse when he'd come to Australia to see her, and at the time, she'd been lonely and vulnerable. She'd wanted to believe it, so she had.

But now that she'd gotten home and seen Ramon, now that she'd relived those emotions she'd once felt for the son of the Rensfields' gardener, she knew that whatever it was she felt for Brad wasn't love. And a marriage without love was surely doomed from the start.

"I care about you, Brad, and I appreciate your friendship, but I can't pull your career out of the toilet, which I think was always your primary game plan. But that's something you'll have to do yourself."

Brad studied the diamond ring in his hand, then glanced up at her. "Will you still talk to your dad about that internship? You said you would. And you owe me, remember?"

She wasn't sure what she'd been expecting from him. Some sign of emotion, she supposed. Even Ramon, who'd shrugged off her parting words and walked away after their breakup, had experienced a twitch at the corner of his eye, a fallen expression.

If Brad loved her the least little bit, shouldn't he be upset over more than his internship?

"So you're calling in a marker?" she asked.

"I need a position this summer, Shana."

She pushed her chair back and got to her feet. "I'll talk to him, but I'm not sure it's going to help."

Then she turned and walked away, seeking the hope and promise of fresh air and sunshine.

As she stepped out of the bar and onto the sidewalk, a

flash of lightning lit the eastern sky, followed by a rumble of thunder. She hoped she was as brave as that homeless man had said she was, because there was a storm brewing.

She braced herself to face it head on and to ride it out.

Craig had hung around the ball fields long enough to gain a growing respect for Ramon. The guy was great with those kids, and they looked up to him. It was obvious that he was making a difference in their lives. Craig was not only impressed but heartened by it.

"All right," Ramon told the ragtag team. "That's all for today. Let's pack up the gear."

As the boys scattered to do as they were told, Ramon turned to Craig. "I know you're busy, and that you said you weren't interested in coaching on a regular basis, but would you like to help me transport the boys to the batting cages on Monday? One of the local business owners has agreed to sponsor the outing, and he's springing for pizza afterward."

Craig wasn't ready to jump into a full-time coaching gig, although he could certainly handle batting practice and pizza. "If we can do it after two o'clock, I'm available."

"Great. Let's meet here."

After leaving the park, Craig no longer had time to drive by the house. Instead, he called Rod Gleason, the contractor, and volunteered to help out on Tuesday and Thursday next week. Rod said that if all went as expected, Craig should be able to start moving in on Friday.

When Craig got back to the church, it was nearly four. He'd just stepped off the sidewalk and onto the parking lot when the Delacourts' Mercedes pulled up beside him, tires crunching upon the grit on the asphalt.

As the engine idled, Daniel lowered the passenger window. "Hey, Pastor. You got a minute?"

"Sure."

"I hadn't planned to stop here, but I thought it was only fair to tell you first since you'll be the most supportive."

"Tell me what?"

"I left the firm today, and for the first time since passing the bar, I feel good about my career. And about myself." His broad smile boasted peace and relief. "You have no idea how much I appreciate that chat we had. Of course, I still have to tell Cassie what I've decided, and I hope she understands why I did it. But if not, I'm ready to face the consequences, whatever they might be."

Stunned that his off-the-cuff talk with Daniel had resulted in a life-changing decision, Craig wanted to both thank him and apologize at the same time. As it was, he did neither.

"You know," he said instead, "I think it would be a good idea if I found something to do tonight, something to keep me out until bedtime. You two ought to have some privacy."

"You're probably right. Shana will be home this evening, which is all right. My decision will have some effect on her, too. But with a wedding on the horizon, and with her starting a new life soon, it shouldn't be too much of a problem."

Daniel's biggest hurdle was going to be Cassandra, Craig realized. Hopefully, Daniel's long overdue decision wouldn't place their marriage in jeopardy.

"Thanks again for talking to me, Pastor. Your advice was just what I needed to hear."

His advice? For the most part, Craig had merely listened. "I'm still not sure what I said that you found so helpful."

Daniel smiled. "It was simple and sage, short and to the point. You told me to follow my heart."

"Sometimes that's all a person can do," Craig said, the truth settling over him.

"Well, I guess I'd better go and face the music." Daniel placed one hand on the steering wheel and the other on the gear shift.

"One question," Craig said. "If you're no longer going to work in the firm, what will you do instead?"

"I'm going to offer my services to the prosecutor's office and take it from there. I might even run for district attorney in the next election. Either way, we'll need to make some financial adjustments to our household budget. But I've got some sizable investments that will help us through the transition." Daniel shifted the car into drive, but didn't accelerate. "It's not like I'm asking Cassandra to move into the poor house."

Craig hoped he wouldn't have to counsel the Delacourts through a divorce, but Daniel had a right to be happy in his job, to feel as though he was making a difference.

"Thanks again, Pastor. I'll see you later." Daniel raised the passenger window, let up on the brake, and continued on his way.

Craig stood in the parking lot for a while, thinking about the power of the simple advice he'd given Daniel.

Follow your heart. Three little words, but not always easy to do.

As he turned toward the church, he spotted Jesse seated on the steps that led to the red doors that opened to the sanctuary.

"Hey, Jesse," he said, as he approached the homeless man. "What's up?"

"Not much. I'm just killing a little time until the bus comes by." He sat up a bit straighter, leaned forward. "I saw you in the park earlier. I'm glad you met Ramon."

"He seems like a nice guy. I like what he's trying to do with those kids."

"I thought you would."

Craig slid his hands into his pockets, warding off the growing chill in the air. "What made you think that I'd like working with him?"

"Because you have a heart for the downtrodden. And you like baseball. Seems like a perfect match to me."

"I never told you that I liked baseball."

"You didn't have to." Jesse stroked his knees, his clean but weathered hands gliding over the threadbare fabric of his khaki slacks. "I could see it in your eyes."

He could?

The night they'd met, Jesse had said he had a gift, yet Craig wasn't entirely convinced and couldn't help asking, "What else can you see?"

"That you're struggling with things."

Craig tensed, giving far more weight to Jesse's "gift" than he ought to. "Like what?"

"The ministry, for one. The assignment you were given."

He'd touched a bit too much on the truth. "What makes you say that?"

"I get the feeling that you're not sure you're doing the right thing."

Craig could deny it, but why should he? A simple chat had led to Daniel's epiphany, although he doubted he could expect one for himself.

"My granddad was called to the ministry," he said, "and over the years, he made a difference in a lot of people's lives."

"Is that what you're struggling with? The need to follow in your grandfather's footsteps?"

"Not exactly, but I would like to think that I'd made a difference in people's lives. My dad was in the special forces during Operation Desert Storm and died a hero, so maybe it's in my blood."

"So why the ministry and not the military?"

The question took him aback. "I never considered joining the military. Of course, I never considered the ministry, either. But when I thought my grandfather was dying, I promised God that if he lived, I'd become a pastor."

"So you're here now because of a promise you made?"

That was about the size of it. Craig gave a half shrug, then nodded.

"Sounds like a bribe to me. You weren't trying to barter with the Almighty, were you?"

"What are you getting at?"

"You might be holding yourself to a promise He never intended you to make."

That possibility had never crossed Craig's mind, and while he gave it some thought, he still couldn't find it in himself to renege on a bargain with God.

"My granddad was healed," he explained. "The doctors never expected him to pull through, and they all agreed it was nothing short of a miracle."

"I'm sure it was." A slow smile stretched across Jesse's face. "Were you the only one praying?"

"No, the entire congregation hit their knees, and word went out to everyone my grandfather had ever even known, everyone whose life he'd ever touched."

Jesse stroked his bearded chin. "Then it seems only logical to assume God had no way of healing the man without responding to your request in the process."

The truth of his statement broadsided Craig. "Are you saying that my prayers were answered by default? And that I never should have become a minister?"

"No, I'm not saying that at all. But I imagine that you're so caught up in the bargain, that you might have missed the actual call."

"Missed it?"

"Maybe you should stop looking at your job as an obligation and consider it an opportunity. Open your heart and listen. And while you're at it, you might ask yourself what you're afraid of."

"What do you mean by that?"

"I mean that there's probably more going on inside your head and your heart than you realize. A fear of failure, maybe?"

"I've never failed at anything in my life."

"Some people make sure that they don't."

The guy was talking in circles, making Craig crazy. He decided to end the conversation, but before he could make some kind of excuse to leave, Jesse slowly got to his feet, grimacing as he did so.

"Are you all right?" Craig asked.

Jesse straightened. "It's just some stiff joints. I predict rain."

Craig smiled and glanced at the darkened sky. "Oh, yeah? Even I could predict that with certainty."

Jesse stooped to pick up a woman's purse that had been sitting beside him, hidden by the bulk of his blue jacket.

"What are you doing with that?" Craig asked.

"I need to return this before the storm hits." Jesse slipped his arm through the shoulder strap, then started toward the bus stop.

"Do you need a ride?" Craig asked. He also wondered where the guy had been staying, although he wasn't sure where he could take him. Certainly not the Delacourts' house, especially tonight.

Jesse offered him a smile. "I'm okay. The bus will be here in a minute or so."

"Do you have shelter from the storm?"

"Not to worry. I'll stay warm and dry."

As big droplets of water began to fall from the sky, Craig remained rooted to the spot, watching the man go and wondering how he'd acquired so much common sense.

Or did he really have a gift?

Chapter 16

By the time Shana returned home, her stomach was churning, and her knuckles ached from gripping the steering wheel.

A part of her wanted to put off telling her mother what she'd done, but she'd decided to get it over with. Her mom was going to have the same reaction today as she would have next week, so admitting to the breakup now would save Shana from days of the pre-confrontation stress.

Her dad's car was parked in the drive, which was a surprise. There weren't many nights that he left the office before dark.

Maybe it was just as well. This way, she'd only need to make the announcement once.

After parking next to the Mercedes in the driveway, she let herself into the house, her movements as stiff as those of a tin soldier.

"I'm home," she said from the entry.

She was met with silence.

That was odd. Her mom usually dropped what she was doing to welcome her back into the fold, and her dad always had a warm greeting.

The soles of her shoes clicked upon the travertine flooring in the entry until she reached the carpet. As she made her way to the living room, she called out again. This time, her father's voice sounded from the kitchen. "We're in here, Princess."

His tone seemed a little flat today, and she was both hesitant and apprehensive, as she joined her parents in the kitchen.

They were seated at the table. Her dad, with his clasped hands resting on the tabletop, offered her a smile that failed to reach his eyes.

Her mom couldn't seem to give her even that much, but Shana could see why—her mom's red-rimmed, teary eyes suggested that they'd been having a heavy conversation.

Shana's first thought was that something terrible had happened to one or both of her grandparents. The second was that Brad had already told his mother, and Mrs. Rensfield had just dropped the bomb.

But that wasn't likely. Brad was more tight-lipped around his parents than Shana was.

"What's the matter?" she asked her mom.

"Nothing, honey." Her mom sniffled, then blotted her eyes with a tissue she'd wadded in her hand.

"That's not true." Shana continued walking to the table, but didn't take a seat. "You're crying, and this time you can't tell me they're tears of joy. This family hasn't been happy for a long time."

The indisputable truth was met with silence.

Finally, her father leaned back in his chair and crossed his arms. "I gave my resignation at the firm today, Shana. I won't be working as a defense attorney any longer, and your mother isn't pleased with my decision."

Her mom dabbed at her nose with the crumpled tissue. "You're giving up so much, Daniel. I can't believe you'd do something like that without discussing it with me first."

"I've given up a lot over the years, Cassie. And as for discussing this with you ahead of time, maybe I should have, but whenever I brought it up in the past, either you or your father shot me down."

"Speaking of Daddy, he's going to be shocked to hear of your resignation."

"This isn't about your father, Cassie. Leave him out of our family discussions for once, will you?"

Shana felt like a voyeur, and for a moment, wondered if she should slip quietly away.

You're braver than you think, the homeless man had said. Not that Shana had put much stock in that crazy encounter, but some of what he'd said had been true.

"What about the money?" Her mother's gaze searched her father's. "We won't have the income we've become accustomed to."

"Money isn't the most important thing in life."

"It is when you don't have any."

"Cassie, we've saved over the years, so we won't be destitute. You can still be involved in your philanthropic endeavors." He glanced at Shana, as if just remembering she was standing there, privy to the marital discord for the first time in her life. "We've set aside plenty of money for your wedding, honey. So you don't have to worry about that."

The wedding? Great. Shana now had the perfect opening for her announcement, but the timing was lousy. Her mom had already suffered one huge disappointment today.

But there had been enough tiptoeing around problems and disappointments in the past, and Shana couldn't continue to play those games any longer. "I hate to drop this on you two now, but we may as well lay everything on the table. I just broke my engagement. I'm not going to marry Brad."

"What?" Her mother's eyes grew wide. "Why not? What happened?"

"Nothing happened." Shana glanced at her father before explaining, saw the questions in his eyes. "I care about Brad, but I'm not in love with him."

"Then why did you agree to marry him in the first place?" her father asked.

Why had she?

They were friends. She cared about him. And he'd always made her laugh.

His unannounced visit to Australia had flattered her, and she'd found him charming. So, with graduation closing in on her and no more reasons to postpone a return home to Fairbrook, accepting his proposal had seemed like the . . . perfect thing to do.

At that moment, the telephone rang—just like the bell in a boxing match, allowing the combatants to take a much needed break.

Her dad snatched the portable phone from its cradle. "Hello? Yes, Frank. Thanks for returning my call." He opened the sliding door and took the call out on the deck.

"Who's Frank?" Shana asked her mom.

"The district attorney. Your father would like to work for him, either as a consultant or as an attorney." Her mother blew out a ragged breath, then slowly shook her head. "I can't believe he did this. It makes no sense at all. Not now. Not at his age. He'll be starting over."

"Maybe he should have worked for the DA all along," Shana said.

Isn't that what he'd told her he'd wanted to do when he got out of law school?

"It would have made more sense than making a move like this now." Her mother sighed again, as though expelling the air in her lungs would relieve the problems at hand. Then she fiddled with the edge of the crumpled tissue, tearing at it. "Your grandfather is going to be shocked."

"Like Dad said, Mom. It's not about Grandpa. It's about all of us. But mostly, it's about Dad and what he feels is the right thing for him to do."

Her mom glanced up. "Of course, it is, but—"

"Oh, wow." Shana finally took a seat. "I *am* guilty of repeating my parents' mistakes."

"What are you talking about?"

"Someone said something to me, but I didn't get it at the time." She raked her fingers through her damp hair. "I get it now, though. It's all falling into place."

"How can you say that I've made mistakes," her mother said. "My whole life has been spent trying to be a good wife and mother."

"I realize that. But I think you've tried a bit too hard to be a good daughter, too."

"What's wrong with that? My parents were good to me, and I owe them that much."

"Do you?"

"This isn't like you, Shana."

"What? Challenging you and your way of doing things? I'm sorry, Mom. I love you, but we've all been forced to live by Grandpa's standards, even if they're wrong for us."

"He's not the bad guy here. He never forced me or you to do things his way."

"He has a very persuasive way about him, and I've just followed your lead. But not anymore. At least, not when I think he or you are wrong."

Her mother massaged her temples, as if she could work out the knots in their relationships.

"You've been unhappy, too," Shana said, her voice soft, sympathetic. "You can't deny it. But this has got to stop."

"What does?"

"Living someone else's life."

Her mom looked up, clearly confused. "Whose life do you think I'm living?"

"I don't know. Your parents'? Dad's? Mine? I'm not sure, but if you were more in tune with what's in your own heart, you'd be a happier person."

And so would Shana, especially if she took that same advice.

Her mom sat up straighter, yet her expression remained the same—cornered and distraught. "To be honest? I'm not even sure who I am anymore. Or what's in my heart. Only that I love my family, and I feel it falling apart at the seams."

"Then maybe it's time you found out who you are."

They sat in silence as the truth hovered around them, just out of reach.

Finally, her mom asked, "What about you, Shana. What's in your heart?"

"I'm not entirely sure." But she had an idea.

Running into Ramon at the park had taught her something. The handsome boy-turned-man still held a very precious place in her heart.

She'd like to date him, if he was the least bit interested. And if he wasn't?

Then she'd head back to Australia and try to play catch-up with her studies. Either way, she definitely had some thinking to do.

Before either could respond, the doorbell rang.

Shana pushed her chair away from the table. "I'll get it."

Unable to help herself, she glanced over her shoulder as she was leaving the kitchen and saw her mom crumble when she thought no one was looking.

She didn't want to see her mother sad or hurt, but she couldn't continue to live a façade of the life she was meant to have.

Be strong, Shana told herself. Break the cycle. It wasn't about her parents, it was about her. About her life, her dreams, her sense of right and wrong.

She proceeded to the foyer and answered the door. She wasn't sure who she'd been expecting, but certainly not the bearded man she'd talked to in the park.

His hair was damp from the light rain that had begun to fall. He held up a purse in one hand and offered a smile. "I'm looking for Cassandra Delacourt. Is she here?"

"Yes, she is." Shana glanced over her shoulder and called for her mother. While she waited for her to arrive, she gripped the edge of the door as though she could hold off the storm from battering her home.

Her mother stepped into the entry. "What is it?"

Shana moved aside, allowing the door to open all the way.

Again, the man lifted the handbag he held. "I found something that belongs to you."

She eased forward and took it from him. "Where did you find it?"

"In a parking lot behind the shopping center on Elm."

Cassandra reached into the purse and filed through the contents.

"It's all there," he said.

"It sure looks that way." She opened her wallet, pulled out a hundred-dollar bill, and handed it to him. "Thank you for your honesty."

"I didn't bring this back looking for a reward."

"Still, it'll make me feel better if you take this." She pressed the money into his hand.

"If you're looking for ways to pay it forward, why not donate your time at the soup kitchen? Dawn and Joe Randolph can always use help."

"Actually," she said, "I already support the church and that particular charity, among others."

The man slipped the hundred-dollar bill into his pocket. "Donations are fine and needed sometimes. But sometimes you need to do some actual foot washing rather than offer to pay for someone's pedicure."

Cassandra stiffened. "What are you getting at?"

"Sometimes you need to do more than write a check. You need to give of yourself to be truly blessed."

Cassandra was speechless, and so was Shana.

Who was that man?

They watched him stride down the walk and onto the street. He walked past each of the cars parked along the curb of their exclusive neighborhood, continuing on foot as rain pelted his hair and clothes.

"I'm going to offer him a ride," Shana said.

"You can't do that, honey. He's a complete stranger. What if he's a drug addict or a serial killer or something awful?"

"I doubt it. He didn't steal anything out of your purse, so he can't be all bad." As Shana started after the man, her mother grabbed her arm. "I won't let you go alone with him. Wait a minute. I'll get your father, and we'll both ride with you."

Shana offered her mom a smile. "Nothing like a little hands-on charity work, huh?"

"He made it sound as though I wrote checks to absolve my conscience, and I don't want him to think I'm heartless. I just hope your father understands what we're doing and why."

"Tell him that we're going on a family adventure."

Cassandra smiled wryly. "This is certainly a first for us, that's for sure."

Shana nodded toward the man. "I'll ask him to wait."

As her mom returned to the kitchen, Shana jogged to the street, calling out to the man. "Mister?"

He turned. "Yes?"

"If you don't mind hanging out for a minute or two, we'll give you a ride."

"I'm not going far. Just to the corner of Fourth and Elm."

Shana had spotted some new apartments near there. "Is that where you live?"

"No, that's the bus stop." He blessed her with a bright-eyed smile. "I thought I'd go to Debbie's Diner for a cup of soup or something to eat."

"We'll give you a ride to the diner. And then we'll treat you to a hot meal."

"You don't need to do that."

"I know," Shana said. "But humor us, okay? Our family is trying to put our lives back in order again, and we could use a new focus."

And if he had some more advice to share, then so be it.

Renee trekked through the canyon, her feet picking up mud and grit along the path that led to the backyards of the houses on Sugar Plum Lane. She was going to work early today. With the clouds gathering, she was afraid she'd get caught in a downpour if she didn't.

She wondered if Kristy had an umbrella she could borrow.

The boys had been great about stocking the tree house with necessities, but no one had planned for a day like this. And tonight was bound to be worse.

The roof of the tree house was sure to leak, and she was going to be wet, cold, and miserable.

She wondered if it would be out of line for her to ask Kristy if she could spend the night tonight. She could tell her that her place was being fumigated. Or that the heater wasn't working.

Kristy was pretty cool and would probably offer to let Renee sleep on the couch.

If she didn't, maybe Renee could take the bus to a motel. Tonight was definitely a good time to splurge on a real room.

She continued her trek, the soles of her sandals picking up more and more muck as she went. By the time she reached Kristy's front yard, the light sprinkles overhead had intensified. In a few minutes, the rain would be coming down steadily, and she couldn't wait to get inside. Her toes were cold, and so were her hands.

When she reached the front porch, she knocked on the door.

Kristy answered, but she wasn't smiling. And she didn't welcome her in.

She crossed her arms like a sentry. "We have a problem, Renee. Some of my things are missing."

Renee wrinkled her brow. "What things?"

"I won't beat around the bush. I'm missing a lot of money. It was in a music box that used to be in the top drawer of my nightstand, but that's gone, too."

Did she think Renee had taken it?

She drew her hands into the long sleeves of her sweat shirt, wishing her whole body could do the same thing. But she stood tall. "I would never steal from you or from anyone, Kristy. I hope you know that."

A frown suggested she didn't.

"That music box was hand-carved," Kristy said. "And it

had a false bottom. It plays "The Blue Danube Waltz." Have you seen it?"

Renee was torn between wanting to clear her name and protecting her secret.

Jason had thought the baby would like the music box, so he'd given it to Renee for that reason.

If she insisted it was a gift, Jason would be questioned. And maybe he'd spill the beans about her, about her situation.

Maybe she wouldn't need much of an explanation if she just returned it. "I know where it is. I'll go and get it."

"What about the money?"

Kristy had said the box had a false bottom, so it might still be inside. "It appeared to be empty, but the money might be right where you left it."

"It had better be. If not, I'll call the police."

More than anything, Renee wanted to tell Kristy that she hadn't taken anything, but she didn't want to get Jason in trouble for going into the canyon and for taking things from his house. "Wait here, Kristy. I'll run home and bring it back."

"So you *did* take it." Anger flared in Kristy's eyes, yet it was tempered by disappointment. "Why would you steal from me? I trusted you."

"But I . . . didn't . . ." It was a gift, she wanted to say. Jason must have taken it without permission, but she couldn't rat on him. She'd sworn the boys to secrecy, and if she told on him, he would probably reveal everything he knew about her to save his own butt. And she couldn't blame him if he did. If she had a mom like Kristy, she wouldn't want to upset her, either.

"If you needed the money or wanted the box, why didn't you just ask me?" Kristy asked, clearly feeling betrayed.

She considered her options. How much was she willing to admit?

That she was young and pregnant and living in a tree?

That she wasn't prepared to bring a baby into this world, no matter how much she meant to love and protect it?

Tears stung her eyes, and emotion clawed her throat. "I'll be right back. Okay? Please don't call the police."

"If all the money is still inside when you return it, I won't report you. But if you kept any of the money . . ."

Who knew what had happened to it.

What if it wasn't in the bottom?

What if Jason left the box lying around and someone else had already taken it before he'd even given it to her?

"Wait here," Renee said. "I'll only be a few minutes."

Oh, God, she thought, as she turned and dashed down the wet walkway to the street. *Please let it all be there.*

It was more of a desperate wish than a prayer.

As she cut between two houses to the path that led to the canyon, the rain poured down on her head, and her feet slogged through the wet dirt that was fast turning to mud.

She hurried toward the tree house. Faster, faster.

Wet strands of hair slapped against her cheeks, and her breaths came out in short, ragged shards that clawed at her chest. She forced herself to run faster, but her steps slowed as big globs of mud stuck to her sandals.

By the time she spotted the tree house in the distance, she was soaking wet and chilled to the bone. But mostly she felt dirty, like she'd done something horrible.

It was so unfair. All she'd wanted to do was stay out of trouble and to keep her baby safe.

Once she returned the music box, she would tell the boys to take back everything they'd ever given her. No way did she want to risk something like this happening again—especially with Kristy, who she'd really begun to like.

As she neared her tree, the wind kicked up, and the sky darkened from both sunset and the storm. She picked up her pace, hoping that a hard run wouldn't hurt the baby.

She couldn't believe this was happening to her—just when she was beginning to think that Fairbrook was all Jesse had said it was, that she'd actually found a place where she fit in. She'd even told Dawn she would meet her at church on Sunday morning and check out the services. And not just because Dawn had said they served donuts and coffee afterward. She'd agreed because Dawn was so nice to her, and she'd wanted to spend time with her and Joe—away from the soup kitchen.

Tears blinded her, and the rain blasted her face. When she finally reached the tree, she began the climb up the wooden slats that had been nailed on the trunk.

Up, up, she went.

As she neared the top, she reached for the edge of the wooden flooring in the doorway, but before she could get a good grip, her foot slipped. Her wet fingers clawed at the wood, but to no avail.

She slipped and fell.

"Oh, God," she cried out loud, just as her back and head slammed onto the ground with a thud.

Upon impact, the wind was knocked right out of her, and she couldn't catch her breath, couldn't yell.

Lightning flashed, and thunder roared in anger.

What had she ever done to deserve this?

When she thought she would surely die from lack of oxygen, she finally gasped. Slowly, her ability to breathe returned, but it seemed that she was sucking in more water than air.

Finally, she yelled for help. But she feared no one would hear her, no one would come.

Her back and head ached something awful, but that wasn't her biggest fear.

It was searing pain low in her belly that scared her the most. The stabbing pain that sliced like a knife across her womb.

Her tears mingled with the rain.

"Oh, God," she prayed, realizing He was her only option and hoping He was really up there. "I don't care about me, but please don't let my baby die."

* * *

In the cozy warmth of the old Victorian house, Kristy waited for Renee to return. She paced the living room, wondering if she'd made a mistake in letting the girl go off alone.

What if she never came back? What if the money was gone for good and she couldn't pay for the new furnace?

Her only peace of mind came from the fact that the boys, at least Danny, knew where Renee lived. So Kristy would have an address for the police report.

She blew out a ragged sigh and raked a hand through her hair. She was sick about this. Not just the theft, but also the fact that she couldn't trust Renee now and once again would need to find another sitter.

There wasn't much left in Gram's savings account, so the money that had appeared out of nowhere had also given Kristy the tiniest glimpse of light at the end of a very dark tunnel.

A whisper of guilt blew over her, as her conscience reared its head, reminding her that the money had actually belonged to Gram's husband. And with his death, ownership had fallen to Gram.

Kristy knew Gram wouldn't mind her using that money to repair the furnace, but she'd also pondered plans to use the leftover on college—all without mentioning her find or seeking Gram's approval.

Even though she didn't think Gram would care one way or the other, she couldn't seem to shuck the uneasiness about her own actions.

"Hey," Jason said, as he entered the living room. "I thought I heard Renee's voice a while ago. Where did she go?"

"She went to get the music box she stole from our house."

Jason bit down on his bottom lip and scrunched his face. "What music box?"

"The pretty one made out of wood, the one I put in a drawer in my room."

"You wanted *that*?"

Renee had said she didn't steal the box, and it didn't take

Kristy long to start filling in the blanks. "Did you take it out of the drawer in my bedroom?"

"Yeah. I didn't think you wanted it. How come you didn't put it out for everyone to see? That's what you do with all the other junk you like."

"Because I'd hidden some money inside of it, and I tried to hide it."

"It was empty when I found it."

She explained how a false bottom worked, yet her heart grew heavy from the assumptions and the unfounded accusations she'd made. She could still see the desperation in Renee's eyes, still hear the fear in her voice. And at that very moment she appeared young, all alone, and backed into a corner.

It hadn't been all that long ago when Kristy had found herself up against a hard wall with no one to turn to, no one to help.

She ran a hand through her hair again, wondering what she should say to the girl. She definitely owed her an apology.

"Don't be mad at us," Jason said. "Renee will give it back."

"I know. That's what she went to do."

Jason strode to the living room window and peered out into the yard. "Did she walk? She's going to get super wet and cold."

Great. As if Kristy needed to feel any guiltier than she already did. She glanced at the clock. Renee had said she'd be right back.

"How far away does she live?" she asked.

Jason turned from the window. "Not too far."

"Maybe I should drive to her house and pick her up."

"You can't drive there, Mom."

"Why not?"

He bit down on his bottom lip again and scrunched his face.

Kristy crossed her arms and shifted her weight to one foot. "Why do I get the feeling that you're hiding something?"

Instead of answering, he seemed to ponder a response. When his gaze finally met hers, he said, "I can't tell you."

"Why not?"

"I promised. Something bad could happen if anyone finds out."

Kristy uncrossed her arms and stepped closer to him. "We've had this talk before, Jason. If someone tells you to keep a secret from your mom, that's your first clue that the secret needs to be shared with me. So you can tell me this one, and I promise to do whatever I can to make sure something bad doesn't happen."

He cocked his head to one side, his eyes brightening. "You'd help her?"

"Yes, if I can."

"But do you promise not to tell anyone else?"

Did she dare make an agreement like that? When she didn't have all the details?

"First you'll have to tell me what the secret is. And I promise not to tell anyone without talking it over with you and explaining why we'd need to do that."

"But someone might take away her baby."

Kristy's heart dropped. "She has a baby? Where is it?"

"In her stomach. But she's afraid someone will take it away if they think she can't take care of it."

"Why would someone do that?"

"Because she's kind of young to be a mother. And because she doesn't live in a real house or have a car or lots of money."

Kristy had thought that the ID she'd flashed had looked phony. "Where does she live?"

"In the tree house we found in the canyon."

Kristy hadn't thought her stomach could plummet any further, and she didn't know what to say. She did know that she would do her best to keep her promise to her son. And that she'd do whatever she could to help in this situation.

The first thing was to get that girl out of the rain.

She picked up the telephone.

"Hey, wait!" Jason rushed to her side and put his hand over the phone. "You promised not to tell."

"Oh, no, honey. I'm not telling anyone. I need to get Charlie to come over and stay with Gram while you and I look for Renee. It's raining, and we can't let her stay in a tree house."

Jason lifted his hand. "Maybe we could let her spend the night here, huh?"

"Of course." How could Kristy let that poor pregnant girl—how old was she?—live outdoors?

She dialed Charlie's number, and when he answered, she asked if he'd please sit with Gram for a few minutes. Then she dug the umbrella out of the hall closet.

As she waited for her elderly neighbor to arrive, she placed a hand on her son's shoulder. "Go get your jacket. The one with the hood. You're going to have to show me that tree house."

Moments later, Charlie arrived.

"I'm sorry to drag you out of your house on a day like this," she told the elderly man, "but it's an emergency. I won't be long."

"Not to worry. This isn't the first time I've had to answer a woman's call of distress. And to be honest, I used to get annoyed when Grace would start in on me with her honey-do list. But now that she's gone, I miss not having the errands she would assign me."

"Thanks Charlie. We won't be long."

"Where are you going?" he asked.

Kristy glanced at Jason and smiled. "I'm afraid that's a secret."

The boy headed for the door, and she followed his lead, as he rushed down the walk and onto the sidewalk. Three houses down, he turned left and ran along a path to the canyon.

"Be careful," she said, trying to keep up.

"I will."

"It's muddy and slick," she reminded him.

Jason dashed around a corner, causing a branch from a bush to swing back and slap at Kristy. She grimaced, but kept going.

"How far is it?" she asked.

"It's right there." He pointed ahead. "Just around this corner."

Suddenly, Jason stopped short, and Kristy almost ran him over. But she soon saw why.

Renee was sprawled on the ground at the foot of a big tree.

"Is she dead?" Jason asked.

Kristy froze in her steps for a beat, as a sense of dread slammed into her. But she shook it off, rushed to the girl's side, and knelt in the mud. "Are you okay?"

Fear was etched deeply across Renee's face. "I fell out of the tree, but I don't care about me. I think my baby's hurt really bad."

"Jason," Kristy instructed. "Run home and call 9-1-1. Then bring the paramedics here."

She reached for Renee's hand, felt her cold, wet fingers. She gave it a gentle squeeze, hoping to transfer a bit of warmth. "I'll do whatever I can to help you, Renee."

"The music box is in the tree house," she said. "I didn't get to see if the money was still in there."

"Don't worry about the money," Kristy said. "I know you didn't take anything. Jason explained everything. I'm going to help you."

Renee's grip on Kristy's hand tightened in desperation. "If my baby lives, please don't let anyone take her away from me."

Chapter 17

As the rain peppered the small window of his office, and the wind blew a hibiscus branch against the glass, Craig sat at his new desk, reached for a mug of lukewarm coffee, and took a disappointing sip.

Everyone else at the church had taken off before the storm hit, but he'd stayed behind, claiming he still had some things to do.

Most of his work, especially the phone calls he had to make, could have been made at home, but he intended to stay away from the Delacourts' house as long as he could.

He glanced at the list he'd made for himself, marking off the item on top: Make arrangements for the youth group to attend Disneyland later this month.

Next up was a phone call to each of the kids, reminding them to get their registration forms and permissions slips for the retreat at Hume Lake turned in as soon as possible since the deadline was fast approaching.

His stomach growled, reminding him that he'd had a very light lunch. As soon as he finished making his calls, he would head to Debbie's Diner and have a bite to eat. After dinner, he might even take in a movie. He hadn't done something like that in a while.

He thought about inviting someone to join him at Cinema Star 10, but the only someone who came to mind was Kristy.

To be honest, it was a tempting thought, and he couldn't help wondering if she was working tonight. It didn't have to be a date. They could go as friends, couldn't they?

The phone rang, dragging him from his musing, and he reached for the receiver. "Parkside Community Church."

"Hello, Pastor. This is Tom Hadley, returning your call."

Tom was a member of the city council. Craig had talked to him about being a part of the Homeless Task Force a couple of days ago, and Tom was working on it. But Craig had just learned that the group of "concerned" citizens had requested a special hearing in an effort to force the church to close the doors on their Parkside location and move the kitchen out of town.

So Craig had called Tom about a half-hour ago, figuring he needed to take a more proactive approach.

"Thanks for returning my call, Tom." Craig leaned back in his seat.

"No problem. What can I do for you, Pastor?"

"I'd like to invite you and the other city council members to join me for lunch at the soup kitchen one day next week."

"You're kidding."

"No, I'm not. I thought it would be a good idea if you got a chance to witness the operation firsthand and to meet some of the people we're feeding before the next meeting of the task force."

"All right. Fair enough."

They settled on Wednesday at one o'clock before ending the call.

Craig would have to give Dawn a heads-up. He didn't want her to alter the menu she'd already planned, though. It was best if Tom and the others saw things as they really were. And while they were there, he would introduce them to some of the soup kitchen regulars, especially Jesse, if he showed up that day.

Jesse had a way about him that made a man examine his preconceived beliefs about himself, as well as the secrets in his heart.

After his last conversation with Jesse had ended, and they'd gone their separate ways, Craig had been left with a lot to ponder.

What are you afraid of? the homeless man had asked. *Failure?*

Craig had scoffed the moment the comment had been made, but afterward, he'd realized it deserved more consideration.

As a kid, Craig had never really been afraid of much—not even things that went bump in the night. Adding that to the fact that he'd succeeded at just about everything he'd ever tried to do certainly mocked Jesse's fear-of-failure theory.

But as time ticked on, Craig had been forced to admit that he actually did have a fear of failure—as a minister—and it was clear why he did.

His granddad was almost bigger than life. So Craig had a lot to live up to, and it would be a real stretch to even come close.

Yet as he faced the truth, another fear presented itself. One he'd refused to admit before.

Prior to throwing out his shoulder, he'd never doubted his ability to make it in the big leagues. But afterward?

He'd been afraid that he would never be one hundred percent again, that he'd always have to baby his arm and shoulder. That he wouldn't make the cut as a pro ball player.

So he'd accepted his fate, thinking that it was all part of some big master plan.

Maybe that's why he'd never asked for a sign that God clearly meant for him to join the ministry. Instead, he'd just accepted it as part of the deal.

So now what?

There seemed to be only one way out of his dilemma.

He bowed his head and opened his heart. "Lord, forgive my doubts. Forgive me for trying to barter or bribe you into healing my grandfather. I tried to play it safe, and I should have asked for divine guidance in my decision. But it's not too late. I'm asking now." He waited a moment, hoping for a sense of peace, for the fog to be lifted in his mind. For a sign that he'd been granted absolution.

Yet he was met with silence—unless one counted the sound of rain spattering the windowpane.

So he took his plea a step further. "Please let me hear the call to the ministry or give me a clear indication that I'm free to try something else."

Before he could utter "Amen," the telephone rang.

He waited a moment, then answered. "Parkside Community Church."

"Oh, thank goodness, Pastor. You're still there." A wave of panic rocked Dawn's voice.

"What's the matter?"

"I just got off the phone with Joe. He's on duty and was called to the scene of an accident a few minutes ago. Renee had a terrible fall and is at the hospital."

Craig gripped the receiver tighter, as though he could get a better handle on the news. "How did that happen?"

"She fell out of a tree. And she's in preterm labor."

What had she been doing in a tree? Craig wondered. Yet it was his second and most pressing question that rolled off his tongue. "She's pregnant?"

"About five months, according to Joe. And she's scared to death."

Craig didn't know what he'd say to Renee or what he'd be able to do, but the compulsion to drop everything and rush to the hospital was much more than just a sense of obligation. It was a demanding need to help, to make a difference—if he could.

"I'll head to the hospital now," he said.

"Good. I'm already en route, so I'll see you there."

After ending the call, Craig shut down the computer and grabbed his jacket from the back of his desk chair before turning off the lights and locking up the church office. Then he hurried to his car, realizing that it was more than an attempt to remain as dry as possible that forced him to pick up his pace.

Ten minutes later, he arrived at Pacifica General Hospital and parked in one of the spaces reserved for the clergy.

He entered through the ER door and scanned the busy waiting room. Much to his relief, he spotted Dawn talking to Joe near the registration window and quickly approached them.

"I'm glad you both came," Joe said. "My partner is wrapping up paperwork, and I can't stay much longer."

"How's she doing?" Craig asked.

"She's being examined now, so I can't tell you much. She's definitely suffered a concussion and a possible spinal injury."

"Is anyone with her?" Craig asked.

"Kristy, Lorraine Smith's granddaughter, is in there now. She's the one who found her and called for help. She asked a neighbor to stay with her son and Lorraine, then she met us here. Renee was pretty shook up, so I'm sure she appreciated having someone with her."

"What was she doing in a tree?" Craig asked.

Joe pursed his lips and slowly shook his head. "You're not going to believe this, but she was living in it."

Craig furrowed his brow. "In a *tree*?"

"Actually, it was a tree house."

"No kidding?" Craig asked. "I knew that she didn't have much money, which is the case for a lot of our soup-kitchen regulars. But I had no idea she was homeless."

"The poor kid." Dawn placed a hand on Joe's arm. "She's going to need a place to recuperate when she gets out of the hospital. If you don't mind, I'm going to invite her to stay in our guest room until she finds something else."

"I don't mind at all," Joe said.

The three of them stood in silence, each pondering the tragedy and the reality of Renee's plight.

"Is she going to be okay?" Dawn asked her husband.

"It depends upon how badly she hurt her back, but I think so. At least physically. She's really stressed about the baby."

"I can understand that," Dawn said. "Will she lose it?"

"The doctors are doing what they can to stop labor, so hopefully that will work. And while I was in there, they were ordering an ultrasound."

"She appears to be awfully young," Craig said. "Do you know how old she really is?"

"In the ambulance, I held her hand and gently coaxed the truth out of her," Joe said. "I'm afraid she's only fifteen."

Dawn's eyes glistened with unshed tears. "That's so sad. She ought to be in school and hanging out with friends at the mall or the park. Instead, she's worried about survival and bringing a baby into the world."

Saddened and pensive, the trio grew silent again.

After a few moments, Dawn turned to her husband. "Does she plan to keep the baby or give it up for adoption?"

"She didn't say."

Craig took a deep breath and slowly let it out. "It seems to me that the baby isn't the only one in need of parents and a home."

Rubber soles squeaked on the linoleum as Joe's fellow paramedic joined them. "It's time to roll out."

Joe nodded and turned to his wife. "I've got to go, honey."

"I'll see you tomorrow," she said. "I love you."

"Me, too." Joe brushed a kiss on her lips. "Are you leaving now or sticking around?"

"I'd like to see Renee as soon as they'll let me in. I want her to know that I'm here. And that I'll do whatever I can to help her."

"Be safe," Joe told her. "And drive carefully, honey. The roads are slick."

"I will."

Before Craig got a chance to tell Joe good-bye, the door

from the exam rooms swung open, and Kristy walked out. She wore a baggy sweat shirt, a pair of jeans, and sneakers—nothing fancy or flattering.

Her red curls, wet and uncombed, straggled along her shoulders, and her mascara had streaked. Yet Craig found her every bit as attractive as he ever had.

"How's Renee doing?" Dawn asked Kristy.

"They've admitted her and put her in a room on the maternity floor. They've determined that the baby wasn't seriously injured in the fall, thank goodness. And they've managed to stave off the contractions, at least for now."

"I'd like to visit her," Dawn said.

"I'm afraid you'll have to wait. They just sedated her and asked me to leave. They want her to sleep."

"Do you know what time I can come in the morning?"

"I'm not sure. Ten o'clock, maybe, although the rules are probably more lenient for family members."

"Does she even have family?" Dawn asked.

"I think we're it." Kristy glanced at Craig, making him feel a part of that "we."

Strange as it might seem, he didn't mind stepping up to the plate.

"That poor girl." Dawn unzipped the purse that hung over her shoulder and reached for her car keys. "I'm so glad you found her, Kristy."

"So am I."

"I'll see you later. Tell your grandmother hello."

"I will."

As Dawn headed toward the exit, Kristy turned to Craig and caught him studying her.

She glanced down at her clothes and back up again. "I must look like a scarecrow caught in a hailstorm. But once the paramedics put Renee in the ambulance, I ran home long enough to change into dry clothes. I didn't dare take time to do anything with my hair."

"Under the circumstances, you look great. I'm glad you were able to be with her."

"There was no way I could leave her alone. This whole experience was pretty scary for her, and I knew she would need someone to talk to, someone who could offer words of comfort and speak to the doctors for her."

"I'm sure she appreciates all you've done."

"It was the least I could do." Kristy chuffed. "I feel this is all my fault."

"Why is that?" he asked.

"I was missing a music box that had some money hidden in it, and I accused her of stealing it. If she hadn't run to the tree house to get the box and return it to me, she wouldn't have gotten hurt."

He hated to think that Renee was a thief, but she'd probably been desperate. And, at least, she'd tried to return it.

"Later, I found out that Jason had given it to her without my permission." Kristy scanned the waiting room as if looking for someone or something. "Speaking of Jason, I need to call home and give him an update. He thinks the world of Renee. I'm also going to let him know that I offered to let her stay in our spare room."

Craig had suspected that there was far more to Kristy than he'd realized, but he just hadn't known how much. In spite of any qualms he might have had, the urge to get to know her better returned, stronger than ever.

Now wasn't the time to readdress that dinner invitation, but when he asked her again, he wasn't going to take no for an answer.

Shana arrived at the Smiths' house on Friday evening, only to find Kristy gone and an elderly neighbor man looking after Gram and Jason. She recognized his face, but had forgotten his name.

Mr. Iverson maybe?

"Kristy called a few minutes ago," the neighbor said. "She should be home shortly."

Shana needed to talk to her best friend tonight. "If it's all right with you, I'll just wait for her."

When the man stepped aside, she entered the living room and spotted Kristy's grandmother seated in a chair, an afghan draped over her lap. "It's good to see you out of the bedroom, Gram."

"I've probably spent too much time in there, so I've been doing what I can to lift my spirits." She offered a smile that was only a shell of those she'd given in the past. "I must admit that a little television in the living room helps a bit."

Shana glanced at Mr. Iverson, who'd apparently been watching over things while Kristy was gone.

"If you'd like to go home," she told him, "I can take over from here."

Mr. Iverson looked at Gram as though requesting her permission to leave.

"That's a good idea, Charlie. Then you can check on the dog. Jason and I will be fine with Shana."

"All right, then. I'll take you up on that offer. When I first came over here, I'd thought it would just be a few minutes. But with all the excitement, it's turned into hours, and I really need to feed my dog."

Gram thanked him for coming over, and as he slipped on his jacket and reached for his umbrella, she added, "You be careful walking on those wet sidewalks."

"I will." Then he let himself out and shut the door behind him.

Shana took a seat on the sofa, and Gram used the remote to shut off the television.

"Congratulations on your engagement," Gram said. "I'll bet you and your parents are not only excited, but busy."

Shana cleared her throat. "I'm afraid there isn't going to be a wedding. That's what I came to tell Kristy."

Gram's expression faltered. "Why not?"

Before Shana could answer, Jason ran into the room and wrapped his arms around her in a big hug. "Hi, Aunt Shana. I thought I heard your voice."

"Hey, Jaybird. I missed you, sweetie." And that was the truth. Shana loved that little boy as though he were her own son.

He ended the embrace long before she was ready to let go. "I'm building a super cool spaceship in my room, Aunt Shana. So I gotta go finish it."

"Before you do," Mrs. Smith interrupted, "I want to know if you ever found that green metal file box I asked you to look for."

"Sorry, Gram. I looked and looked in that bedroom upstairs and in the closet, but I couldn't find it. And it's not in the tree house. I checked when I got mom's music box and the money."

"I can't imagine where it is." She frowned and looked at Shana. "We've been losing things around here lately. I wish I could make it up those darn stairs and look around myself. I'm sure I could find everything that's missing."

"Is there anything I can do to help?" Shana asked.

"No, I'm afraid not. I'll have to ask Kristy to look for it when she gets home."

Jason, who apparently decided he was no longer being quizzed, dashed out of the room.

Shana watched him go, a longing in her heart so strong, so warm, that it nearly brought tears to her eyes. "I adore that boy."

"I know. I hope you have one just like him someday."

The tears that had been bubbling at the surface burst forth and spilled over. Using the length of her index fingers, she brushed them away.

"What's the matter?" Gram asked.

Shana tried to smile and shrug off the incredible sadness, the ache. "I love that little boy so much it hurts."

"Are those happy tears?" Gram asked.

Shana wanted to agree, but she couldn't seem to use her mother's old excuse. Not after the heartfelt promise she and her parents had just made to be honest with their feelings from now on.

Yet she couldn't bring herself to share her dark, ugly secret, either, and the floodgates opened, releasing a stream of tears that she struggled to wipe away.

For the past seven years, she'd kept her secret, her pain, close to the vest. The only one who'd ever known about it had been Brad, which is why she'd felt a bond with him. Why she'd wanted to do what she could to help him.

"I might be old and out of touch," Gram said, "and my body is certainly useless, but I still know heartbreak when I see it."

Shana was tempted to open up to the woman who'd been a better grandmother to her than the one she had, but the burden had been shoved so deep inside that she wasn't sure if it would ever come out.

Or, if it burst free, whether it would destroy her completely.

"Do you want to talk about it, honey?"

"I don't think I can." Shana had never even told Kristy, although she'd been tempted to many times over the years.

At first, she'd been too ashamed. And then Kristy's whole life had fallen apart, and Shana hadn't had the heart to dump any more on her. As the years wore on, she'd never found an appropriate time to share.

Maybe she was still too ashamed.

"Sometimes it helps to share a burden," Gram said, the warmth in her maternal smile reaching deep in her tired blue eyes. "And I'm good with secrets."

She might not be with this one.

Yet in spite of Shana's best efforts to shove the dark memory back where it belonged, it rose to the surface and wadded in her throat. The tears streamed down her cheeks, and she feared she would explode if she didn't open her mouth.

"I . . . uh . . ." She sucked in a wobbly breath, then forced it out. "I did something I'm ashamed of. Something unforgivable."

"It may feel shameful, but forgiveness is a lot easier than you think."

Shana desperately wanted to believe her, and as she looked into those tired old eyes, as she sensed the compassion and wisdom that had accrued over the years, the truth tumbled out. "Seven years ago, I got pregnant."

Gram didn't respond right away, but when she finally spoke, she asked, "Did you lose the baby?"

Shana wished that she had. Then she would have been able to deal with the loss that had haunted her nearly every day of her life.

"No one knows about this," Shana said. "Not even Kristy. But I was so afraid of facing my parents, of disappointing them, that I . . ."

So close. So very close.

Like a small child jumping into the arms of a loving parent in the deep end of the pool, Shana closed her eyes and let go of her apprehension. "I had an abortion."

There. It was out. And now Shana was sorry that it was.

Gram had never been able to have children. Would she find Shana's act abominable? Would she recite biblical platitudes and point her finger at her for such an unforgiveable sin?

Maybe Shana had chosen the wrong person to tell. She stole a peek at Gram, only to see that same expression she'd worn moments earlier.

"You're apparently struggling with this," Gram said.

"I am. It's been seven years, and it was the biggest mistake I've ever made. I know that other people have chosen the abortion path and never blinked an eye afterward. But it was the wrong thing for me to do. And it's been killing me ever since." Shana was afraid to look the woman in the eye, afraid to see the condemnation. "I want you to understand something. At the time, I'd felt backed into a corner. I hadn't been able to face my mother, so I took the easy way out. And now I can hardly face myself."

"Have you prayed about this? Asked to be forgiven and released from the guilt that's crippling you?"

"More times than you can imagine. I've begged, cried, and apologized over and over, but it hasn't helped."

"Then it's not God's forgiveness you need. It's your own."

"You're probably right, but I can't seem to do it, Gram. Deep in my heart, I wanted that baby. And not a day goes by that I don't imagine what it might have looked like."

"What's done is done, Shana. You have to let it go."

"I've tried, but I can't."

"Mistakes and sins are a dime a dozen. We all make them. God's forgiveness comes easy, but it's our own that's hard. Stop punishing yourself, honey."

"You make it sound easy."

Gram scanned the room, then pointed to the floor, where a green plastic Army man lay, left behind by the child who'd been playing with it. "Can you hand me that little toy soldier?"

"Sure." Shana picked it up and gave it to her.

As Gram held the toy in one gnarled hand, she said, "This represents your guilt, troubles, and worries—everything you struggle with. God wants to take it from you and throw it into the deepest part of the sea."

Shana wished it could be that easy.

The elderly woman handed it back to Shana, her frail fingers still wrapped around it. "Here. You be the Lord and take it from me. It's too much for me."

Shana reached for the little man, but Gram continued to hold it. In order to do as she was told, she would have to pry it from Gram's arthritic fingers, but she didn't want to hurt her.

"Take it," Gram said, her voice steady and firm.

"I can't. You won't let it go."

"That's what's happening to you. You're burdened by guilt, and you've asked God to take it. He's willing, but He's not going to jerk it out of your hands. You have to release it, Shana."

"I'll try."

"That may not be enough. The next time that guilt comes back, threatening to rob your joy or your peace of mind, you just give it right back to God." Lorraine opened her hands, palms up. "Many people clasp their hands when they pray, and that's fine. But in this case, why don't you open your hands to remind yourself to let go and to show God you're serious about giving it up."

That might help, Shana thought.

"Let's pray together." Gram bowed her head, and Shana followed suit.

She clasped her hands, then caught herself and rested her palms up in her lap, her fingers extended.

"Lord, you forgave Shana the very first time she approached you with a heart broken with guilt. But she's punishing herself, which grieves you. She's lifting that guilt now, Father, giving it all up to you. Take it from her and grant her the peace you've longed for her to have. Then wrap her in your everlasting love and grace."

Gram continued to pray, and for the first time in years, a sense of tranquility and acceptance settled over Shana, freeing her from the bondage of her own making.

When Gram said "Amen," Shana did too.

"Thank you," she told the woman, meaning it from the bottom of her heart.

"Don't thank me, honey. Thank God."

"I will, but I was struggling with this for so long, that I wasn't able to accept His forgiveness. I needed you to put it all in perspective for me. Thanks so much for being here, for listening, for understanding."

Gram grew silent, pensive. "You know, life is a journey. Sometimes the scenery is lovely, and at other times, the sky is dark and gloomy, the road full of potholes. But along the way, there are lessons to learn. And those lessons come in the strangest ways."

"I'm not sure I know what you mean."

Gram smiled. "For the past few years, I've been traveling on a bumpy, treacherous road. I was so tired and wanted to quit my trek, to throw up my useless hands and just give up. But thanks to an unexpected lesson I received a few days ago and one I just had today, a streetlight has come on. I see a turn in the road and a glimpse of the beautiful scenery ahead."

"What lesson was that?" Shana asked, realizing she'd just had a streetlight moment of her own.

"In a dream, a bearded man came to my bedside, and I told him that I wanted to die."

"I'm glad that you didn't," Shana said, realizing she might never have learned the lesson she'd received tonight if Gram hadn't been here.

"I'm glad, too. Apparently, the man was right."

"What did he say?"

Gram smiled, one that radiated warmth and joy. "That I still have work to do on earth."

Chapter 18

The next morning, at five to nine, Dawn reached for two blue plastic Wal-Mart bags and climbed out of her Honda Civic. After locking the car door, she strode toward the main lobby of Pacifica General Hospital, avoiding the shallow puddles as she zigzagged her way to the front door.

The damp sidewalk and water droplets glistening on the lawns and foliage were all that remained of the rain that had battered the community overnight and moved on at sunrise, leaving the sky with only a splatter of clouds, the air fresh and clean.

She glanced at her watch. Joe would be getting off duty soon and had promised to meet her here. They'd talked on the phone last night and had agreed to do whatever they could to help the poor kid.

The automatic doors swooshed open as she entered the lobby. Up ahead, at an information desk, a silver-haired gentleman watched her approach.

"Can I help you?" he asked.

"I came to visit Renee . . ." Dawn paused. She wasn't sure if the girl's last name had ever come up, but if it had, she'd forgotten, which left her feeling remiss now. She and Joe had both been drawn to Renee from day one—probably because they'd sensed she was too young to be on her own. It broke Dawn's heart to think that she'd been living in a tree, and she wished she'd asked more questions. "I'm sorry. That's all I know her as."

"Then it'll take me a while to look her up." The man turned to the computer at his desk and, using the index fingers of both hands, began poking at the keys slowly and methodically.

He wasn't kidding; finding Renee could take him all day.

"I'm not sure if this helps," Dawn said, "but she was in Maternity last night."

Hopefully, they hadn't moved her. Several years ago, before her hysterectomy, Dawn had carried one of the babies she'd lost, a little boy, to four months. When she'd miscarried, the nurses had moved her to another floor so she wouldn't have to be around all the newborns and happy families while she was grieving. Since Joe had mentioned that Renee's only concern was for her child, Dawn knew what she must be going through.

"That does help," the man said, as he went back to his hunting and pecking.

Dawn turned her head and scanned the lobby, noting a few people seated on chairs in a waiting area, as well as several lined up at a coffee cart that provided light snacks and beverages. A gift shop staffed by hospital volunteers was still closed, although a woman in a pink smock and white slacks was inside near the cash register.

On her way to the hospital this morning, Dawn had stopped to buy some items she thought Renee might need—a toothbrush, toothpaste, deodorant, shampoo, lotion. She'd even purchased a nightgown and slipper socks.

"I found a Renee." The man squinted as he studied the screen. "I can call the nurses' desk to make sure it's the patient you're looking for."

"She suffered a fall and was admitted last night," Dawn added. "The paramedics brought her to the ER."

A click sounded, and Dawn glanced over her shoulder to

see the pink-smocked woman unlock the doors to the gift shop. She wondered if she should pick up some flowers or chocolate for Renee while she was here. Joe had said Renee was really shaken up yesterday, so something cheery might help.

After the man made the call to Maternity, he reported that Renee Delaney appeared to be the patient Dawn was looking for, and that she was in room 422.

"Thank you." Dawn turned away, but instead of walking to the elevators, she veered to the right and entered the gift shop, a small room that offered a variety of toiletry items, as well as magazines and knickknacks.

A refrigerator display case in back held several small flower arrangements and a few potted plants. She looked them over briefly and chose a bud vase with three yellow roses.

On her way to the cashier, she paused in front of a shelf of stuffed animals. She reached for a teddy bear, then decided she'd better wait. If Renee had lost the baby during the night, the stuffed animal might make things worse. Dawn knew firsthand how badly a woman could grieve after losing an unborn child.

As she waited for the cashier to ring up the flowers, a short, matronly woman entered the shop and went right for the display of stuffed animals. She reached for a fluffy yellow duck.

White lettering on the back of her turquoise T-shirt said:

IF I HAD KNOWN HOW MUCH I WOULD LOVE MY GRANDKIDS, I WOULD HAVE HAD THEM FIRST.

The thought that she and Joe would have neither, tweaked Dawn's heart. She closed her eyes and tried to shrug off the painful reminder.

You'd think that over the years, after three miscarriages and a hysterectomy, she would have gotten used to the idea that she and Joe would never hear the pitter-patter of little feet in their own home. They truly had resigned themselves to that fact, but at times it still hurt.

"Will that be all?" the cashier asked.

"Yes." Dawn reached into her wallet and withdrew her Visa.

As the woman ran the card, Dawn glanced at a display rack that held bracelets. They weren't fancy or expensive, but they were just the kind of thing a teenage girl might like.

A silver chain adorned with heart-shaped charms caught her eye, and she fingered it. She wondered if Renee had ever received a gift for no reason at all, one of those little surprises that told her someone cared.

Dawn suspected that, if she had, those occasions had been rare, and her heart broke for the young girl who should have had a mother or father to love and guide her.

That baby isn't the only one in need of parents, Pastor Craig had said last night.

The truth of Craig's words struck like an unexpected wallop.

Dawn and Joe had planned to let Renee stay with them after she was discharged from the hospital, but that poor child needed more than a warm bed. She needed love, security. A real home and family.

"Wait," Dawn told the cashier. She removed the bracelet from the rack. "I'd like this, too."

After paying for her purchases, she took the elevator to the fourth floor. All the while, an idea began to fill her heart with hope. She would have to call Joe to run it past him, but only as a marital formality. Joe, who'd come from a family of seven, was an even bigger softie than Dawn was when it came to kids.

An LVN sat at a desk in front of the double door of the maternity wing. When Dawn told her who she was and why she was here, the nurse buzzed the security lock, granting access.

Dawn made her way to room 422 and peered through the

open doorway. The patient's back was to the door, but Dawn would recognize that blond stringy hair anywhere.

Again, her heart ached for the girl who should be stretched out on a bed in her very own bedroom, munching on a bag of potato chips, sipping a Coke, and texting her BFF about the cute guy in English class.

"Renee?"

The girl rolled over, presenting her face, as well as red-rimmed, watery eyes.

Dawn sensed bad news, and her heart sank. "How are you doing?"

"Okay, I guess." A tear slid down her cheek, but she didn't bother wiping it away.

It tore Dawn up to see Renee so sad, so all alone, but she managed a smile. "Are you up for company?"

"Sure. Come in."

Dawn placed the roses on the tray table and set the bags at the foot of the bed. "I brought some things you might need, like a toothbrush and toothpaste. And I thought you might want some flowers for your room."

"Thanks. They're really pretty."

"Is there anything I can do to help?"

Renee slowly shook her head. "I don't think so. The nurse told me they're going to call social services. That's what I didn't want to happen. I don't want them to take my baby away."

"They can't take your child, honey."

Renee's gaze latched onto Dawn's. "How do you know? They're going to put me in foster care again. And what if that family doesn't want a little baby? Or what if they want the baby and not me? What if they try to make me give her up? I can't do that, Dawn. The baby is the only family I've got. And she needs me." She swiped at her tears and sniffled. "I know I'm just a teenager, but I love her already. And when I thought that I was going to lose her, I wanted to die."

Dawn knew the feeling too well, and it saddened her to see

this poor child who'd had enough disappointments in life face the same thing. So she placed a gentle hand on Renee's cheek. "Let's hope for the best, okay?"

Renee's bottom lip quivered, but she nodded.

Some things were out of Dawn's hands, but she'd do whatever she could to help. "For what it's worth, I won't let anyone put you or the baby in foster care."

"How can you stop it? The court makes those decisions, and that's all there is to it."

"I know a way around that."

Renee studied her, both hope and skepticism etched on her brow. "What is it?"

"I haven't talked to Joe yet, but I'm certain he's going to agree." Dawn brushed a strand of hair away from Renee's forehead, revealing pretty blue eyes and a freckled nose. "We've wanted a family for a very long time."

Renee sucked in an emotion-laden breath and held it a beat before slowly letting it out. "I know what you're going to say. You and Joe want to adopt my baby. And that's probably in the baby's best interests for me to agree. But I can't give her up. You might think this is weird, but it's almost like she's already here. I think about her all the time. I even talk to her."

"The baby doesn't need a mother. She already has you. And it's clear to anyone with eyes and a heart that you love her more than anything in the world."

Renee wrinkled her brow. "Then what's your idea to fix everything?"

"What the baby doesn't have is grandparents. I'll need to talk to Joe, but I know he'll agree. If we adopt you, we'll have the daughter we always wanted. And, as a blessing on the side, we'd have a grandbaby to love, too."

"You want to adopt *me*?" Renee asked, the words not quite sinking in. "I'm practically already grown up."

"You still have most of your teen years left. You ought to be in school, not stressed about providing a roof overhead and the basic necessities." As Renee took it all in, Dawn reached into her purse, pulled out her cell, and dialed her husband's number. "Hi, honey. It's me."

"Where are you?" he asked.

"I'm visiting Renee at the hospital."

"Good. I'm almost there now. How's she doing?"

"She's hanging in there. But do you remember that temporary home we talked about providing her?"

"What about it? Doesn't she want to stay with us?"

"Yes, but I want to offer her a permanent home. I want us to be her parents."

Joe paused, but only for a moment. "I'd like that, too, honey. Ask her what color she'd like me to paint her bedroom."

A smile broke across Dawn's face, and she turned to Renee. "We're game if you are."

"Are you kidding?" Renee blinked back a flood of tears as she appeared to struggle with both disbelief and relief. "You really want to be my parents?"

"With all our hearts."

The morning sun peered through a couple of bent slats in the mini blinds, and birds chattered in the branches of the maple tree outside the bedroom. Apparently, the rain that had battered the community last night had moved on its way.

Kristy glanced at the baby monitor that rested on the bureau and allowed her to hear any sounds coming from her grandmother's room downstairs. Usually, Gram woke before dawn, needing a glass of water or to use the bathroom.

But she hadn't last night.

At just after nine o'clock, Kristy rolled out of bed, slipped on her robe and slippers, and headed down the hall to check on Jason, only to find his bed empty. She wondered what he was doing.

Watching television quietly, she suspected.

As she made her way downstairs, eager to put on a pot of coffee, she yawned. Rarely did she get a full night's sleep, and after the drama in the canyon and at the ER, she found it surprising that she had.

She planned to call the hospital and check on Renee. Hopefully, everything went well during the night.

In the living room, Jason sat on the sofa, watching cartoons.

"Good morning," she said, her voice still sleep-laden.

"Oh, hi, Mom." Jason, who wore his Spider-Man pajamas, smiled. "What's for breakfast?"

She hadn't given it any thought yet. "How about pancakes?"

"Cool." His attention immediately returned to the television screen.

As she continued her morning bed check, she headed down the hall to Gram's bedroom. With each step she took, she grew a bit uneasy. One of these days, she feared that she just might enter the room and find that Gram had gotten her wish, that she'd passed away.

As she reached the doorway, she peered inside to see her grandmother on her back, her eyes open and staring at the ceiling.

"Good morning."

Gram turned her head to the side, her gaze lighting on Kristy. "What day is this?"

"It's Saturday. Why do you ask?"

"Because Craig usually stops by on Wednesdays, and I'd really like to see him today."

A wave of apprehension strummed over Kristy. "Is something wrong? I can certainly call and ask him to stop by if he can."

"Nothing's wrong," Gram said, although her face was all scrunched up as though she was perplexed. "But I had another one of those dreams and I need to talk to him about something."

"I didn't realize you'd been having recurring dreams."

"It's the second one I've had, but it was so real I could

swear it really happened. Last night, I dreamt that the bearded man came and spoke to me again."

Again? The first time, Jesse had actually been in the house and had carried on a conversation with her. At least, that's what must have happened.

"What did the man say to you this time?" she asked.

"He said that he was leaving. And that he had a message for me to give Pastor Craig."

After practice, Ramon waited for the boys to pick up their gear and meet him at the dugout. Their first game was on Wednesday evening, and since they would face National City, last year's intercity league champs, he wanted to give them a pep talk before sending them home.

He'd hoped to see Craig this morning, but he'd been a no-show. Not that the pastor had actually promised to help out at practice today, but he'd said he would try to stop by. Something must have come up.

"Give it back," Simon yelled.

Ramon glanced up and spotted Jamal and David playing keep-away with the catcher's mitt. "Hey, you two. Knock it off."

David appeared to really give Ramon's order some thought and tossed the mitt back to Simon, which was a sign that they were finally becoming a disciplined team.

And that was good. Most of the boys had short fuses, so Ramon's primary goal was to teach them self-discipline. They already had too many cards stacked against them, and he didn't want their tempers to get them in trouble.

Ramon scanned the park, still thinking Craig might show up, but spotted an attractive blonde instead. It was Shana, and she was heading his way.

If he didn't know better, he'd think she'd come by just to talk to him. But that kind of thinking would only lead to disappointment.

Still, he headed for the third-base fence, keeping his thoughts and his imagination in check.

"Going for another run?" he asked, even though her clothing—a pair of black jeans and a freshly-pressed lime green blouse—didn't lend themselves to exercise.

"Not today." A light ocean breeze whipped a strand of hair across her face, and she swiped it away. "I know that you're busy now, but do you have a few minutes after practice? I'd like to talk to you."

He tried to read her expression, but a serious demeanor wasn't giving him any clues. "We're just wrapping things up now. If you give me a couple of minutes, I'll be right back."

"No problem. I'll wait." She tucked the rebellious strand of hair behind her ear, and while she offered him a smile, her lips weren't fully cooperative.

Ramon took a few minutes to talk to the boys, telling them they'd be practicing again on Sunday afternoon and insisting they stay out of trouble, that the team needed each of them. Then he excused everyone but the Sanchez boys. Their terminally ill grandmother had taken a turn for the worse, so Carlitos and Luis were staying with Ramon this weekend.

"I need to talk to a friend," he told them. "You can either wait for me in the dugout or sit in the car."

"Can we listen to the radio?" Luis asked.

"Sure." Ramon reached into the front pocket of his jeans, removed the keys to the Jeep, and tossed them to the older boy. "If you guys can keep from arguing over which station to listen to, I'll take you to Burger Alley for a late lunch. And if not, you're stuck with bologna sandwiches at the house."

"We won't fight." The younger boy gazed at Shana, who waited at the fence. "Ooh, coach. Your friend is really hot. But she looks all mad."

Ramon glanced at Shana, noting that her serious expression hadn't faded in the least. He didn't think she was angry, but something was clearly bothering her.

As the boys headed for the Jeep, Ramon returned to the fence, where Shana waited.

He offered her a smile, and she tried to return it, but something weighed heavily in her eyes. Worry? Stress? It was hard to tell.

Maybe she *was* mad.

"What's up?" he asked.

"I, uh . . . broke my engagement."

Ramon wanted to let out a whoop, but bit his tongue and held his reaction in check. "I'm sorry."

"You are?"

No, he wasn't. And he decided she deserved the truth. "I was just trying to be polite. I'm not sorry at all. For the record, I've never liked Brad and think you can do a whole lot better."

She didn't respond, so they continued to stand in silence.

"What caused the breakup?" he finally asked.

"I didn't love him."

He was really glad to hear that.

"I wanted to," she added. "But no matter how hard I tried, I couldn't force myself to have feelings that weren't there."

He knew what she meant. He'd never found another woman who'd been able to stir his heart like Shana had, but he was unwilling to make that admission.

They remained cocooned in silence, and he assumed she hadn't yet gotten to the heart of the conversation she meant to have.

"I need to confess something," she said.

"What's that?"

He had no idea how long his question hung suspended in the air they breathed, but about the time he assumed she wasn't going to respond at all, she did.

"When you and I dated in high school, I fell in love with you. So I know what real love is supposed to feel like."

She'd had a weird way of showing her love to him. The

day she'd ended things between them had been the worst day of his life, but he couldn't bring himself to admit it.

"Our breakup wasn't my idea," she added. "My parents thought I was too young to be so serious about a guy."

Ramon tried to guess where she might be going with this, as she studied her feet, her teeth biting down on her bottom lip.

He wanted to tell her to forget about it, that all of that was in the past. That it didn't matter anymore. But how could he say that when right this minute it seemed to matter a whole lot?

Hoping to make things easier on her, he said, "I can understand your parents' concern."

"You can?"

"You were only fifteen." Yet he'd always suspected that there'd been cultural and socioeconomic differences at play, too. "Were they upset about you dating any guy? Or was it just me?"

Her eyes filled with tears. "Mostly it was you."

He wasn't surprised, yet the truth still slammed into him, making him hurt all over again.

"My parents, especially my mom, pressured me to break up with you. And at the time, I was afraid to challenge her."

"So you're telling me that even though you loved me, you ended things between us because your mother told you to?" Ramon had a hard time understanding that kind of blind obedience.

"For almost as long as I can remember, I've done whatever they asked me to do. I'm not entirely sure why. Maybe because of their devotion to me during my illness. Maybe because I feared that if I didn't dot each I or cross each T that the cancer would come back." She inhaled deeply, as if the extra oxygen would infuse her with the strength to go on, then slowly let it out. "That doesn't sound very noble, does it?"

He ought to be angry, offended by her parents' prejudice and her obedience, but for some crazy reason, he wasn't.

Instead, he didn't want her to suffer about something she couldn't go back and change.

"You were a kid," he said. "Kids are supposed to obey their parents."

"I know that, but I should have fought for you. For us."

He wished she had.

"Deep inside, I'd hoped you would put up a fight and provide me with the strength to rebel."

And he hadn't. He'd just nodded when she'd told him she didn't want to see him anymore and, in an effort to be macho and hide his tears, he'd walked away from her.

"For what it's worth," she said, "I've finally begun to stand my ground. My parents, or rather my mom, wasn't happy about me breaking up with Brad, but I refused to back down."

"I'm glad. I always thought you were a lot braver than you let on."

Her lips parted, and her gaze snagged his. "You're the second guy to tell me that in the past couple of days."

He wanted to ask her who the first guy was, but he didn't think it was any of his business.

"So that's what you wanted to tell me?" he asked. "That you loved me back then?"

"There's more." She took another one of those fortifying breaths, and he wished he could do something to make this conversation easier for her. "After we broke up, I found out that I was pregnant."

This time Ramon's jaw dropped, his brow furrowed, and his stance stiffened. "Why didn't you tell me?"

The tears that had been welling in her eyes overflowed. "Because I didn't think you loved me. Because I didn't want to burden you."

He caught her face in his hands and caressed her cheeks with his thumbs. "I loved you, too, Shana. I hurt so bad when you ended things, but I never thought that I truly deserved a girl like you. So I let you go to make it easier on you and to save my pride."

As the tears continued to stream down her cheeks, her lips quivered, and his heart broke all over again.

"What happened to the baby?" he asked. "Did you give it up?"

"I . . ." She closed her eyes. While standing statue still, she placed her hands against the railing, palms up. She remained like that for a moment, then opened her eyes and caught his gaze. "I had an abortion."

The news knocked the wind and the words out of him.

"I'm sorry," she said, as though understanding the myriad of emotions blurring in his heart and mind. Yet she couldn't possibly understand, not when he didn't.

He felt betrayed, hurt. And he felt cheated—not just out of a child, but out of the knowledge he'd deserved to know, the decision she'd made for both of them. He struggled not to be angry, not to blame her for keeping a secret like that.

She'd been a kid, he reminded himself. And he'd walked away without letting her know how badly it had hurt to lose her. How he would have done anything to keep seeing her if he'd thought they'd actually stood a chance.

"I'm so sorry, Ramon. Please forgive me. I really wanted the baby, but I was so afraid back then. I didn't think I had anywhere to turn."

"You had me."

She bit down on her bottom lip so hard that he feared she would break the skin. "I didn't know that."

No, she hadn't.

He raked a hand through his hair, trying to wrap his mind around what she'd done.

And why.

They should have faced that trial together, and the decision should have been made as a couple.

She placed her hands on the fence, her fingers gripping the chain link. "There's wasn't a day that went by that I didn't wish I could have gone back in time and done things differently, but I couldn't."

It was clear that she not only wanted his forgiveness, she needed it. And while he wanted to give it to her, it wasn't that easy.

Of course, nothing about their relationship had ever been easy.

"Your parents probably wanted to string me up," he said.

"They didn't know. About any of it."

"You went through that alone?"

"Not completely. One day, I went to the Rensfield estate looking for you, but Brad told me you weren't home. I started crying, and he asked why it was so important for me to find you."

"Did you tell him?"

"Yes, and then I fell apart. He held me while I cried and promised to take care of everything."

"He suggested the abortion?"

She nodded. "He even paid for it out of his allowance so my parents wouldn't find out. But instead of feeling better, I felt worse. It was only recently that I was able to forgive myself. And I came to you to ask you to forgive me. It seems like the right thing to do."

That's one of the things he didn't like about Brad. The guy would mess up, then buy his way out of it. This time, he'd stepped in and offered Shana an easy way out. And she'd been desperate, vulnerable.

Now, as he saw the emotion welling in her eyes, she appeared vulnerable again. And just as alone.

It tore him up to see her that way. How could he blame her for a decision she'd made seven years ago, even if he should have had a say about it?

He wanted to slip his arms around her, to hold her close, but the chain link stood in the way, just as her parents and their cultural and economic differences always had. But fences didn't have to be permanent.

Rather than taking the time to walk back to the dugout and open the gate, he hopped over the railing, wrapped his arms around her, and drew her close.

He'd meant to offer her compassion as well as forgiveness, but when he caught a whiff of her soft floral scent, when she fit into his arms in a way that no one else ever had, he brushed his lips across hers—softly, tenderly.

She kissed him back, and when common sense returned and he pulled away, her gaze locked on his. "Is it too late for us?"

Maybe. He refused to put himself in a position where he had to prove himself worthy of anyone's love.

"A lot's happened in the past seven years," he explained. "For one thing, I'm going to be a foster parent to two boys. So that in itself would complicate our lives, especially if your parents—"

She placed her fingertips over his lips, silencing him with a gentle touch. "It's not about my parents. It's about us. And if those boys are a part of your life, then it's about them, too."

Something in her eyes told him that she was willing to fight this time around. That the risk he'd be taking might be worth it.

"Those boys are lucky to have you," she added. "And I'd be lucky to have you, too. Is there any chance at all that we could start over?"

There might be some rough spots along the way, but he would try his best to forgive and forget.

He slipped his arms around her waist and pulled her close. "I was a fool to let you walk away once, Shana. But it won't happen again."

Chapter 19

Craig slept better than he had since coming to Fairbrook, although he wasn't sure why. Maybe because he was looking forward to a full and productive day that would wrap up tonight following the meeting he'd scheduled with the board of elders.

Ramon had called a practice this morning, and Craig had volunteered to help unless something came up, which it had. After Renee's accident last night, Craig had decided to stop by the hospital before doing anything else.

He knew Ramon would understand.

Now there was a man who followed his heart and put his faith in action. Not only had Ramon given his time to help kids with two strikes against them already, but he'd also offered to take Luis and Carlitos into his home, which was a lot of responsibility for a single young man to assume.

Ramon, it seemed, had a calling, and he'd taken the ball and run with it. Craig wished he could say that he was doing what he was meant to do with his life—and doing it well. But he didn't think he'd ever be the man his granddad was.

As Craig left the den and approached the kitchen, the rich aroma of coffee and the sound of water gurgling through the filter and into the carafe grew stronger.

"Good morning," he said to Daniel, who stood before the cupboard, reaching for a mug.

Daniel glanced over his shoulder and smiled. "It *is* a good morning, isn't it?"

As far as Craig was concerned, the jury was still out on that. But at least the storm had passed. "How did things go last night?"

"It was bit rough at first, but I think Cassie is resigned to the change my leaving the firm will make in our lives."

"That's good to hear."

Daniel removed two mugs from the shelf and handed one to Craig. "You'll never guess what we did last night."

Craig didn't have a clue. When he'd gotten home from the hospital, the house had been empty.

Fortunately, Daniel didn't intend for Craig to actually guess. "Cassie, Shana, and I had dinner with a homeless man, if you can imagine that. What an interesting experience."

"Was his name Jesse?"

Daniel reached for the carafe and filled his mug with coffee. "How did you know?"

"I met him, too." Craig held out his cup, and watched Daniel fill it. "He's unique, isn't he?"

Daniel nodded. "He gave each of us something to think about."

Jesse had given Craig a few things to consider, too. But instead of providing any solid answers, he usually left Craig with more questions to ponder. "He's an ace at making a point in as few words as possible."

"I know what you mean. Last night, after dinner, Cassie, Shana and I decided to volunteer at the soup kitchen on Sundays so that Joe and Dawn can have a day off."

"I'm sure they'll appreciate that."

"Jesse also suggested that I talk to you about me speaking on behalf of the church at the next city council meeting, as well as any upcoming hearings. So all you need to do is say the word. During my transition, I'll have a lot more time on my hands."

"A respected attorney who knows how to make a convincing argument will be a valuable addition," Craig said. "And as a side note, there's a special meeting with the board of elders at five tonight. If you can join us, that would be great. But if not, I'll fill you in when I get home."

"I'll try to make it." Daniel strode to the sliding glass door that led to the patio and rolled open the shutters, letting in the morning sun. "I'm also going to meet with Todd Forrester this afternoon. He's involved in a nonprofit group that encourages underprivileged kids to participate in sports. Most of their parents are incarcerated, so they're all at risk. And by getting involved in that particular organization, I might be able to make a difference beyond the courtroom."

"I've heard about that group," Craig said. "There's a baseball team in Fairbrook that's part of the intercity league, and their first game is on Wednesday night. I'm probably going to help coach them." Craig took a sip of his coffee. "That's something else Jesse put into motion. He can be pretty convincing with his thought-provoking, heart-searching comments."

"Jesse's not the only one who tosses around things to think about," Daniel added. "Thanks again for telling me to follow my heart. It's made a big difference in my life."

"You're welcome, but it was just a comment."

"People don't always need a sermon, Pastor. Sometimes they just need somebody to listen and to care." Daniel took a sip of his coffee. "We still have a lot to work through as a family, but I think we're all on the same page now."

"I'm glad." Too bad Craig couldn't apply that same follow-your-heart advice to his own life. He would, if he could, but he wasn't sure what his heart was telling him to do. Each time he tried to examine what felt good and right and true, Kristy came to mind.

"Do you suppose you could find time to talk to Cassandra sometime this week?" Daniel asked.

"I've got some things to do this morning and I'm booked tight this afternoon, but I'm sure we can find time to talk after dinner."

"Not here at the house," Daniel said. "Cassie wants some pastoral counseling. She could make an appointment with George, but she'd rather talk to you."

The fact that Cassandra would choose Craig over the senior pastor took him by surprise, but he nodded as though it made perfect sense.

"It's not like she needs any long-term counseling," Daniel said, "but I think a chat like the one you had with me would do her a world of good. She's been living under her father's thumb for years and needs to follow the beat of her own drum for a change. Besides, Jesse told her you'd be the perfect one for her to talk to."

While Craig appreciated Jesse's faith in him, he still couldn't quite embrace it. For as long as he could remember, he'd been trying to live up to the larger-than-life standards his dad and his granddad had set, yet he'd somehow fallen out of step, and his heart just wasn't in it. But that was his secret and not something he would or could admit to anyone.

"I'll talk to Cassandra at dinner," Craig said. "We can make an appointment to meet at the church whenever it's convenient."

"Good." Daniel unlocked the door that led to the patio. "I'm going to drink my coffee outside. Do you want to join me?"

"Sure." But before Craig could take two steps, his cell phone rang.

When he answered, he recognized Kristy's voice on the line and found himself smiling.

"Is there any chance you could stop by the house today?" she asked. "My grandmother would really like to talk to you."

"Sure. I'll stop after I visit Renee at the hospital."

"Good. How's she doing?"

"I'm not sure. I think I'll give Dawn a call. She'll probably be able to give me an update."

"Tell Renee that I'll try to stop by this afternoon, if I can get someone to sit with Gram and Jason."

"I will." Craig glanced at the clock on the microwave. "But it probably won't be until noon or later."

"Thanks, Craig. I really appreciate that."

When the call ended, he disconnected the line, yet his thoughts remained on Kristy.

He'd told Daniel to follow his heart. And Ramon seemed to be following his. Maybe Craig ought to do the same thing— but not in a selfish, I-want/I-need sort of way. Instead, he would listen to his conscience and trust the Word of God.

As wrought iron scraped against concrete, Craig glanced outside and saw Daniel pulling out a patio chair so he could sit at the glass-topped table. Before joining him, Craig would call Dawn. If Renee had lost the baby, Craig wanted a heads-up before dropping by the hospital.

After three rings, Joe's voice answered.

"Hey, it's Craig. Is Dawn available?"

"Not at the moment. The obstetrician is in Renee's room right now, so I stepped out to give them privacy."

"How's it going?"

"The doctor wants to keep her one more day as a precaution, but labor has stopped, thank goodness. And he said the baby is fine."

"That's good news. Tell Renee that I'm coming by to visit her later this morning."

"By the way," Joe said. "I'd like to thank you."

"For what?"

"Working a miracle in our lives."

Craig had no idea what he might have said or done that would cause Joe to make that kind of assumption. "What do you mean?"

"You told Dawn that the baby wasn't the only one who needed a mother, and it set her to thinking. I've got a call into

Sam Dawson, the attorney who handled my uncle's probate. We're going to have him handle the legalities."

"What legalities?"

"Dawn and I are going to adopt Renee, and we couldn't be happier. It's a dream come true for all of us. That poor kid hasn't had a very good life so far, but Dawn and I are determined to give her the loving home she deserves. It's a blessing for all of us."

Craig could see why he'd consider that a miracle, but Craig had only made an observation. The miracle had happened when the Randolphs took his comment to heart and decided to do something about it. "I'm glad everything worked out."

When the call ended, Craig no longer had a pressing reason to rush to the hospital. So, under the circumstances, if Lorraine wanted to see him, he probably ought to swing by her house first. At least, that's the excuse he gave himself for bypassing the practice at Mulberry Park and altering the schedule he'd planned for today.

But there'd been no explanation for plucking a red rose bud from the bush in the Delacourts' front yard and taking it with him.

Kristy ignored the doorbell the first time it rang and, expecting Jason to answer, continued to wash the breakfast dishes. When it gonged again, she called her son's name, assuming that one of his friends wanted to play.

Still no response.

So she dropped the dishcloth into the sink full of warm, soapy water and headed to the entry.

She called Jason one last time, realizing he was probably in the bathroom and unable to hear her, and continued to the entry.

Needless to say, when she swung open the door and spotted Craig on the porch, her jaw dropped and her heart skipped a beat.

"I'm early," he said.

He certainly was. She wished she'd done more than clip her hair up, that she'd put on something other than worn jeans and a faded yellow T-shirt. That she'd slipped on a pair of shoes. Dabbed a splash of perfume on her wrists. Swiped a bit of lipstick on her lips.

He held a rose in his hand, which she assumed he'd brought for Gram. It was a deep, burgundy red, and she suspected he'd gotten it from someone's garden.

A boyish grin dimpled his cheeks, softening the sharp angles of a masculine jaw. "I had a change of schedule. I hope that's okay."

"Of course. It's fine." She stepped aside and allowed him into the living room.

He surprised her by handing her the rose. "I saw this growing in the Delacourts' front yard and thought you'd like it."

She took the stem, trying not to grab a thorn, and her pulse slipped into overdrive. "Thank you."

The gesture was both unexpected and sweet, and on impulse, she took a deep whiff, savoring the heady fragrance.

"I'd still like to take you out to dinner tonight," he said, "so I hope you've reconsidered."

There were a lot of reasons why she should decline, but right this moment, with Craig's gaze locked on hers and pheromones swirling overhead, she couldn't seem to think of a single one.

"I know you're concerned about what people might think or say, but I don't care in the least. If anyone has any qualms about us dating, they need a refresher course in forgiveness and second chances."

He made it sound so easy that she couldn't help believing that it was. "I'd have to find someone to stay with Gram and Jason."

"See what you can do. If no one is available, I'll bring dinner here."

"You drive a hard bargain."

"I want to spend more time with you, Kristy, and I'm willing to do whatever it takes to make that happen." He tossed her another grin, and her mind scrambled to think of someone she could ask, someone who wouldn't think she was over-stepping neighborly expectations.

Ellie Rucker, who lived across the street, might not mind, although it might be too much for her.

"What did your grandmother want to talk to me about?" Craig asked.

"She said she has a message for you."

"From whom?"

"An imaginary Jesse, I think. He was here one evening, but she'd been asleep when he arrived, and he left before morning. She mentioned a dream she'd had about a bearded stranger, so I think she must have really talked to him that time. But since he hasn't been here since then, last's night's visit must have been a dream. When she woke up, she insisted upon talking to you. So humor her, okay?"

"All right."

Kristy nodded toward the hallway. "Come on, I'll take you to her."

As they approached her grandmother's bedroom, Kristy called out, "Gram? Pastor Craig is here to see you."

Gram turned her head and looked toward the doorway. She brightened when she spotted the handsome minister enter behind Kristy. "Thanks for coming."

"How are you feeling?" Craig asked.

"Tired of being in bed and unable to move, but I've come to realize my dancing days are over."

Kristy moved to the foot of the bed, allowing Craig to stand at Gram's side.

"You might think I'm daffy," Gram told the man, "but I can't help that. I've been having this recurring dream, and last night it was especially real."

"Kristy mentioned that. So why don't you tell me about it."

"All right. The strange thing is that each time I've had the dream I was lying in this very bed. It's almost as if a long-haired, bearded man really is standing at the foot of my bed, just like Kristy is now."

"What did he look like?" Craig asked.

"His hair and beard were stringy and mostly gray. And his eyes were the color of a summer sky. He wore old clothes, but he had on a new blue jacket that looked a lot like the one I'd given my late husband before he died."

"Did the man tell you his name?"

"He never introduced himself. Why do you ask?"

Craig glanced at Kristy, then back at Gram. "I was just wondering."

"Anyway, when he came to me again last night, he had a message for you."

A hint of skepticism clouded Craig's eyes, but Kristy could understand why. If Jesse really had a message, he would have come right out and told Craig face-to-face.

"He had a message for me?" Craig asked.

Gram nodded sagely.

"What was that?"

"He said to tell you that you've been following in the wrong footsteps."

Craig stiffened. "That's an odd thing for him to say."

"I thought so, too," Gram said. "So I quizzed him, and he said that your grandfather had a path to follow. Your father had one, too. But that you needed to blaze your own trail."

"Thanks for passing on that message," Craig said. "I'll keep it in mind."

"He also insisted I tell you something else," Gram said. "You weren't just called, Craig, you were chosen. And you're right where you need to be."

The skepticism in Craig's eyes gave way to surprise, yet he didn't respond.

Surely he wasn't taking those words seriously.

"I think it's scriptural," Gram added. "You know, many are called but few are chosen?"

Craig crossed his arms and sobered, clearly pondering what Gram said, yet appearing to be confused by it, too. "Is that all he said?"

"For the most part, yes. He also mentioned that he'd been called home."

A bevy of goose bumps fluttered along Kristy's arms. Going home was the terminology Gram had always used when she'd wanted to die.

This was all too weird, but the imagination, especially while the body slept, could be amazing.

"That man said my job on earth wasn't over yet," Gram added. "But it would be one day soon. And at that time, he would see me again."

Kristy had asked Craig to humor Gram, and he seemed to be doing just that. If she didn't know better, she'd suspect he truly believed he'd been given some kind of message via a dream.

They chatted a few more minutes, then Craig glanced at his watch and told Gram he had to take off.

"Thanks for coming by," she said.

"No problem. I'll see you later this evening."

Gram arched a brow. "Tonight?"

Craig grinned. "Kristy is going out to dinner with me."

"Well, now. Isn't that a lovely surprise."

"Isn't it?" His gaze locked on Kristy's again, turning her inside out. And she had to admit that, yes, it was a nice surprise.

As she walked Craig to the door, he paused in the entry.

"If I didn't have my doubts, I'd think she really had talked to Jesse last night."

"Why?"

"Because Jesse always has a way of knowing things no one else knows. And because I've been struggling with my call to the ministry. I'd made a promise to God and felt bound to keep it. So my decision to attend the seminary had been an obligation I owed, not a true calling."

She found his candor both surprising and refreshing. "I

would have never guessed that you'd had any reservations. You're a great minister."

"Because I help out at the soup kitchen? Or because I visit the shut-ins on a regular basis?" He seemed to chuff silently. "Any lay person could—and *should*—be doing that."

"Okay, I agree. But when I talked to you about the guilt I'd been harboring for years, you told me to talk to Gram about it, and I followed your advice. For the first time since I got pregnant, I have peace and a sense of direction. Sure, things aren't always easy, but there's light at the end of the tunnel. I don't have any idea when I'll be able to register for a few classes at the junior college, but I know that I will. And while I may not go to medical school, I can certainly become a nurse. Who knows what the future might bring?"

"Thanks, Kristy. In the past day or so, several different people have mentioned that I've helped them come to grips with problems in their lives. Maybe I have something to offer the people in this community after all. I just have to . . ."

". . . blaze your own trail?" she asked.

He smiled. "Yeah. Maybe so."

Before she could respond, the back door opened and slammed shut.

"Mom?" Jason called.

"I'm in the living room."

Footsteps sounded, growing louder, as Jason padded into the room. In his arms, he held a familiar blue quilted jacket.

"Where did you get that?" she asked.

"It was on the back porch all folded up like a present."

"Isn't that the one Jesse was wearing?" Craig asked.

"I think so." Kristy took the jacket from her son, felt the material and checked the inside tag. "Yes, I'm sure it is. When I gave it to him, he said he'd return it."

"Maybe he was here after all."

"Here and gone home," she said. "This is all so . . . weird. In fact, things have been weird about that guy from the first moment I saw him. I can't explain it."

"Scripture might."

"What do you mean?"

"Do not forget to entertain strangers," Craig said, "for by so doing some people have entertained angels without knowing it."

"Do you think Jesse is an angel?"

Craig paused for a moment, as though struggling with the notion, just as Kristy was, then gave an open-handed shrug. "I'm not sure what I believe."

Epilogue

Six months later, Kristy stood before a full-length mirror in the church choir room, wearing a white gown and veil. She'd purposely chosen a color that seemed appropriate, even though there might be a few in Fairbrook who would question her choice.

She felt like a princess today, one who was pure and cherished. One who was worthy.

The daughter of a king.

In spite of any mistakes she might have made along the way, in spite of those she might make in the future, Kristy now realized her value—thanks in large part to Jesse.

His arrival in Fairbrook had been a real blessing to many.

No one had seen him since the day he'd returned the blue jacket and left it on her back porch. He'd moved out of their lives as simply and silently as he'd moved in. Yet the homeless man—or had he been an angel?—had touched the lives and the hearts of everyone with whom he'd had contact.

Well, at least he'd touched those whose hearts were open.

"Are you ready?" Shana asked, as she approached the mirror and smiled at their images—the happy bride and her maid of honor.

"Yes." Kristy turned to her best friend. Just last month, when Shana and Ramon had exchanged vows in this very church, Kristy and Craig had stood up with them.

They'd had some things to work through first, but it was clear that they loved each other. Shana's parents had also been surprisingly supportive of their union and had accepted Carlitos and Luis as part of the package.

Several months ago, Ramon had mentioned that Brad had a cousin named Matthew, and that the two Rensfields might have been involved in a cover-up to avoid a paternity suit.

Kristy had considered following up on that lead, but only for the briefest of moments. Craig wanted to adopt Jason, and she couldn't imagine her son having a better, more loving father.

"Kristy," Gram said, her face beaming with love and pride, "you look absolutely beautiful."

Kristy's heart swelled to the point that it might overflow with love. "Thanks, Gram. So do you."

Her grandmother, whose wheelchair had been adorned with silver ribbons and white roses, wore a blue gown they'd found in a Nordstrom bag in the closet, a dress she'd purchased before her stroke and had never had the chance to wear. Her eyes danced with joy.

A knock sounded at the door, and Shana answered.

Dawn entered the small room carrying Jessica, Renee's two-month-old baby in her arms. "Pastor George said it's time. So whenever you're ready . . ."

Renee, who was dressed in the same style gown as Shana and would walk down the aisle first, brushed a kiss on little Jessica's cheek. "Is she being good for you, Mom?"

"So far so good. If she starts fussing, your father said he'd take her out of the church and give her a bottle. He never has been very good with a camera, and I want to get some pictures."

Jessica, who Renee had named after Jesse, was just about the prettiest baby Kristy had ever seen, with big blue eyes and dark curly hair.

And speaking of pretty babies . . .

"How's Jason doing?" Kristy asked.

"He's with Craig and the groomsmen," Dawn said. "You can't believe how cute he is in that little tuxedo."

"I can't wait to see him."

Dawn glanced around the room and smiled. "I love weddings. And this one feels like a dream come true."

"I know what you mean," Kristy said. "I want to pinch myself half the time, just to make sure I'm not dreaming."

"Are you ready?" Shana asked Kristy.

"I've never been more ready." She was a princess, the daughter of the King.

And the future never looked so bright.

ENTERTAINING ANGELS
Judy Duarte

ABOUT THIS GUIDE

The suggested questions are included
to enhance your group's
reading of Judy Duarte's
Entertaining Angels

DISCUSSION QUESTIONS

1. When Jesse met Craig at the Fairbrook city limits sign, he said, "Things aren't always what they seem." People often make false assumptions, which can be damaging to themselves and to others. Kristy made one such assumption when she accused Renee of stealing. As a reader, you knew the truth ahead of time. Did you have an emotional response to Kristy's false accusation? Did she lose favor in your eyes? Why or why not?

2. While reflecting on the time when she and her mother had been homeless, Kristy remembered what it felt like to be seen as an apparition rather than a real person. *But we're here,* she'd wanted to shout. *And we're hungry. Don't pretend you can't see us.* Some people avoid making eye contact with those who make them feel uncomfortable. We've all been guilty of it at one time or another. Why do you think that is?

3. Jason missed not having a father, Danny's dad was in prison, and Tommy's father left his wife and kids for another woman. While the kids discussed absent fathers, Renee reached over, patted Jason on the knee, and said, "My dad hasn't been in my life for almost as long as I can remember. And the way I see it, sometimes having a dad can be more trouble than it's worth." What were your thoughts about that discussion? Do the details surrounding a father's absence make it any tougher or easier for a child? Was Renee reflecting upon her own experience?

4. Jesse said, "Life's a journey with twists and turns and potholes. . . ." Later, after talking to Jesse, Gram told Shana, ". . . life is a journey. Sometimes the scenery is

lovely, and at other times, the sky is dark and gloomy, the road full of potholes. But along the way, there are lessons to learn. And those lessons come in the strangest ways." Whose journey had the most impact on you while you were reading? How does this relate to your own life?

5. In the author's first novel, *Mulberry Park*, many of the characters saw their faith shattered along life's journey. In *Entertaining Angels*, many of the characters had their dreams shattered. Choose one character and explain what you learned about how he or she handled losing his or her dream.

6. Jesse used a fairy tale about a princess who forgot her own value. Then he told Kristy not to sell herself short. How did that fairy tale speak to you?

7. The author addressed several similar conflicts, including lost dreams and altered game plans. Which of the characters struggling with regret and disappointment did you relate to best, and why?

8. Lorraine (Gram) told Shana, "Mistakes and sins are a dime a dozen. We all make them. God's forgiveness comes easy, but it's our own that's hard." Then she used a plastic Army man as an analogy while talking to Shana. "You're burdened by guilt," she said, "and you've asked God to take it. He's willing, but he's not going to jerk it out of your hands. You have to release it." What things (or old baggage) do people tend to hang on to?

9. The following are Jesse-isms. Choose one that hits home with you and share why: (a) Things aren't always what they seem. (b) Donations are fine and are needed some-

times, but you need to do some actual foot washing rather than offer to pay for someone's pedicure. (c) You can't do anything about someone else's attitude. You can only change you own. (d) God doesn't give a person a dream without also giving the power to make it come true. But that doesn't mean it won't take a great deal of work on your part. (e) A wise man once told me that the essence of mental health is knowing you have options. (f) You're doomed to make the same mistakes that your parents made if you don't make some changes—mistakes that will make you unhappy for a very long time. (g) Sometimes confrontations are the only way out.

10. Have you ever encountered a stranger who touched your life in an unexpected way? Have you ever wondered whether you've been visited by an angel?